LOST LOVE ON 6TH STREET

Lolu Sinclair

ISBN: 978-1-965155-00-4 (TPB)

ISBN: 978-1-965155-01-1 (KIN)

lostlust.com

1

ELEANOR

I thought summers in Chicago were hot. But my first week in Austin has been searing.

However, the chill of this basement is so sharp it's already reached my bones. It comes with the job of archiving photos, which is why I packed both my cardigan and a wool blanket in my backpack despite the heat outside.

The woman leading me through the winding aisles of black binders looks over her shoulder at me and grins. "I thought Midwesterners were used to cold." Her southern twang is subtle, but present.

I pull my cardigan tighter around me.

"Used to it, sure. I'm not the type to wear shorts in thirty-degree weather, though," I say.

She laughs. It's a lovely laugh. Tripping and high-pitched. The kind that would draw your attention in the middle of a crowded bar.

Her name is Jolene. When she introduced herself, it took everything in me not to ask if she was named after the

Dolly Parton song. She seemed used to that question, because while shaking my hand, she added, "And no, not like the song."

It must be exhausting to be a blonde named Jolene and work at a museum dedicated to preserving Austin's music history.

I hadn't heard of the Reeder Music Library until I came across the job listing a few months ago. But the second I saw the architecturally lavish granite building in pictures, I couldn't wait to work here.

It doesn't matter if I'm stuck in the frigid, brightly lit basement where style has been sacrificed for practicality. The carpets alone look like they knew the likes of the Roosevelt administration.

Regardless, I'm happy to be here.

"Here's your workstation," Jolene says as we emerge from an aisle.

My workstation isn't much more than a glorified card table and folding chair, but that's to be expected from a small museum. All the money goes into the exhibitions, the preservation, and the salaries. I should be grateful I don't have to sit on the floor.

"And, to save your butt from freezing off," Jolene announces, going over to the chair. She lifts a flat brown cushion. "It's more comfortable than it looks."

I smile. "Thank you."

"So, as we discussed on the phone, we're looking at trimming the fat on our collections." Jolene holds up her hands with long nails like spikes. I wonder how she's able to wear examination gloves with nails like that. "I know, it doesn't sound nice. But there's only so much we can keep."

In the business of museums, this process is called deaccessioning. It serves a dual purpose: it clears out storage while bringing in a little extra money since pieces are often sold to collectors.

"The first week or so, I'll double check your work just so we're on the same page about what belongs in our physical collection. Any reproductions can be scrapped. And anything that doesn't have a description needs to be researched before we decide to part ways with it. Think of it as . . . *refining*."

I nod. "That's a good way to put it." I've been working in this industry since I graduated college nearly ten years ago. It might not be the most thrilling work, but not everyone who studies photography gets to continue working in the industry. So, I'm grateful.

"This is your issued laptop," Jolene says, gesturing to the dinosaur of a Dell on the table. "As you go through the collections and identify what needs to be deaccessioned, you can scan it into the database."

I drop my bag by the leg of the table. "Sounds good to me."

"I know it's not the most exciting job," she says with an apologetic smile.

I shrug and plop down into the chair. "It's only three months, anyway."

"True, although being down here too long can make you go stir crazy. Just make sure you touch some grass during your breaks," Jolene says, leaning on the end of one of the aisles.

I laugh. "There's grass around here?" I ask. "I thought the sun dried it all up."

Jolene rolls her eyes. "Okay, Eleanor. That's fair. But you'll get used to it. I did."

I open the laptop. All the graphics are blocky and antiquated looking. What version of Windows does this thing even *run* on? I pull off my glasses and rub the lip of my cardigan over the lenses. Maybe that will help. "You're originally from here?" I ask.

"Me?! Heavens, no," Jolene says. "You think with an accent like this I'm a born and bred Texan?"

I smile sheepishly. "I'm afraid southern accents kinda blend together for me."

"Right, you're a northerner," she says. The tease in her voice is playful and kind. For a boss, she seems like the exact type you'd want. "I'm from Tennessee. Outside of Nashville. Which I know makes the whole 'Jolene' thing even more confusing, but don't take it up with me, alright? Wasn't my choice."

I adjust my cat-eye glasses back onto the bridge of my nose. "What brought you here, then?"

"Same thing as you. Work. Museums are hard to come by this day and age. Not to mention museums focusing on music that are a bit more nuanced than the Rock and Roll Hall of Fame. No offense."

"None taken," I say with a quirk of my eyebrow.

Jolene shrugs. "Not sure your opinion on Cleveland."

I burst with a laugh, unusually loud for the quiet din of an archive. "Oh, we all hate Ohio."

"That's what I thought," she says. "Anyway, I had a similar job here as you do. Short term, temporary. And then I stayed."

"So, you like it here?"

The apples of Jolene's cheeks tighten as she smiles. "Love. It became home faster than I knew what to do with. My mama is still begging me to come back to Tennessee, but . . . something about Austin. I can't walk away from it."

"What do you think it is?" I ask. I haven't had a chance to learn much about my new city. I've been getting set up in my new apartment the museum has rented for me, a small studio with thin walls and Ikea furniture. Since I don't have a social circle here yet, I have to go out adventuring by myself. And that scares the bejeezus out of me. Stranger in a strange land. I'll get over it eventually.

Hopefully.

Jolene folds her arms over her chest, the corner of her lip quirking upward. "I think you'll have to figure that one out for yourself."

I have half a mind to ask whether she's practiced that line. But instead, I give her a single nod. "Alright. Challenge accepted."

She ticks her head back through the aisle. "If you need me, I'll be in my office. Seriously, for anything. You have a question or observation. Need a couple minutes just to chat. A distraction . . ."

"Got it," I say. "Thanks, I will."

Jolene disappears down the aisle, leaving me alone with stacks of binders and this ancient laptop. I take the first one and begin to go through it. I've done some preliminary research on the Austin music scene to get an idea of the history and various things I should know. But there's no better education than going through a book of photos, no matter how banal they are.

What Jolene didn't mention is that the binders she's having me go through are a mess. Things are out of order, some photos aren't even contained in plastic sleeves, and others have been bent and bruised through improper handling.

I take my time, going through the first binder page by page with my gloved fingers, scanning each photo into the database while trying to match locations and faces to other photos in order to update the description.

Sure, there's a lot of representation of the country music scene, but there's so much more than that. Polaroids of Stevie Ray Vaughan and his guitar, Number One. Images from backstage at Austin City Limits. A group of guys on stage in very few clothes, apparently a noise rock band from the '80s called Scratch Acid. Who knew it was so easy to make history? Make good music, take off your shirt. And sometimes your pants.

Jolene didn't have to warn me that the work would be drudgerous. To me, it's not. I'm discovering a whole world I never knew, one I couldn't have known in such detail by googling late into the night back in Chicago.

I grab the second binder. I can work through a couple of pages before lunch. The first page is more of the same, the second has some pictures of reggae performers who aren't named in the caption. I'll have to go through the database on that one.

However, before I can tear my eyes away to begin my search, the final photo on the page grabs my attention.

I narrow my eyes at a picture of a young woman. It's got a yellow-orange date stamp. *05-26-1993*. She's got a guitar case in her hand, one arm up in the air, and a massive grin on her face as the wind whips through her dark shoulder-length shag haircut. She wears a time-period-appropriate flannel over a heroin chic slip dress with Doc Martens. A dark-haired Liz Phair.

In the background is a big star-shaped sign with "The Lo" clearly written, but the rest of the venue's name was cut off.

There's no description attached to the photo. No name. No location.

I lift the plastic sheath and grab the photo edge. It's paper—not photo paper—printer paper. Like it's been photocopied. How did it get here if it's not even an original?

Mysteries like this abound when it comes to archiving. It's my job to solve them.

I pull the photo the rest of the way out and hold it with both hands, trying to find any other discernible details. She must be a musician. Except she doesn't look familiar to me. Perhaps if I double-check it with the database—

"How's it going?" Jolene interrupts my concentration, emerging again from the aisle.

It's difficult to pull my eyes away from the photo, but I manage it. "Um. Good. Actually, do you recognize anything about this photo? There's no description and, well, two heads are better than one."

Jolene crosses to the table and peers down at the photo. "Well, that's the old Lone Star," she says.

"The Lo." Makes sense.

"But other than that," Her brow furrows. "How did this get in here?" she says, more to herself than to me. "Just toss that one, Eleanor. No one will want a copy."

My heart drops into my stomach. The beauty of photographs is the ability of film to capture ephemeral moments and make them everlasting. This might not be the original photo, but what if the original is gone? "I'll keep it," I say. "If that's alright."

Jolene cocks her head to the side. "You want to keep it?"

"Uh. Yeah, there's . . . just something about it."

Her confusion turns into endearment. "It speaks to you?"

I half-laugh. "I guess, yeah, you could say that. I'm curious."

7

"Say no more. I get it. That's why we're here, right?" she says, opening her arms to gesture to the caverns of binders.

"That's true," I say. I hate to admit it, but I've definitely judged a book by its cover. Jolene is tall, blonde, and made up for a night on the town. Doesn't seem like the type that would want to scuttle photos away in the basement. But who is to say that all archivists should be like me? Bookish and quiet? "You'll have to tell me what got you into museums initially sometime," I say.

Jolene looks down at her watch. "How about I take you to lunch, and we can trade stories?"

"Deal," I say.

Before I leave, I carefully place the photo into my bag, right next to my padded camera case.

A mystery to visit later.

2

LUKE

I tuck my phone between my shoulder and ear, squeezing tight so it doesn't fall to the tile floor of the convenience store. The fluorescents are starting to nag at my eyes. "Okay, tell me again what they want?"

My assistant, Randy, replies with detailed intensity, "They specifically want 7-Eleven brand gummi bears. Not worms, no name brand. 7-Eleven gum—"

"Got it," I say, snatching every bag of 7-Eleven brand gummi bears off the rack. "Anything else *specific?*"

Randy chuckles. "I think we got everything else on the rider."

"We better have," I grumble before dropping all the bags onto the counter and adjusting the phone into my hand. My neck aches from being crooked. "This is the last time I work with the band from Brushy Creek."

"You always say that."

"And this time I mean it. They say they're from Austin, but they're all from—" I jab my card into the reader, not bothering to look at the price, "bougie suburbs and think they're so fucking special." I rip the card out.

Randy sighs. "If they're bougie, why are they requesting 7-Eleven gummi bears?"

"Don't argue with me, Randy."

He chuckles. "Luke, take it easy, alright? It was an easy fix."

A missing item from a rider is usually an easy fix. Mostly because they're *usually* reasonable asks. Chips and salsa. Coconut water. Sugar-free Red Bull. Not specific 7-Eleven brand gummi bears.

I take a deep breath. I could have sent Randy and dealt with other things, but I wouldn't have been able to focus. I jogged all the way here. Needed to get my energy out. I left him to deal with all the last-minute details before the venue opened to the audience.

"Yeah. You're right," I say with finality.

"Need a bag?" The older man asks from behind the counter.

I shake my head, giving him a pathetic and apologetic smile. I look like such an asshole right now. Blame up-and-coming cowpunk band Fried Polyester.

With my spoils in hand, I bolt out of the 7-Eleven and begin striding down 6th Street at a steady clip. "Alright, I'm on my way."

"Great. I'll let them know."

I hang up the phone and shove it into the pocket of my suit jacket. I ought to make this band pay for my dry-cleaning bill. This suit is custom after all. *Breathe, Luke.* It's all a part of the job. A job I love in a city I love. I can handle this.

Being a music promoter isn't always easy work, but it's rewarding. I get acts from across the country, across the fucking world, streaming into Austin's best venues. It's a hustle and grind every day, but that also means every day is different.

I could never see myself doing anything that required me to sit at a desk, in a cubicle, or fill out spreadsheets. That's what corporate America is, right? And don't get me started on becoming a real estate agent. I've already got the wardrobe for it, but trying to sell homes to people who are hung up on the type of hardwood floors they want is not my cup of tea.

No, my home is on 6th Street, Austin's nine-block strip of clubs and music venues. Beautiful vintage buildings line the streets, neon signs to boot, and crowds wander between the sidewalks and streets indiscriminately.

I've been pounding these streets since I was just a kid, being dragged along to jazz clubs and blues sets with my dad, eventually sneaking into the harder shows with my friends when I was underage.

Yep. 6th Street is where I belong.

Even if I'm having to track down a specific type of gummi bears for a smarmy band from *Brushy Creek*, Texas.

"Hey, Luke!" a familiar voice shouts.

I tick my head over my shoulder to get a better look. Everyone's always yelling out "Hey, Luke" around here. I'm a fixture of the scene. Whether it's musicians, venue owners, hell, even concertgoers, I've got my own little fan club.

Before I can find the face of whoever called out my name, I slam into someone. Something rigid jabs into my belly and I yelp in pain.

Bags of gummies fall to the ground at my feet. *Fuck me.*

"Oh my gosh, are you okay? Did I hurt you?" the woman asks, delicately touching my arm.

I'm about to swear and be more of an asshole than this person deserves considering I was the one who wasn't looking, but I go mute when I lay eyes on her.

11

She's not just a woman, but a beautiful woman. One with lots of dark, corkscrew curls, high cheekbones, and big brown eyes magnified behind the lenses of her glasses. I've always been a sucker for girls with glasses.

In her hands is a camera. A nice one. I must have been jabbed by the lens. I touch the aching spot on my ribs. "I . . . uh . . ." Of course, that's the moment I spot who called out my name, an older club owner, one of the more old-fashioned types. He's across the street, snickering at my pain with the bouncer. I ignore him.

She drops the camera, so it hangs around her neck. "Let me help you with . . ." She crouches down and picks up a bag of the gummies. "Your gummies."

I drop to my knees. "No, I've got it, I'm the one who ran into you." I scoop up as many as I can before she can get to them. "I'm sorry, I wasn't looking."

"No, it's my fault," she says. "I had my head down. I was looking at my . . ."

Our eyes meet; she doesn't manage to finish her sentence. I can't tell if she's embarrassed or maybe she's sizing me up the way I just did her.

"Anyway, here," she says, dropping her gaze and shoving the couple bags of gummies she collected into my arm.

"Thanks," I say.

We both stand up. It feels weird to move along and act like this encounter didn't happen, despite the mortification.

"That's a lot of gummies," she says.

"I—um, yeah, they're not all for me. I'm prone to cavities anyway," I say.

She offers me a laugh and a shy smile. "I would never judge a sweet tooth."

"No, seriously, they're not for me, they're for a band I'm working with." A lock of my hair has fallen on my forehead, and I don't have a spare hand to put it back in place. Apparently, I needed more gel before I left the house.

Her eyes skitter along 6th Street. "You're in the music industry?"

"Everyone is around here," I reply. I give her another up-down, not in a lustful or inappropriate way. Just . . . her attire really isn't 6th Street on a Friday night. It's more like cute librarian. Long airy skirt and a scrunchy type of top with embroidery. She'd fit into the San Francisco music scene of the '60s. By twenty-first century Austin, Texas? Not so much. "Except for you," I say.

The woman takes half a step back, unsure. "How do you know that?"

"Just guessed," I say. "I know all the faces around here. I can tell the locals from the suburbanites from the tourist . . . so which one are you?"

She chews on the inside of her cheek. "I guess I'm a wannabe local. I'm new in town."

"Oh, well . . ." I smile my winningest smile. "Welcome to Austin."

"Thanks," she says brightly. "You're a local, I take it?"

"Born and bred," I reply.

Her eyes alight. "Then maybe you can help me with something."

"Depends," I say, but I'm close to committed to moving heaven and earth to help.

"I'm looking for The Lone Star. Or at least the location of it. I saw it's closed on Google Maps, but I thought I'd be able to see where it used to be . . ." she trails off, once again looking around at the scenery.

13

I'm used to 6th Street on a Friday. Vibrant and alive, downtown Austin's throbbing pulse. It's where I'm in my element, where I'm most comfortable and at ease. That is unless I'm talking to a beautiful woman I ran smack into. That's when the thrum courses through my veins, and the sounds of the street become less of a backing track and more about the rhythm of how I move.

Been a while since I've been on pins and needles like this.

But this woman's managed to do that to me. And I don't even know her name.

"I think I might have gone too far . . ." she says carefully, looking at the bar front beside us.

"Yeah, The Lone Star closed recently but it's still in operation under a different name—The Yellow Rose. It's a few blocks that way," I say, gesturing with my gummi-filled arms.

She flips around and scratches her hand through her crown of curls. Adorable. "Damn, I knew I missed it."

I step beside her, tilting my head down the street. "You're in luck. I'm going there. I can walk you."

"You're going there? Really? You're not just being nice," she asks, a teasing smirk on her lips.

"No, seriously, I'm promoting an event there tonight. That's why I have all these gummies."

She frowns. "Is it some weird Willy Wonka thing?"

"No, no, nothing like that. I'm a music promoter, I just . . ." I let out a groan of frustration. "Let's just say musicians are temperamental and when you forget one thing from the rider, that's the one thing they notice."

"Interesting," she says, leaning her head back enough that the dying sunset casts a golden glow over all her features, illuminating her olive-toned skin. "I always expected, you know, sex, drugs, rock'n'roll."

I nod. "Yeah, you'd be surprised by how banal and specific the requests are sometimes."

She laughs through sealed lips, then glances down the street. "Well, I don't usually go walking with a man whose name I don't know."

"Ah, where are my manners?" Good old southern hospitality is elusive when under pressure. "I'm Luke. Would offer you my hand, but—"

"You've got your hands full. I could help actually if you—"

I pull my bounty away from her. "No, no. Not necessary. What kind of gentleman has a woman carry his gummies for him?"

"Is this a weird Austin thing I don't know about?" she asks.

I chuckle. "No, promise, gummies aren't a requirement for understanding Austinite culture."

The conversation stills for only a moment, a moment long enough for me to feel like I might never breathe again. Everything about her is *arresting*. I work too much to date and even while I'm working, I'm sometimes swamped with women on all sides. As much as I hate to admit it, I use my flirting prowess to get ahead from time to time.

Something about her.

"I'm Eleanor."

Something about Eleanor.

"Well, Eleanor, let me take you to The Lone Star."

We walk side by side, the conversation stilted with the newness of our connection. I'm not on my game, not my best self. "So, where are you from?" I ask.

"Chicago."

"Chicago? And you haven't melted?"

"We have hot summers in Chicago," she says through a laugh.

"Great music town," I say.

She nods. "Oh, obviously."

"I mean, if I didn't love Austin so much, I'd consider taking things there. Maybe Seattle, although that's more of a dream of the nineties than anything."

"Ah . . . Nirvana fan?" she asks.

I decide to spare her the ramblings of a music addict. "You know, that scene feels . . . mythological almost."

As we walk, the seas of people seem to part for us without any effort.

"So, what brought you here?"

"Work," she says.

When she doesn't offer more in explanation, I bring it upon myself to pry. "Ah. What kind of work?"

Eleanor holds up her camera. "I'm a photo archivist at the Reeder Music Library."

"No way."

"Way," she says. "At least temporarily. My contract is only for three months."

"You didn't like Chicago?" I ask.

She shakes her head. "No, I love Chicago. I went to school there . . . so it was time for a change."

I'm kind of jealous of her. Though I've never had an impulse to leave my home turf, there's a what-if about the world beyond. The past however many years have been all about my job, not about the adventure of experience.

"Who knows if Austin will be my landing pad? I'm trying it on for size," she says.

And what a nice size that is.

"Actually, that's why I'm interested in The Lone Star. Because I saw something at work, and I just wanted to check it out."

"Oh?"

"Yeah, lemme—here, I'll show you."

I feel bad for making her keep walking as she roots around in her bag, but I'm worried that Fried Polyester's manager might rip my head off. Twenty-two-year-olds have no respect, and they also have no shame. They let it rip when they're mad.

"Ah, here it is." She pulls out a crisp piece of paper and holds it out in front of me since I can't hold it. "I saw this and, I don't know, my boss said I should toss it, but . . ."

Her words drift away as I focus in on the photo. That's The Lone Star alright. And that's . . .

"I couldn't find any information on the person from the database, so I . . . I don't know, I know it's crazy, but I wanted to see if I could find out some information by talking to people. She just deserves to be immortalized."

I rip my eyes from the photo and clear my throat. "We're here."

3

ELEANOR

We stop suddenly in front of a club. I scan my surroundings. Looks a hell of a lot different than the picture, but then again, it's been almost thirty years. I shouldn't be so surprised.

There's a line pouring out the front door, waiting to get in. And the marquee reads "Fried Polyester." Naming a band is an interesting art form, that's for sure.

"Sorry, do you mind holding a couple of these so I can . . ." Luke inclines his stubbled chin toward the picture.

"Sure, of course." I take a few of the bags to free up one of his hands so he can take a closer look at the picture. His fingertips brush my hand in the process, and I try to pretend it doesn't feel *amazing*. Not sure if that's because it's been a long while since I've had any physical touch from a man or if it's because of Luke himself.

I have to admit, I'm shocked he's giving me the time of day like this. Must be that good old Texas charm. In Chicago, guys in suits wouldn't have even looked at me. And frankly, the only reason I would have looked at a guy like him back home was if he was standing in my way at a cross walk, not paying any mind to where his body was in space. The finely pressed suits and slicked-back hair were a certain type back home.

However, Luke isn't like that. He's a different breed altogether. He cares about his appearance without trying to look like a buttoned-up banker. He'd stick out like a sore thumb back home in his tailored tweed suit. Though there's product in his golden-brown hair, it still looks like a breeze could brush it out of place. And his smile, while charming, isn't ridiculously white.

I watch as he takes in the photo. His height could cast a shadow on me. Must be nearly a foot taller.

His eyes work across the image, and I can tell it's not just a picture to him either. He scrutinizes, peruses, and maybe even wonders.

"You want to figure out who this is?" he asks, eyes rising to meet mine.

His baby blues are devastating. I nearly lose my spot in my own brain. "Um. Yeah. You know, I'm a historian in a way. And I'm just curious what the story is. It's not for work, this is my own personal quest."

Luke's intense gaze turns genial again. He smiles and hands back the photo. "That's admirable of you."

I try to ignore the knife to the gut. Admirable. Like it's *cute*.

"I'd like to help you."

Wait. "What?" That's not condescending like I thought he was trying to be.

"I've been in this scene a long time. I know a lot of people, could get you the right contacts and—" Luke does a doubletake and slides his phone out of his pocket. "Listen, I've gotta get these gummies to the band."

I nod. "Right, well, let me give you my number and we can—"

"Davy!" Luke calls out to the man at the door and points at me. "I want her put on the photographer list."

I shake my head in shock. What is happening? "The photographer list?"

"Yeah, you stay, take some pictures and we'll talk afterward," Luke says as if it makes the most sense in the world. "Unless you've got plans or a date or something."

"A date? No, I don't—"

"Perfect. Here, I'll take these." He scoops the gummies out of my arms. "And I'll see you after the show, okay?"

Luke starts to step away. I follow on his heels. "Wait, I'm not an event photographer. It's just something I do for fun, it's not like . . . something I *do*."

It used to be the thing I wanted to do most in the world. The trade I learned in college. Like I said, I'm lucky to have a job in my industry. Photojournalism, though, isn't the easiest field to break into. So, I settled for behind the scenes. I'm happy with that. Photography is just a hobby now.

"What do you mean it's not something you do?" Luke asks, the smile on his face effervescent. "You've got the camera. You take pictures, right?"

"Well, there's a lot of different kinds of photography," I say. Wedding photography is different from music photography is different from nature photography. But I'm getting ahead of myself. "It's a generous offer, but really, I wouldn't know the first thing about concert photography."

Luke doesn't respond right away, he just nods. "Okay, well . . ."

I start to pull out my phone to type in his number.

"Davy, put her on the VIP list," Luke says to the doorman.

"What?!" I squeak.

"Name's Eleanor," Luke goes on.

Davy starts scribbling on his clipboard. "Eleanor what?"

Luke nods at me. "Eleanor what?"

I stare at him. I was looking forward to a small jaunt down 6th Street after my first week at the museum and then a quiet night in with a bottle of wine and a good book. I hate to be the stereotype of a girl with glasses who works in a museum, but if the shoe fits.

"You can't fight with me now," Luke says in a low, gravelly tone, his eyes locked on mine.

My body goes numb.

Holy. Cow.

"Hayes," I say. Instead of no.

Because even I can't refuse an adventure when it falls into my lap.

"Eleanor Hayes," Luke says. Should be for Davy the doorman's benefit. But it's all for me. My full name from his amazing lips. "Make sure she's not paying for anything, alright? She's my guest."

Davy nods curtly before pulling out a walkie talkie to deliver the information to lord knows who.

Before I can attempt to fight, Luke disappears into the club, bags of gummies piled in his arms.

I stare at the spot that he left empty in front of me.

I don't know if Luke knows this town, but it certainly seems like he runs it.

"Ahem," Davy clears his throat. He's pulled the red velvet barrier away. "Eleanor Hayes? VIP?"

I glance at the long line of Fried Polyester fans glowering at me.

I've never been a VIP.

Could be fun.

* * *

The VIP section is no joke. Instead of being tangled with the masses in the club proper downstairs, we get to watch it all from a balcony. No one is pushing anyone to make room, rubbing our sweat on each other, no threat of beer spilling down the back of my shirt. Not to mention, the floor isn't sticky. It's slick, dark wood, which compliments all the red velvet seating. It's more like a lounge than a concert venue.

I notice a yellow-labeled beer in many audience members' hands that I've never seen before. It must be a local thing.

Up here, the mood is calm and relaxed. Even the bartenders seem at ease. Rather than dealing with a line of patrons eager to get their drinks before the set starts, they are circulating the floor to take orders and deliver drinks.

I've posted up at a high top in the corner, my camera tucked deep in my bag so as not to incur side eyes from event security. For events like this, you need to be an approved photographer. Sure, I wouldn't mind taking a few snaps here and there during the show but being a concert photographer is a totally different thing. You have to be at the edge of the stage with your ears packed with plugs to make sure you don't lose your hearing. Not to mention, it can get dangerous if things get out of hand.

It's a shame, though. I have a great view of all the techs tuning the instruments, with apathetic expressions on their faces and draped in hot pink and dark blue lighting.

The bartender with purple hair tied on the top of her head comes over to me. "One Yellow Rose of Texas for you."

I take the drink. When it came to picking out a cocktail, I felt it was only right to choose the signature drink of The Yellow Rose. "Thank you so much."

"'Course honey. Need anything else?"

I smile. Not gonna lie—being called honey by a stranger is different, but it's kind of sweet. "Well, I actually have a question. Do you know anything about the band?"

"Fried Polyester?"

I hold back a laugh. Sounds even funnier out loud. "Yeah, I—a friend invited me tonight, I'm just along for the ride." Calling Luke a friend might be a stretch, but there's no better way to describe someone I nearly maimed with my camera earlier.

"Oh, they're goooood," she says with a slow nod and a big smile.

"Yeah? What kind of music do they play?"

"Cowpunk."

I blink. I know there are lots of . . . interestingly named music genres. Zydeco. Shoegaze. Acid Jazz. "Cowpunk?"

"Yeah! It's like country and punk mixed together. You'll like it."

I wilt at the sound of "country." I'm in Texas, after all; I should have known that's what I'm in for. But like many Midwesterners, "I'll listen to anything but country" is a mantra. That being said, I've never really given country music a fair shot.

"Oh, don't make that face. You haven't even heard it yet," she says, eyes glimmering. "Just strap in and enjoy. I'll come check on you during the set and see how you like it."

The bartender waltzes off to her next table. I appreciate everyone's positivity around here. Maybe she's right. I ought to give it more of a chance. Country isn't a bad word. Right?

I sip my Yellow Rose of Texas. Lots of tequila. I have to be careful with these if I want to drive home later.

I watch the stage as a few guys lumber around tinkering with the instruments. I've never understood why the musicians don't do the final tune-ups of their instruments. Wouldn't you want to make sure everything is perfect? It seems like it's just a tactic to get the crowd riled. Which it does. The crush of people downstairs starts cheering.

I continue to sip my drink, watching as the scene plays out on stage. The techs are acting like they don't even hear the crowd. Tuning up the bass guitar, whacking the drums . . . someone even runs a spoon along a washboard.

God, what the hell am I in for?

At the back of the stage, Luke appears. He's totally out of place compared to the raggedy jean-wearing techs. His arms are crossed over his chest as he speaks in a low voice to one of the techs, gesturing toward the microphone set up at the front.

Damn, I'm a sucker for watching men in their element. And given the poise and focus Luke exudes, he is *in* his element.

He starts to turn and then gives a final look at the stage. His blue eyes cut right through the low club lighting. And a smile ticks onto his lip before he disappears behind the dark curtains.

Instinctually, I pull the picture out of my bag once more and put it on the table. I stare at it, willing it to tell me more about the captivating singer. I wonder if this woman ever performed on this stage. I wonder if there was a crowd waiting on pins and needles for her just like this one. I hope she's happy wherever she is.

For a second, I'm struck with the silliness of this situation. I know nothing about Luke. I don't even know his last name. I don't know what his personality is when he hasn't just met someone. Why am I waiting around to let him help me when he's just a stranger? I'm a city girl. I know better than this.

Before I can let my thoughts push me into an anxious spiral, the house lights dim, the stage lights go up, and a group of guys lumber onto the stage. Trucker hats, flannel, blue jeans. Yep, exactly what I pictured.

When they're all set at their instruments, they begin.

It's nothing like I expected or could have imagined. Fiddle mixed with heavy bass and guitar, lyrics about bad childhoods and the world ending, familiar drumbeats subverted to a '70s sound.

Yeah, the bartender was right. This is good.

And I think if I'm going to hack it in Austin, even just for three months, I'm going to need to reserve my judgments. Because so far, this place is pretty cool.

4

LUKE

The band is flying, the crowd is eating them up. I've paid Fried Polyester's manager and stole a bag of the gummies as retribution. For the most part, my work is done. Now I just need to be on high alert for any funny business. The last thing a music promoter needs is drama at their event. Well, second to last thing. The *last* thing they need is the band walking out. But we've already made it this far. I think we'll be fine unless someone throws a beer bottle.

I sneak out of the backstage area and check on the bar. No one's been overserved, everyone's in good spirits. Then, I take a look at the balcony, narrowing my eyes.

At first, I'm not able to spot Eleanor, but then there's a glint of something in the corner and I realize it's the light bouncing off her glasses. She's hidden in shadow, but she's leaned over her table, watching the band with all the attention she can muster.

I'd say she's enjoying it.

I make my way up the stairs to the balcony, giving the security friendly nods and pats on the back. It's much quieter up here than the floor and for that, I'm grateful. You can actually hear yourself think up here, maybe have a conversation if you're lucky.

The VIP crowd at my events is always a mixed bag. Some people show up dressed to the nines, others are just fans who didn't want to deal with the annoyance of general admission. It's very Texas, a mishmash of everything our fine state has to offer. Beauty queens and blue-collar workers.

I head to the bar, knocking my knuckles against it to get Cressida's attention. "How's business, Cress?"

Cressida turns to me, a sprig of her violet hair sticking out of her bun. "Tips are shit."

"Aren't they always?"

She smiles and leans on the bar, showing off her cleavage. "What can I get you, Luke?"

It's an old routine at this point. She's been on the scene a bit longer than me and bounces from venue to venue depending on who is offering better pay. Old friends, nothing more, even if she does like to shimmy her chest up to the bar and tease me with it. "What's my friend drinking over there?"

Cressida peers around me, her eyebrow raising. "That's your 'friend?'"

"New friend," I say. "And I know that sounds like a euphemism, but—"

Cressida snorts and grabs a glass to start on a fresh cocktail. "I know, Luke. New month, different girl."

My insides twist. "That's not totally true."

She looks at me from under her long, dark lashes. I can hear her without her speaking. *You're joking, right?*

I straighten out my jacket. "For your information, it's been a while since I've dated anyone."

"I never said *dated*."

I bite my lower lip. Been a while since *that,* too. Just because I don't have time for a relationship, doesn't mean I don't have time for other extracurriculars. But in the past couple of years, the whole "new month, different girl" mentality that Cressida has pinned me with has lost its luster. I'm 35, and I'm not getting any younger. I want it all. Want the job, want the family.

I just haven't figured out how to balance that quite yet.

Cressida slides a Yellow Rose of Texas onto the bar followed by a Shiner Bock. She snaps the metal cap off with her bottle opener. "Enjoy, pretty boy."

I give her a smile. "Put it on my tab."

"Bah," she replies in annoyance, tossing a manicured hand my way before moving on to her next customer.

I turn to head over to Eleanor's table and find myself pinned by her stare. She smiles and wriggles her fingers at me.

I smile back and stride over to the table, placing her drink next to her empty glass. "I heard you were drinking a Yellow Ro—"

"What kind of beer is that?" she asks, jabbing a finger toward my bottle of beer.

I glance down at the yellow label. "Uh . . . Shiner Bock?"

"Shiner *Bock*?" she repeats, leaning closer, her voice rising in volume.

I chuckle. "Yes, Shiner Bock. It's a Texas beer."

Her eyes shimmer as she looks at the beer. "Oh, like how Pabst is a Chicago beer. Well, it's from Wisconsin, but. Yeah."

"You want to trade?" I ask. I'm not one for overly sweet cocktails, but her piqued interest is too cute to withhold from her.

Her eyes widen, brows jumping over the frames of her glasses. "You sure?"

"Here, take it." I switch my beer with the cocktail and settle into the chair beside her.

Eleanor's cheeks flush. "That's nice of you."

I swig her cocktail. Not too bad actually, though the cinnamon of Southern Comfort reminds me of too many mistakes in my 20s. "I want you to get the full Texas experience. If you're only here for three months, ya know."

"Sure," she says, then swigs the beer. I love a woman who drinks beer. The glasses and beer-drinking combination is too much for my heart to handle. She purses her lips, tilting her head to the side. "Huh. It's sweet."

"It's Shiner Bock."

She laughs, then tips the mouth of the beer toward the stage. "They're good."

I rest my arm on the back of my chair and gaze down at the band. Yeah, they might have been a pain in the ass before the show, but that's the whole punk attitude. "I saw them at a little club a few months ago and I thought they could handle a bigger venue. They've got a cult following, as you can see."

"Cowpunk, right?" she asks.

My mouth falls open. "You know a lot about music?"

"Oh, no, *no*," she says adamantly. "I mean, not the way you probably do. The bartender told me about them. Gotta be honest, I wasn't sure I'd like it."

"I sense a but coming on?"

Eleanor giggles and presses the mouth of the bottle to her mouth. I try not to stare at her pretty lips as she takes a sip, but it's hard. They're not particularly pink or red, but they're full and contrast nicely against her skin tone. Lips like hers have secrets and I don't mean the kind she could whisper in my ear.

She leaves me hanging a couple more moments, watching as the lead singer of Fried Polyester swings a cowboy-booted foot onto an amp and yells about walking miles for gas. "*But . . .*" she finally puts me out of my misery. "I'm really enjoying their music. Actually."

"Good, I'm glad," I say in earnest. I place my foot on the rung of her chair. Just a little bit closer. See how she reacts. "Would have hated to have forced you to stick around for a show you didn't even enjoy."

Eleanor tucks a chunk of curls behind her ear, keeping her eyes downcast on the table. She's shy. And curious. And ethereal.

Driving me crazy.

"So, um, anyway, the picture." Eleanor grabs the picture and places it on the table.

I clear my throat and shift my foot back to my chair. "Oh, yeah. The picture." I'd nearly forgotten about that.

She places it on the table in front of me. "So, The Lone Star isn't The Lone Star anymore. That's one thing . . . can you tell me anything else just by looking at this?"

I pull the picture closer to me and take it in. I'm not a sleuth. Not like Eleanor might be. But I'm going to do my damndest to come up with something else to give her, else I'll look like a fool or a womanizer for keeping her around. I chew on my lower lip and look everywhere on the image except the woman's face. My eyes land on the orange date emblazoned in the corner. "Okay, well '93 . . . that was in Kenny Zapeta's time."

"Kenny Zapeta?" she repeats.

I slide the picture away. Don't want to linger for too long. "Kenny Zapeta, he owned and managed The Lone Star for a while. A couple decades if I'm correct. Sold it in the early aughts."

"Do you think he'd have any information about this woman?" she asks eagerly. "I mean, I'm assuming she's a musician. And from the looks of it, she looks so excited. I guess it's a stretch, but maybe she performed here."

I cock my head to the side and let my eyes linger on Eleanor for a long moment. Thankfully, the crowd has erupted in cheers for the latest song, which gives me a few moments before I can say anything. Eleanor is sat up straight in her chair, her whole body straining with desire to solve the mystery.

When the crowd settles down and Fried Polyester moves into their next song, a ballad, thank fuck, I say, "You really want to figure this out, huh?"

"Yes, absolutely."

"Why?" I ask. "What do you get out of it?"

Eleanor's face slackens. "I . . ."

"That's not meant to be judgmental, I'm genuinely curious."

"Me too! I'm a genuinely curious person. Some people can be curious and let things go. I . . ." Her hands tighten around the Shiner Bock. "I need answers. At least as many as I can get."

I find myself smiling again. "I think we have that in common then," I say. "Being genuinely curious."

It's not often that a woman's gaze makes me feel bashful, but Eleanor's warm brown eyes strike me to my core. I look away, thankful my stubble can hide any flush on my cheeks. "Anyway, Kenny runs a record shop here in Austin. A collector's paradise."

Eleanor whips out her phone. "What's it called? I'll go check it out and see if I can talk to him."

I rub my hand over my chin. "Naw, I'll go with you."

"Uh, what?"

"Yeah, Kenny's, you know, he's a curmudgeon. He probably won't take kindly to an out-of-towner walking in and asking him random questions. No offense."

Eleanor furrows her brow. "Well. I don't want to ask you to give me any more help than you already have. This is more than enough for a lead."

"Trust me, you're not putting me out. I'd be happy to accompany you."

Eleanor's lips twist to the side. "Why is this starting to feel like I'm a woman in the '50s who needs to be chaperoned?"

"That's not my intention, not at all, just . . ." Damn, I'm bungling this. "Listen, I know this town. I know the music and the history of music in this town. Sure, I might not have my own personal archive, but I know how to get answers. How to ask the right questions. I know the right people, and I know how to get the ins we—you might need to figure this out. I'm not going to say you need me, but . . ."

Eleanor lifts one of her shoulders and gives me a look that basically says, "Don't step in it."

"I think I could be a good resource for you," I say, holding my hands out. "I'm not trying to take charge or anything. This is your project. Just take this as my official application to be your sidekick."

Sidekick? Seriously, Wyatt? Sidekicks don't get the girl, especially when the girl is the person you're a sidekick to.

"That is a compelling argument . . ." Eleanor says, pooching her lips out and narrowing her eyes as she strokes her chin like she has a goatee. "Okay. Deal."

She sticks her hand out toward me for a handshake. The second I accept it I have to tighten every muscle in my body for fear of turning to jelly under her touch.

Blessedly, by the grace of God, I make it through the handshake without totally losing it. I slide both my hands under my thighs to keep from trying to touch her again. Have to recover.

"So," Eleanor says, grabbing her beer bottle and looking at me with a raised eyebrow. "When do we start?"

5

ELEANOR

I should have known he'd be late. Hell, I've been waiting for twenty minutes already. I'm this close to accepting he's blown me off completely.

I thrum my fingers against the steering wheel and stare at the little record shop. It's a dingy, old place. Lots of character. All the signage is clearly made by hand and hasn't been updated in god knows how long. It could all use a fresh coat of paint.

When I parked in front of the store, I was suddenly very grateful that Luke offered his help. This is the type of place you have to know what you're doing to enter without looking like a rube.

Now, though, I've been here so long I'm convinced the owner is going to call the cops on me for loitering.

I look at my phone one more time to check the clock. Twenty-*one* minutes late. And not even a damn text message to apologize or to let me know he's backing out.

I should have known he'd be like this. He snowed me at the concert last night and really made me feel like the only woman in the world. Of course, that was after he had a flirty back-and forth with the bartender. I couldn't hear what they were saying, but the way she was leaning over the bar told me everything I needed to know.

He's used to the attention of women. And now I've played right into his hand, let him know I wouldn't mind spending more time with him.

I've been played for a fool.

Part of me wants to U-turn out of the parking lot and head back home. But the drive out here was long, especially in Austin traffic. Traffic in every city blows, but at least in Chicago I understood the driving culture. Here, I feel like I'm getting honked at for every little thing. Just existing on the freeway seems to be an affront to other drivers.

I've come this far. Curmudgeon be damned, I'm not leaving empty-handed.

I get out of the car and head into the shop. I notice the scent of the store first: aging paper and comforting must. The shop is almost completely silent except for the crackling of vinyl playing through the speakers. There are other people here but they're all quiet. The bright orange and yellow walls—which should be warm and welcoming—seem more cautionary, warning me that I don't belong.

Luke was right about this place. It's a collector's haven. Which means everyone here is dower and serious as they sort through the records, looking for their find of the day.

I pull my purse over my shoulder, the weight of my camera reminding me of my plight. At the end of the long room of records is the checkout counter. It's a foot off the ground which makes the man behind the counter look more like a judge than a cashier, the keeper of all the collectible records lining the walls behind him.

This must be Kenny Zapeta. He's an older guy with errant hairs poking out of his ears and a grouper-like frown on his lips.

Yeah, Luke wasn't lying. He's intimidating, to say the least.

I approach the counter, ignoring the stares of the patrons as I go. They can smell I'm an outsider. Sharks ready to go in for the kill.

When I arrive in front of the counter, Kenny doesn't look up from the newspaper he's reading.

"Excuse me?" I say, much softer than I mean to.

Kenny doesn't move. He must not have heard me.

"Excuse me?" I say again. "Mr. Zapeta?"

"Huh?!" He rips the paper down from in front of his face and leans over the counter to lord over me. "What do you want?"

I should have picked out a few records as a cover. Then as he was checking me out, I could have subtly asked my questions. "Um . . . I'm sorry to bother you, but—"

"What do you want, Miss?" he asks again. More insistent. More annoyed.

I reach into my bag, my hand gripping onto the picture. "You used to own The Lone Star. Correct?"

"Who wants to know?"

I want to know! Obviously, I want to know or else I wouldn't be asking. I decide to plod ahead though I feel my cheeks burning with the heat of a billion suns. "I'm interested because—"

Before I can place the picture on the counter, Kenny swings a hand in my direction. "Bah. If you're not going to buy anything, leave me alone."

I wish I wasn't so sensitive, but the way he's treating me makes me want to cry. This situation is already embarrassing enough without getting tears involved. "I'm sorry, I'm not trying to bother you, but—"

"Look, kid," he begins with an annoyed sneer.

Thankfully, he doesn't get a chance to finish that sentence because a familiar voice cries out from the front door. "Kenny!"

I turn on my heels to see Luke waltzing into the record shop, and *holy cow* he looks just as put together as he did the other night but in a completely different way. Instead of slick music promoter, today he's giving hipster cowboy. White t-shirt overlaid with an open navy button down, blue jeans, whiskey-colored cowboy boots—and to top off the whole look—a *fucking hat*. Broad-brimmed and black.

I didn't know I had a cowboy fantasy until this very moment.

"Wyatt," Kenny barks. There's still an edge in his voice but it's a helluva lot more affectionate than the way he spoke to me. "To what do I owe the pleasure?"

Luke removes his hat as he walks down the long record shop, revealing his golden hair. His boots clack against the floor with every step. I lean against the counter in an effort not to topple over. He smiles. "I see you've already met my friend, Eleanor!" he says with a gesture in my direction. His blue eyes flick to me for a second, long enough for me to read the apology in his eyes.

"I, uh . . . this is your friend?" Kenny asks.

Luke puts his hand on my shoulder and turns me back toward the counter so we both face the overlord of the record shop. I can't ignore the feeling that zips down my spine at his touch. "Yeah, you haven't met Eleanor yet? She's a big deal."

I scoff. "Luke . . ."

"What? You are!" he says with a glimmering smile.

Don't know where he got that idea. Further proof I need to keep my wits about me around Luke Wyatt. He's too charming for his own good.

"Where you from?" Kenny asks me.

"Chicago," I answer, though my voice gives out on the second syllable.

Kenny nods curtly. "Yeah, thought so."

"Hope you weren't giving her too much of a hard time, Kenny."

Kenny grunts. "I give everyone a hard time."

Luke laughs and I force myself to laugh too. He goes on, "We wanted to come ask you a couple questions about the good ol' days."

Kenny cracks a smile. I didn't know the man was capable of smiling. "Oh yeah? What do you want to know?"

Luke glances in my direction. "Well, Eleanor is new in town. She's working at the Reeder Music Library."

Kenny appraises me for a moment, and the tension in his forehead softens. "Is that right?"

Though the man still scares the bejeezus out of me, I manage to smile back. "That's right."

"What kind of work?" Kenny asks.

I blink at him, letting the silence linger long enough that Luke has to jab me in the side with his elbow. "I'm a photo archivist!" I blurt.

"Oh. That's nifty," Kenny says, crossing his arms over his chest.

"That's what I said," Luke says. "Anyway, she and I crossed paths, and she had some questions about a piece in the collection that I can't answer, and you know if I can't answer it that means it's a real mystery."

Kenny nods once. "True."

"Why don't you show him the photo, Nor?" Luke asks.

Nor...? He's calling me by a nickname now? People usually opt for El or Ellie. Nor is a new one. And to be honest, I kind of like it.

I realize I haven't let go of the picture in my bag this whole time. I slide it out of its compartment and place it on the high countertop before Kenny. He whips a pair of glasses out from the front pocket of his shirt and slides them on, magnifying his otherwise beady eyes.

I glance at Luke. He ticks his chin toward me. *Go on.*

I clear my throat. "We don't have any information other than the location and the date. I'm assuming from the photo she's a musician, but there aren't any matching images in the museum's database and . . ."

"Mmm," Kenny cuts me off with a low grunt. "Can't help you."

I'm not the only one who is stunned. Luke also seems to be taken aback, brow furrowing and lips dropping down. "What? *You* can't help? Kenny, The Lone Star was yours!"

"Not then it wasn't," Kenny says without explanation, removing his glasses. He points the folded spectacles at the photo. "That year it wasn't mine."

"What's that supposed to mean?" Luke says, a smile remaining on his face despite an edge of annoyance in his voice.

Kenny clears his throat. "Someone else was looking after it. I had to take a break to, uh, deal with the bottle, if you know what I mean."

I raise my eyebrows. Well, that was an unexpected admission from a crotchety old guy.

"Been sober for almost three decades now if you can believe it," he says with a soft smile.

"That's amazing," I say without considering whether I should speak or not. "Congratulations."

The older man gives me a soft nod. "Thank you."

I might not have any new information on the photo, but I've endeared myself to the record shop overlord and I'll call that a win.

"So, someone was babysitting it for you, Ken?" Luke asks.

"Yup."

Both Luke and I stare at Kenny, waiting for more of an explanation. When we don't get it, Luke presses, "*Who?*"

"Bobby."

Seems to me Kenny is trying to ignore the question, but Luke immediately blurts, "Sutton?"

"Yup."

Jeez, this guy really *does* know everything about everything around here. Music-wise, that is.

"I had no idea he was running The Lone Star," Luke says.

Kenny lets out a loud guffaw. "Yeah, and we'd like to keep it that way. Bobby might be a master of the sax, but he can't run a business for shit. Anyway, he had it that year."

"Well, thanks Kenny, you've been a great help." Luke swipes the photo off the counter and hands it over to me.

With utmost care, I put it right back where it's been living in my bag so there's no possible way for it to crease.

"You're a liar, kid," Kenny says. "Now buy something or get out."

This time, when he says it, there's a joking lilt to his voice. I can't help but smile.

"On it, boss," Luke says and puts his hat back on. I have to suppress a swoon. "Ready, Nor?"

I give him a small nod. "Thanks again," I say to Kenny before stepping off.

"Yeah, yeah. Any time," he mutters. And I think he means it, which is sweet and unexpected.

I follow Luke through the main lane of the record shop; when we're only a few feet from the door, Kenny calls out, "And Wyatt?"

Luke turns his head and lifts his chin toward Kenny in question.

"Make sure you be a gentleman to your *friend*, huh?" Kenny says—a knowing look in his eye.

My cheeks heat up.

"Have I ever been anything but?" Luke replies with an easy smile.

I duck out of the store before anyone can see me blush.

6

LUKE

Eleanor rushes out of the store, and I follow quick at her heels. "Well, that didn't go the way I thought it would," I say, once I'm in step with her.

She throws me a smile, then looks away, her curls falling over her face.

"I'm sorry I was late," I offer.

"It's okay."

"I had to deal with some business. Had a meeting, it ran over, anyway, that's no excuse," I say. I hate when I can't follow through on my commitments. My line of work has my schedule doing gymnastics most of the time. Being late is a cardinal sin in my mind, something my father pounded into my brain when he was alive. A man sticks to his obligations, even if they're as small as meeting up with a woman at a record store to ask questions about a photo.

Especially when that woman is as intriguing as Eleanor.

"It happens," she says without fanfare.

She's making the whole conversation thing a little difficult right now. No problem. I'll manage. "I hope he didn't give you too hard of a time," I say. "He's rough around the edges but—"

We stop in front of a car which I realize is hers when she starts shoveling through her bag for her keys. "It wasn't too bad, but I'm glad you showed up when you did."

I gnaw on my lower lip for a moment. "You busy right now?"

Eleanor stops searching and finally looks up at me. "Why?"

"I owe you," I say. "For being late."

She smiles, eyes rolling upward. "No, Luke, really, it's fine. You helped me out with Kenny. You did your part of the deal, so—"

"No, no, no. Kenny made me promise I'd be a gentleman, and I am nothing but," I say. "Let me buy you lunch."

Eleanor's eyes widen through her glasses.

"For the trouble," I clarify, though if she didn't mind it being a pass, I'd let it be one. "Besides, I know the best taco joints in the city and if you're going to be living in Austin, you need to know the right spots for tacos."

Eleanor glances at her car, then back at me. She smiles. "Okay, fine. I'll allow it."

* * *

Eleanor and I sit across from one another at a picnic table, narrowly shaded by an umbrella emblazoned with the Coca-Cola logo. The smell of sizzling meat wafts through the air and is making me salivate.

"Best tacos in Austin are served in a dusty parking lot, huh?"

I glance around the parking lot. "What's wrong with the parking lot?"

Her lips curl up and she shrugs. "I don't know, I guess I never would have come here on my own."

"Well, you're going to love it, I promise," I say before swigging a sip of my Topo Chico.

Eleanor triangulates her fingers on the tabletop. "So, Bobby Sutton . . ."

"Yeah?" I say.

"Who's that?"

I take off my hat and place it on the table, running my fingers through my sweaty hair. Summer in Austin doesn't mean I can't look put together. I'm built for this kind of weather. "He's a jazz musician. One of the best in the city and has been for I don't even know how long."

"And he owned The Lone Star?"

"He *ran* it," I correct. "But even I didn't know that until I heard it from Kenny."

She looks off at the line of patrons forming in front of the truck service window. "So, you really do know a lot about this city, huh?"

I smirk. "The music scene at least. Were you questioning that?"

Eleanor shakes her head. "No, I just didn't know exactly what I was getting into with you inserting yourself into my investigation."

"Okay, Nancy Drew. Didn't realize you were going full on sleuth mode here . . ."

Eleanor takes her cup of horchata and sips it, a sneaking smile on her lips.

My mind lingers on that word—"inserting." "Look, I'm sorry if I've forced myself into this, I was just trying to help."

"I'm just giving you a hard time," she replies. "I appreciate it. Seriously."

Our eyes meet for a moment and my heartbeat quickens.

"But I can't help but wonder why you're so interested in helping a stranger figure out some details about a photo that has nothing to do with you," Eleanor says with a shrug of one shoulder.

"The photo has nothing to do with you either," I remark.

"But it's my job to figure out these kinds of things. In fact, this meal would have been a tax write-off because of that if you'd have let me pay," she says.

I laugh. She's starting to loosen up just a bit and her humor is devastatingly witty. I'm not used to that. "Wouldn't have been very gentlemanly of me," I say, raising my eyebrows.

"Ugh." She waves her hand to me, playfully frustrated.

"And besides, you've got it all wrong, Eleanor," I go on. "You're not a stranger. You're a friend."

Eleanor frowns. "We barely know each other."

"Well, yeah, maybe in Chicago knowing someone as long as we've known each other would still be considered stranger territory. But you're going to have to get used to the way things work around here," I explain.

She inclines her chin. "Southern hospitality, hm?"

"Exactly. Around here, you're a friend until you're not. So don't start being an asshole."

Eleanor laughs, her bare shoulders rising. She's wearing a loose yellow top with spaghetti straps that gives me a beautiful view of her collarbone. Somehow, she's managed to avoid the sun enough to keep her complexion cool and untanned. Not sure that will last for long, though. "No promises, Luke."

I lean on my elbow, slide my thumb under my lip, and let my eyes fall to the wooden slats of the table. It's cliché to say you like the way a woman says your name, but it's a cliché for a reason because I can't ignore how nice it sounds when she says it. "Anyway, like I said, I know a lot about the scene around here. Not just because it's my job, but I've grown up around it. I used to come into town and sneak into venues with my older sister because I was underage and . . . the music around here was my life. So, when I come across something I don't know much about, well, I can't help but be interested in finding out the truth. You know?"

Eleanor regards me for a moment with her brown eyes that flare a bit brighter in the sunlight than they did the other night. "Yeah, I get it."

"If you don't want my help," I say, raising my hands in surrender, "then we can have our lunch and I'll leave you alone. Never going to force something on someone, especially not the pleasure of my company."

She giggles. "You certainly think highly of your company."

"I'm a damned delight, Eleanor."

"And humble too."

"Very."

She laughs harder and I can't help but grin that I've made her smile.

"But if you think my expertise might be valuable, I'm offering myself to you," I say and find myself falling silent when I realize just how intimate that sounds.

She spins her cup of horchata slowly. Is she nervous? Do I make her nervous the way she makes *me* nervous? The only difference between the two of us in that regard is that I keep throwing shit out, trying to see what sticks while she remains quiet and poised. Almost unreadable. Then she says, "Okay, well, what would you suggest our next step be?"

I like the sound of that. *Our* next step. I'm not out of the race yet. "We gotta talk to Bobby Sutton obviously."

"I take it you know him from the way you talk about him?"

"Know him. Sure. But I know a lot of people."

She frowns.

"Knowing people is different than knowing how to catch people. However, you're in luck. I know how to catch Bobby Sutton."

"Are we laying a trap or trying to get information?"

I place my forearms on the table and lean closer to Eleanor. "Aren't they kind of one in the same, Nancy Drew?"

She blushes along her cheekbones. Gradually it spreads down her face. "Okay, fine. We have to catch him. And how do we do that?"

"Well, he plays sax in the house band at Franklin's every Thursday night. We can go this week." I grab my Topo Chico and take a swig.

"Like a date?"

I nearly spit the carbonated water out. It jabs up in the back of my throat, threatens to spill out my nose. I swallow the water down to the best of my ability, grabbing the edge of the table as I do so. The burn remains at the front of my face. "Uh, what?"

"Just checking that you don't have some ulterior motive for helping me," Eleanor says calmly.

Well, if my reaction was any indication, I'm probably not selling that I'm not exclusively enjoying her company for the history lesson. "Not a date. Not what I meant."

"Okay. Good."

Damn, okay, that settles that. She's not feeling it. And that's fine. To be expected honestly. She's all smart girl and all she sees probably is pretty boy. I'm sure she'd do better with a professor or lawyer or something. I will eliminate this crush as expediently as I can. If I can. "We're just going for research. Friends. You know. Like today."

"Like today. Right. That's why you paid for my meal," she says. Is that a smirk on her lips?

"I am indiscriminate with my kindness, Eleanor," I say. "But if you have such a problem with it, you can buy drinks Thursday."

She tilts her head to the side. "Fine. It's a deal."

From the truck, a woman calls out, "Order 58!"

I scramble for the receipt in my pocket, already swinging my legs out from under the picnic table. I confirm the number and get to my feet, grabbing my hat and plopping it on as I go. Can't risk a burn in the twenty-foot walk from the table to the truck.

When I get to the window, I show the lady my receipt. As she slides the tray toward me, she asks, "You want verde with that?"

"If you don't mind," I say with a small nod.

"Give me a second." She steps out of sight, and I'm left alone with the tray.

I turn back toward the table to give Eleanor a look when she's hopefully not looking. Just because nothing's going to happen doesn't mean I can't look.

However, I should have known better. Because she's not just looking at me, she's got the lens of her camera trained on me. Who knows how many pictures she's taken already?

I try to smile at the lens but find it impossible to make eye contact with it, dropping my head forward slightly and focusing on a stripe of white on the black asphalt.

When I return with the tray, Eleanor flips her camera around to show me the photo in the viewfinder. "I'm sorry," she says sheepishly. "I couldn't resist."

Sure enough, she caught me right when I was looking back at her, the brim of my hat dipped down, eyes cutting through the space between us like daggers. My throat constricts a bit. To see myself through someone else's eyes is strange. Not sure I like it. "Photographer's gotta take her photos, right?" I say, then shove the tray between us.

Eleanor flips the camera back toward her and looks at the screen. A small smile creeps across her face.

My pulse begins to rise.

"I like it. Quintessential Austin. Maybe?" she says with a hopeful gleam in her eye.

I chuckle. "You're getting it, Nor. Now come on. Eat while it's hot."

7

ELEANOR

When Luke parks, I'm not sure we're in the right place. It's a relatively quiet street. Mostly warehouses, or warehouses converted into luxury apartments. Not nearly as lively as 6th Street. Luke told me Franklin's was a little out of the way, but this seems a little too out of the way.

"Uh. Are you sure we're in the right place?" I ask, peering out the window.

Luke laughs. "I've been to Franklin's a million times. You think I don't know where it is?"

"It's just so quiet," I say.

He unbuckles his seatbelt, pushes his door open, and sticks one long leg outside. "It's Austin's music scene's worst kept secret."

I sit in the car a few moments longer and scan the street. "Seems like a pretty well-kept secret to me," I mumble to myself.

Luke is still a stranger to me. And while he's been nothing but kind, what if I'm making a mistake trusting him? I haven't gotten a single bad vibe from him. Not even on the drive over here. But now my anxiety is reeling. I shouldn't have let him pick me up, shouldn't have let him drive me in his car, shouldn't—

Down the street, I spy a door opening and orange light pouring out onto the street. A couple stumbles out, giggling and grabbing for each other's hands, totally intoxicated by the night they've had.

I let out a taut sigh. Alright, maybe I was overreacting.

My door opens and Luke drops his hand down for me. Okay, *gentleman*. I look up at him as I take his hand, mumbling a soft, "Thank you."

He helps me to stand, and closes the door of his slick black Audi behind me before leading me onto the sidewalk and toward the building the couple just emerged from. "This way."

When we arrive at the door, I realize it *is* indeed marked with a small sign over the door, albeit it's quite faded. The pale letters in Franklin's are now ghosts of their former selves, specifically the "L" which is almost invisible.

Continuing his streak as gentleman, Luke opens the door for me. "After you."

We have our IDs checked by the bouncer and then descend a long, warmly lit staircase side by side. On the walls are pictures upon pictures of musicians from years past. I admire them as we go.

"I bet you'd like these for your collection," Luke says with a cheeky smile.

I smile in kind. "You read my mind."

The lower we go, the louder the music gets. The plangent croon of a trumpet solo, soft rapping of the drums, and a bleating piano. I feel like I'm back at the Green Mill where I'd spent many a night in Chicago.

By the time we arrive in the doorway of the venue, the song is peeling into its last notes and people are already clapping. Though no one is smoking, I can't help but feel the room is smoky, a haze looming over everyone. The small stage is across the room, crowded with musicians of all ages, a full jazz band. Cabaret tables litter the space, most of them full of lovers and friends. Across the ceiling are delicate chandeliers, and along the rightmost wall is a bar with mirrors arching behind the bartenders and rows and rows of liquor bottles.

"Tables look full. Should we grab a seat at the bar?" Luke asks me.

I nod. "Sounds good." That feels a little less intimate too. That way, we aren't leaned over a tiny little table. Better for my heart. Since our lunch the other day, I haven't forgotten how he nearly choked on his mineral water because I dared to ask if he was asking me on a date. That made it very clear that he sees me firmly as a friend, just the way he'd described me to Kenny.

That's fine with me. It's better if we remain colleagues through this process anyway.

We wind through the little tables and find two bar seats beside one another.

Luke pulls the chair out for me; this man never quits with the gentility, does he? Before I can utter a thank you, he mutters, "You look really nice tonight, Eleanor."

My heart lunges into the back of my mouth. "Really nice" isn't a flirtatious choice of words, but knowing he's even taken a moment to look me over and take in my outfit means a lot considering how I fretted over it before he picked me up.

In the days leading up to today, I studied Pinterest boards of Austin street style and even had Jolene direct me to some boutiques that might give me a fighting chance at fitting in.

Of course, that meant I blew my budget for the month on this airy, boho floral number.

"Thank you," I say as I settle into my seat, holding back a, "So do you," for fear my voice might pitch a little too high and I'll sound silly. But it's true, he looks nice. Of course he does. That seems to be Luke Wyatt's prerogative at all times. Tonight, he's opted for a rust-colored jacket over a black dress shirt. I don't think I've ever been on a date with a guy who is wearing a suit coat.

Not that this is a date.

"What would you like to drink?" Luke asks.

"Gin and tonic," I say.

He grins. "Why am I not surprised?"

"What's that supposed to mean?"

Luke holds up his hands. He's got broad palms. Hard to ignore the idea of how they'd feel sliding around my back. "Just feels very Chicago of you."

I scoff. "You've never been to Chicago, have you?"

"Once."

"It shows."

He laughs, all his teeth visible. I laugh too.

"Okay, gin and tonic, got it." He lifts his gaze toward one of the bartenders.

I hurriedly reach into my bag for my wallet. "Don't pull a fast one. This is on me."

"Oh, of course, how could I forget?" Luke smirks.

I ignore the pretty way his lips contort and whip out my cardholder.

"Just hope you brought cash . . ." he trails off.

I furrow my brow. "What?"

Luke directs a finger to a sign hanging behind the bar. Sure enough, in red, vintage-looking font, the words, "Cash Only" are written.

My jaw falls. "I . . . who carries cash anymore?"

He chuckles and pulls out his wallet. "You're in luck. I do."

I drop my wallet back in my bag. "You hustled me."

"See, most people would say hustling is trying to take money away from you, not the other way around," Luke says, leaning in just close enough that his breath brushes up against my ear.

He smells amazing. I don't know much about the notes of certain types of colognes, but it smells expensive and leathery.

However, he doesn't linger long. The bartender comes over and takes Luke's order. I watch him hand over some crisp bills in payment.

Across the room, the band begins their next song. I glance at the group and smile to myself. "You think I could take some pictures?" I ask Luke.

"Don't see why not," he replies.

I take my camera out of my bag and begin to adjust the settings to the lighting of the room.

"You take that thing with you everywhere, huh?"

I push my eye as close as it will go to the viewfinder what with my glasses in the way, squinting, cheek tensing. "Why wouldn't I?" As I try to find my focal point, I land on a tall and lanky Black man with graying facial hair and gaunt cheeks who licks the reed of his saxophone in preparation to play. His eyes are shaded by a porkpie hat. I jerk my camera down. "Is that him?"

Luke follows my gaze. "Sutton? Yep. That's him. Looks like he's getting ready to blow the house down."

Bobby Sutton plays a few notes on his tenor saxophone, almost like an unfamiliar, yet welcomed caress.

I pull my camera back up and snap a few shots of the band with Bobby as the focal point. Then I drop my camera down for a few moments to take in the scene.

"Drink?"

I jolt my attention over to Luke who holding my gin and tonic. "Oh, yes. Sorry."

He frowns as I take the drink from him. "For what?"

"I always do this," I say, lifting my camera up for emphasis and then placing it carefully on the bar. "I've been told I'm not very good company, what with the camera and all."

"You don't need to apologize on my account," Luke says.

Perhaps it's because I've been inundated with accents ever since I arrived in Austin, but Luke's is just starting to settle over me. It's very slight, but it's there, the way his vowels scoop into the back of his mouth. A drawl, they might call it.

Very sexy.

"In fact, I like watching you. Makes me reconsider what I'm looking at, you know? I'd love to see the world the way you see it," Luke goes on.

I'd like to ignore how that comment makes my heart flutter. I spent a good deal of my early twenties learning that people *didn't* want to see the world the way I saw it. Rejection after rejection for shows and publications and competitions, over and over. "I can't help but feel you probably have better ways to spend a night out rather than waiting to talk to a jazz musician with me," I say before swigging my drink. Gotta get some of this liquid courage pumping ASAP.

"You seem pretty intent on me *not* enjoying time spent with you, Eleanor," Luke says. "Is that a Chicago thing too?"

"No, I just . . ." I roll my eyes and sigh. Fine. I'll just say it. "Luke, you're a catch. And to be on a not date with a woman on a Thursday night feels like it might be a waste of your time."

Luke's eyebrows lift and he laughs to himself, almost sadly. He sips his whiskey neat and leans back on the bar, looking out at the band. His profile is beautiful and would make for a great photograph if we weren't mid-conversation. The hard edge of his jaw, a straight, definitive nose . . .

"I do my best to be honest," he says, not drawing his eyes away from the band. "And honestly, Eleanor, I wouldn't be here if I didn't want to be." He pulls his chin over his shoulder to look at me. "And I'd appreciate it if you took my word for it this time."

I nibble on my lower lip and nod. "Okay. Sorry."

His seriousness splits with a signature smile. "And stop saying sorry."

I huff, shoulders falling. "I'm a disgrace to feminism."

Luke laughs, extends his arm out along the bar behind me. Almost like he's embracing me, but not really. The ghost of an embrace. "You're mean to yourself. For no good reason."

Though the music is calling my attention, the tenor sax of Bobby Sutton approaching a fever pitch, I am trapped by Luke's eyes. We are only a few inches away from one another. Something so intimate about a darkened bar, smoky liquor, and jazz.

If this was a date, this would probably be an appropriate moment for a chaste kiss or a subtle touch. Instead, we maintain our respectful distance and merely look.

Except there's nothing *mere* about the look he's giving me. Nothing at all.

The moment is interrupted as an older woman who was heading toward the door stops and leans into the space between us. "You two are so cute together," she says, clasping a hand to her chest.

I sit up stock straight, at a loss for words.

The man on her arm tries to pull her away. "Come on, Marlene."

Luke hums and gives her a nod of courtesy. "Thank you, ma'am."

Her eyes find mine, smile dimpling her cheeks. "You keep an eye on that one. When your back is turned someone might swoop in and steal him away."

"Not while I'm around," I say, getting a little push of inspiration.

The woman, Marlene, laughs and lets her husband drag her toward the door. I watch them go, both of them on a cloud of intoxication and laughter. They seem like the type who've known each other a long, long while.

I crave something like that.

Luke leans in toward my ear again. "I think I'd be more worried someone might swoop in and steal you away, Eleanor."

I look up at him. His plush lips are only an inch away.

A kiss would change everything.

Instead, I box him on the shoulder playfully, sending him back into his own air space. "Don't be ridiculous."

Luke laughs and we settle back into a comfortable silence as the music swells around us, taking complete control of our minds and bodies.

And I can't help but feel that I'm right where I belong. Even if it's just for tonight.

8

LUKE

If this was a date, I'd have Eleanor hold my hand as I lead her through the crowds, past the stage, and through the "Performers Only" door. That way I couldn't lose her, and she wouldn't be lost in the crowd.

But despite the observations of well-meaning older folks, this isn't a date, and we aren't cute together. We're friends. Colleagues maybe. On a mission. She's made that abundantly clear.

"Are you sure we're allowed back here?" she asks.

I glance back at her with a smirk. "We would have been thrown out already if we weren't."

Like the rest of Franklin's, the backstage area hasn't been updated since the place opened. Which means that instead of any sort of fancy greenroom, all that's back here is a lounge area with rickety old couches, most likely salvaged from a back alley somewhere, and a few private areas cordoned off with curtains.

The air is laced with the smell of ancient cigarette smoke and dank carpets that needed to be replaced years ago. However, it's a good smell, like gasoline, one you can't get enough of even though it should be unpleasant.

I go straight to the back where Bobby's room is. Bobby is a stalwart favorite here at Franklin's, all across Austin even, and as such, gets the star treatment. At least when it comes to being a local musician.

Stopping in front of the curtain, I let Eleanor catch up to my side.

She looks up at me through the lenses of her wire framed glasses, brown eyes wide and nervous. No wonder she looks at the world through a camera or sticks herself into the depths of the Reeder Music Library. Her default seems to be skittish. Until she gets comfortable or has one of those bursts of wit.

That's why she needs me around for this project. We complement each other. Charisma paired with diligence.

Not to mention I have my own reasons for being interested.

"Ready?" I ask.

Eleanor runs her fingers through her curls, pushing them out of her face. One of them sprigs onto her forehead, but she doesn't seem to notice. "Do I look okay?" she asks.

"You trying to be a groupie or something?" I ask.

Her lips and nose squinch together. "I'm trying to make a good impression," she hisses.

I touch her shoulder, her bare shoulder. The blood running through my palm pulses. "It'll be great. I'll do the talking, alright? All you need to do is show him the picture and . . ." *Look pretty.* "Be yourself."

Eleanor smiles gratefully and I take that as my permission to rap my hand against the curtain. "Bobby!" I call out. "You've got some fans out here!"

"Is that Wyatt?" Bobby cries back in response. "Come on in!"

I pull the curtain back and usher Eleanor through before stepping in after her and letting the curtain flutter shut behind us.

Bobby is sitting up against the wall in a folding chair, running a polishing cloth across his tenor saxophone. Though he's getting up there in years, he has the smile of a hopeful teenager and the brightness in his eyes to match. And when his fingers bounce across the keys so spry and agile, you'd think the man was meant to be immortal. "Well, well, well, you didn't tell me that I had such pretty fans, Luke."

Eleanor laughs, unable to quell her flush. I'm glad she takes it as a compliment rather than an affront to her intelligence.

"Bobby, this is my friend Eleanor," I say with a gesture in her direction.

Bobby's eyes flick to me for just a moment. "Friend, huh?"

"Colleague better for you?" I offer.

The older man laughs, hard enough for his head to fall back and his chest to wheeze. He rubs his free hand against his thigh and then extends his hand to Eleanor. "Name's Bobby. You from around here, Eleanor?"

"Chicago," she says as they shake.

"Oh, Chicago. I can hear it in your voice," he says. "How'd we measure up to what you got up there?"

Eleanor shakes her head. "Oh, wonderful. Better than."

"Better!" He points one of his fingers at her. "I won't tell Mayor Daley you said that."

She laughs. "Good thing he hasn't been mayor in over a decade, then."

"Ah, I'll have to brush up on those Windy City politics," he says with a grimace, returning to polishing his sax.

"Surprised to see you out there, Wyatt. Been a while since you've been able to pop in."

I slide my hands into the pockets of my pants. "Been busy with work."

"Sure, sure," Bobby says. He pauses in his work for a moment. "How's your ma doin'?"

I gulp. I should have predicted he'd be wanting to check in about life stuff. I wouldn't mind answering his questions if Eleanor wasn't here. But we're still relative strangers. "She's good."

"You're visiting her, I hope?"

"As much as I can," I reply.

Bobby tsks and puts some elbow grease into buffing his instrument. "You know, your old man was gone way too soon. Way too soon."

Eleanor looks over at me, but I ignore her gaze. I don't want to see the question in her eyes, or worse, the pity.

"Yeah, we miss him," I say with a finality I hope gets the point across I don't want to talk about it. "Listen, Bobby, Eleanor and I are on a bit of a mission, and we were hoping we could get your help with it."

He pauses again and places the saxophone between his legs, leaning on it. "A mission? Well, I would never come between a man and woman on a mission. Shoot."

I give Eleanor a look and though her expression is still resonating with the information she's just learned, she catches on fast. She reaches into her bag and produces the photograph. "I work at the Reeder Music Library as a photo archivist, and I came across this photo a couple weeks ago. Trying to get more information on it for our database."

"And Wyatt couldn't help you? He's basically an encyclopedia when it comes to this sort of thing."

I chuckle and lean on the wall, crossing my arms over my chest. "For once, I've fallen short."

"For once," Bobby mutters and laughs to himself as he takes the photo and appraises it, looking down his nose and narrowing his eyes. "'93, huh? That's when I was taking care of The Lone Star for—"

"That's what Kenny told us when I asked him about it," Luke says.

"We'd like to figure out who the woman in the picture is. You know, what's her legacy? Maybe even get into contact with her," Eleanor says, excitement growing. "I don't know. There's just something about it that makes me want to know more."

Bobby is quiet as he scans the photo. Then, his dark brown eyes rise to meet mine. His expression is . . . confounding. Eyes focused in on me as if he's studying a painting, lips parted just enough to make me wonder if he's about to say something that will ruin everything.

My stomach twists. I'm terrified he's about to blow this whole thing for me. Cut the mystery short and, consequently, my time with Eleanor.

"Do you know who she is?" Eleanor asks, breaking the silence.

Bobby snaps away from me, his friendly smile replacing that gut-churning expression. "I've been around a long while, Eleanor. She looks familiar, sure, but do I know who she is?" He shrugs. "Would take a miracle to unlock that part of my memory. Hell, that was almost thirty years ago."

He hands the photo back to her. Though it's a minute change, I can tell the disappointment is causing her to collapse in on herself. "Oh."

"You think she might have performed at The Lone Star back then, though? She's got a guitar," I say, hopping to attention again.

Bobby nods. "It's possible. But you know how many people walk down 6th Street carrying guitars that have no business carrying them?"

"True," I say. I've been handed more demos than I know what to do with while working a job.

"There must be a schedule somewhere, right?" Eleanor offers. "A ledger that lists who might have performed there? I mean, it's not a small venue by any means. There must have been a way to record things."

Bobby's lips dip down in consideration. "You're not wrong. I still have all the paperwork from that time."

Both Eleanor and I leap with excitement.

"You do?" Eleanor says with a hopeful gasp.

"Hold your horses, missy," Bobby says, holding up his hand. "Like I said, thirty years is a long time. I've got thirty years of shit up in the attic. Much to my wife's chagrin. I never throw anything away, that's a fact. But I never . . ." He slides his fingers across some of the keys on his saxophone. "Never really organize it either."

"Oh, come on, Bobby," I say. "You know how important it is to keep traditions alive around here, right?"

"I do, I do," he says.

"Then, who knows what kind of story could be missing here," I say with a gesture toward the picture in Eleanor's hand.

Again, Bobby looks at me. This time, his gaze is hardened. "Have you ever thought that sometimes the only reason we love stories is because we lose some of them?"

63

I've never dealt with an unaffable Bobby. This is the first time I feel myself teetering into a territory I don't want to travel with him.

"You're right. Stories matter because our histories are too rich to catalogue everything," Eleanor swoops in. "But perhaps some stories deserve to be discovered too. Don't they?"

Bobby looks at Eleanor with a lot more softness than he does me. Which I appreciate. I'd hate for her to be pushed away from the edge in his eyes. "They do. You're not wrong there. I can appreciate that."

Eleanor looks to me, almost for permission to continue. I tick my chin in her direction. *Go on.*

"The history of music here in Austin is vast and incredible. I mean, I've been here a little over two weeks and I already feel overwhelmed by its richness. I understand it's difficult to conceptualize sorting through your history in order to provide me with more context. But I'm just a baby when it comes to all of this, you know?"

I watch her as she speaks, her conviction elegant and poised, yet not at all forceful. She's earnest. Moreso than me.

"I know it's a big ask for a picture that might mean nothing. I mean, for all we know, this could just be a tourist or a relative nobody. But she has a story too, right? We all do."

Bobby's nodding along with what she's saying.

"I'd even offer to organize your attic for you if it would give me an opportunity to at least see if we can figure out who this woman is," she says.

Bobby's head droops forward as he shakes it. "Now, that's the most ridiculous thing I ever heard."

Eleanor's face falls.

I hold my tongue, unsure what to say.

"No, no, not going to have a young woman organize my attic just to find . . ." He sighs heavily. "I'll take a look tomorrow and you two can come by for dinner. Mandy will cook. We can see what we come up with, alright?"

The relief is so great that Eleanor smiles into a gasp. "Really?"

Bobby's eyes flutter shut, and he smiles. "You have my word."

"Oh, thank you. Thank you so much," she says, clutching the picture to her chest.

"Don't thank me yet. Who knows what I'll find up there? Might get bit by a spider and wind up dead before dinnertime," Bobby says.

We say some quick goodbyes before Eleanor and I step out of Bobby's domain. There is a buzz between us that keeps us silent until we've weaved back through the club, up the stairs, and into the Austin night air.

Eleanor takes a few steps toward the car, then stops, whipping around and letting out a hefty sigh. "Woah."

"Yeah, woah," I say.

"That was—that's something, isn't it?"

"Definitely something," I say. I can't shake the weird look Bobby gave me when he saw the photo. Almost like he saw right through me.

Eleanor pulls her bag further onto her shoulder. "Um, I'm sorry about your dad, by the way."

I wince, gritting my teeth. "S'fine."

"That must be hard."

I don't want to talk about it. My dad's sudden death a little over a year ago. Heart attack. It's not unusual for men in my family, especially when they give up the ghost of paying attention to their cholesterol. Still . . . one day you're talking to your dad about spring training over the phone, and the next you're trying to console your mother in the emergency room.

It's a mindfuck, to say the least.

"Yeah . . . it's fine," I say. *Change the subject.* "You're really passionate about this picture, huh?" I ask.

Eleanor takes a step back as if my words had that much force. "We've had this conversation, haven't we?"

"Well, yeah, but you haven't put it in the words for me like you did for Bobby. Unless that was just a very well-crafted argument, in which case you should consider becoming a lawyer."

"Oh, god, no, I'd be terrible at that," she says. Then, she lifts her face to the night sky and smiles. "I don't know, I think I'm just in so far at this point I need to know about her. I can't explain it, but it feels sort of like my purpose. Cosmic, maybe."

I don't have words to respond. Her beauty is ethereal and timeless. I've never been captivated by someone quite like she's captivated me.

Eleanor looks at me, a sheepish smile on her face. "I think I've had a little too much gin."

I laugh, stripping away both the uneasiness of the club and the questions I have if I'm doing what's right.

I don't say it aloud. Can't. But if Eleanor's cosmic purpose is to find the story behind this photograph, then my purpose is to get her there with the information and connections I have. To let the story unwind for her.

All in due time.

9

ELEANOR

I rub my fingers together, desperate for them to warm up. The archive gets colder throughout the day as the world outside heats up. Jolene's informed me the system controlling the temperature is set to do that, but I can't imagine it needs to be so frigid I can nearly see my breath.

Just a little bit longer . . .

Another binder, another day. I am moving through the photos at a steady rate, but I underestimated how much uncategorized material the archive had.

I zip up my fleece (yes, *a fleece* in Texas), and burrow my nose into it as I stare down at another muddy shot of Austin City Limits, so overexposed I can't tell if it's Robert Plant or Allison Krauss or both.

"Eleanor?"

I look up; Jolene is poking her head out from the center aisle. "What's up?" I ask, my voice muffled by my sweater.

She cocks a smile at me. "Are you really that cold?"

"No," I say drolly.

She laughs, tinkly like a glockenspiel. "You're so funny."

I smile, though it's hidden in my sweater. Through these two weeks, I've become quite fond of my boss. She spends a lot of time talking my ear off instead of doing *her* job. That's how I've basically heard her whole life story. I like people who overshare in the name of closeness. I've never been like that, but I'm a good listener and find those who like to expose themselves gravitate toward me for that very reason.

Makes having a job that much easier when you like who you work with.

"Anyway, there's a man asking about you at the front desk," she says.

I frown and glance up at the clock. "He's early."

"So, you *know* him?" Jolene's eyes brighten and she smiles.

"Um, yeah."

"*Um, yeah.* How can you be so calm about it?" she says, putting her hand on her hip.

I close the binder. Not going to be getting much more work done today now that Jolene has me locked in a conversation. Robert Plant/Allison Krauss will have to wait. "Because he's a friend?"

"A friend? You're letting yourself be friends with a guy who looks like that? How do you have that much self-restraint?" Jolene squeaks. "Unless you don't swing that way, in which case, that's totally fine."

I giggle. "I do swing that way. But Luke's just a friend."

"Luke?! God, even his name is sexy."

I get up from my workstation, shaking my head. "You're ridiculous."

"You're ridiculous! Guys don't just show up at your place of work asking for you if you're *friends*."

"Hate to break it to you, Jolene, but they do. He's helping me figure out the story behind that photo I found on my first day. You know, the one of the woman outside The Lone Star."

Jolene's eyes widen. "Damn, seriously?"

"Seriously," I say and fish my bag off the ground to start packing up my stuff.

She edges up to the front of my table. "But how did you meet *him*?"

"On 6th Street. Accident. We quite literally bumped into each other," I say, smiling fondly as I remember the tumble of gummies onto the ground, the excitement of that Friday night around us.

Jolene slaps her hand against her forehead. "And you're telling me you two are just friends? That's a meet cute if ever heard one."

She's not wrong. But it's already been determined. We are working on a project together. Nothing more. And that's fine. Even after last night, sharing drinks and listening to jazz. It's *fine* that we're just friends. I'm totally *fine* with it.

Okay, I'm not fine with it, my insides are mush when I think about Luke. However, I don't need that complication. I've moved to a new city, started a new job, and taken on a passion project.

Not to mention, he'd be much more interested in someone like Jolene.

"I can introduce you if you like," I say.

Jolene's head jolts back. "You're insane. If I were friends with a man like that, I'd never let my friends get a hold of him."

My insides warm at the idea Jolene considers me a friend. Southern hospitality is a very real thing. "Well, fine. Your loss I guess."

"Where are you going then?" she asks as I step away, following at my heels down the bank of binders. "For your research project."

"We're going to the house of a local musician. Bobby Sutton. Heard of him?"

Jolene snorts. "Of course I've heard of Bobby Sutton."

"Yeah, well, he ran The Lone Star at the time of the photo, and he might have some documentation to give us information on who the woman in the photo is. If she was a musician or . . ." I trail off as Jolene's smile grows. "Why are you looking at me like that?"

Jolene looks away like she's been caught doing something she wasn't supposed to. "I was just thinking that your story would be really neat to share during the next exhibition."

I frown. "The '90s exhibition? I thought that was trying to emphasize the grunge and punk scenes."

"It's about the *'90s*. Sure, they're trying to capitalize on Gen Z's new appreciation of Nirvana, but you know, they have to paint the whole picture. And besides, maybe she *was* in a grunge band and is just on the softer side," Jolene says.

I chuckle. "That would be surprising, to say the least." The woman in the photograph gives more Joni Mitchell than Kim Deal.

"I'm just saying because, I know your tenure here is supposed to be temporary, but who knows? If you're able to offer more than your contract stipulated, people upstairs might be able to find you a more permanent position here."

My stomach flips at the notion, which is surprising. When I accepted this job, it was comforting to know that I wouldn't be stuck here forever. A short tenure at a small museum in a big city, then onto the next.

However, in just the two short weeks I've been here, there's something exciting about the idea of having a reason to stay.

Maybe it's the mystery, the richness of a new and strange city. Or maybe it's the fact that I've been welcomed here. By Jolene, by Luke . . .

"Then I don't have to train someone new," Jolene adds, folding over her middle and rolling her eyes as far back as they'll go. "God, you have no idea how annoying it is to *train* someone."

I laugh. "Well, I'll do my best not to disappoint you, Jolene." I open the door to the stairwell.

"Hey, have *fun*. That's the most important thing. I mean, with a guy like *that—*"

"Bye, Jolene!" I call out over my shoulder, laughing to myself as I head up the stairs and out into the main lobby where Luke is standing against the far wall, waiting. When he hears the door open, he raises his eyes to mine and the stillness of his expression breaks with a warm smile. He kicks himself upright and strides over to meet me in the middle of the lobby.

"You're early," I say.

"Trying to make up for my previous lateness," he says.

I chuckle. "You're lucky my boss is a cool boss."

"Ah, the blonde who said she was going to get you? Yeah, she seems like the cool boss type."

My shoulders tense. Is that meant to be suggestive? Is the cool boss type somehow someone he would want rather than a lowly, temporary employee? I try to cast those thoughts aside as we emerge from the frigid museum into the Austin summer heat. This is the only moment in my day I actually *like* the heat. In only a minute or two, my body will be begging for the chill of the archive again.

Luke's car is right on the curb in the standing zone, blinkers blinking.

I grab the passenger side door, but Luke intercepts me. "Uh-uh-uh," he chides. "My job."

I step back and allow him to open the door for me, shaking my head. "I can open my own door."

"I know you can," he says, throwing me a smile over the roof of the car. "But you don't have to. That's the difference." Luke climbs into the car out of sight while I try to control my raging heartbeat.

Thank god I can blame any blushing on the beating sun overhead.

When I get into the car, Luke immediately thrusts a condensation-soaked iced coffee into my hand. "I don't know your order, so I went off vibes. Iced horchata latte."

I bug my eyes out. "That sounds . . . amazing."

"I also . . ." He reaches into the back seat and retrieves several brown pastry bags. "Have snacks if you're hungry."

I laugh in disbelief and excitement. I grab the bag that smells of cinnamon. "Mm. Coffee cake. My favorite."

Luke makes a fist and pumps it in the air. "Score."

"You really didn't have to do this," I say.

"You bet I did. We've got a long drive in rush hour traffic ahead of us," he says. "Now buckle up, princess."

Somehow the word "princess" in his accent doesn't sound at all condescending. In fact, I like it.

Buckled and ready to go, Luke pulls onto the street and begins the drive down to Bobby's.

"You think we'll get anything out of this trip?" I ask, breaking off a piece of the coffee cake loaf.

"Something has gotta turn up in all of Bobby's mess," Luke says, eyes fixed to the road through a pair of aviators.

I nibble on the coffee cake. Heaven. "Mm. Needed this."

Luke says nothing, just smiles to himself, eyes not leaving the road. It's pleased him to please me.

I like that.

"Apparently, if things go the way we'd like, they might use the photograph in the next exhibition at the library," I say.

Luke does a double take. "Seriously?"

"I mean, that hinges on us actually figuring out who the woman is and if she's even important, but the next exhibition is all about the '90s and given the date of the photo, it would fit right in."

"Next best thing to having your own photographs shown I'm sure," Luke says.

I shake my head. "I mean, I haven't even—that's not what I'm—" I decide to move on from his comment without acknowledging it in a cogent way. "My boss said it might merit a long-term position at the library. Which would be cool."

Luke grins at the road, which is dissonant given the stop and start traffic we're already in. "You're already taking a shine to Austin, huh?"

"I guess two weeks isn't enough to tell. More like a glorified vacation," I say, then break off another piece and pop it in my mouth.

"Naw, I think when you know you know," Luke says.

I let that sentence hang in the air. I've heard that sentence used often in reference to all sorts of gut feelings. Mostly love and romance. And though I've put up a mental wall between Luke and crush territory, I can't ignore the warmth in my chest.

Luke looks over at me when I don't respond. "You know?"

I can't bear to meet his gaze. "Yeah, I know what you mean."

"Austin's the best city in the world," Luke says.

"Maybe that's why I'm liking it so much. I'm seeing it through your eyes."

He leans his head back on the headrest of his seat. "And I've been told I have very nice eyes."

More warmth burning through my ribs. His flirtations are getting bolder and more consistent. Unless that's just the type of person he is. I've met people like that, where you think they're flirting with you, but when you ask someone if they would agree, they tell you, "Oh, he's just like that."

Luke is the definition of "he's just like that."

I have decided not to take it personally. I will take the way he speaks to me at face value. And he should do the same. "Yes, well, I am enjoying looking through them so far."

Luke's smile falters and his teeth land on his lower lip.

I think I've taken him off-guard.

A moment later, Luke flicks on the radio and turns it up, drowning out any thoughts of what's been said.

10

LUKE

"You weren't kidding, Bobby," I say, looking at the piles of boxes. I turn myself sideways, making myself as slight as possible to sneak through a gap between the boxes to follow the saxophonist. "This place is a labyrinth."

Bobby laughs from *somewhere* in the attic. I know I'm walking in his general direction, but the way his voice bounces off the rafters makes it impossible to locate exactly where he is unless I have eyes on him. "You should have seen it this morning. Less of a labyrinth and more of a clinch."

"Must be some amazing artifacts in here," Eleanor muses, only a few feet ahead of me. She ducks under a beam which means I'm going to have to practically crouch under it.

"Artifacts? I'm not a dinosaur yet, am I?" Bobby scoffs.

She looks back at me with a pursed smile and wide eyes. She's more relaxed than she's been the whole time I've known her, which I guess is to be expected. The more time you spend with someone, it's inevitable that you'll get more comfortable with them. But I think it has something to do with the milieu of this meeting too. The cramped quarters, the threat or promise of hidden treasures. That's Eleanor's whole gambit. She does it all day in the basement of the Reeder Music Library. Her curiosity is probably propelling her forward.

Not to mention her newfound inspiration to stick around in Austin.

I had to veil my abject excitement in the car. She's right that two weeks isn't really enough to know if you're in the right place. And two weeks isn't enough to know you've met the right person either.

So why did my whole body get lighter at the thought of her remaining in my city?

Remaining close to me?

Eleanor and I finally reach Bobby at the back of the attic. He's cleared out a little piece of space for himself back here: a roll top desk which is also filled to the brim with documents, pictures and the like, and a little wooden chair. We're surrounded by fans plugged into a precariously ancient power strip, making the stuffy attic air moderately tenable. Thank god. When we first climbed up here, I thought I might suffocate by the time the night was over.

Bobby points to a stack of boxes. "These are the boxes with stuff from The Lone Star era."

Four boxes for a short stint running a nightclub in the '90s? Yeesh.

"I think this one is photos and things," he says, knocking on one of the middle boxes. "But—" He holds up an aged finger, long and strong from years tickling the keys of his saxophone. "I'll do you one better."

Bobby turns and begins to scrap through the papers on the desk.

Eleanor and I stand side by side, silent, exchanging a look now and then as he searches . . . and searches . . . and searches.

"Doggone it! I had it a couple hours a—ah! Found it!" He pulls up a big green book and holds it into the air. "This is the Rosetta Stone of my time at The Lone Star. My Book of Kells. My Leningrad Codex. You get it, right?"

Eleanor nods vociferously. "Yes, yes, absolutely."

I keep my mouth shut and nod though I understood *maybe* half of what he said.

Bobby holds the book out toward Eleanor. She poises her hands underneath the book to receive it as if it's sacred. "Hopefully you'll get some information out of this puppy."

Eleanor pulls the book into her chest, her eyes bright behind her glasses. "Thank you so much for helping us with this."

"All I did was move some boxes around. And now, I leave you to it. Too damn hot up here," he says, waving a hand to dash it all away. "If you need anything else, try not to let me know, huh?"

Bobby shuffles back through the maze of boxes until he disappears.

"Well. Guess we should get started," Eleanor says.

"Guess so," I say, sliding my hands into my pockets. "You want to go through the photos or the ledger?"

Her lips twist up at the corner. "I think I'll take the photos. That's my realm of expertise, isn't it?"

"Sounds good," I say.

She passes the book off to me with the same amount of gravitas she received it with. I can't believe I'm nervous over touching a godforsaken book that probably has more worthless scribbles and scrabbles than anything of particular interest, but this is Eleanor's territory. She's given so much respect to mine. It's my turn to show her respect in kind.

Eleanor goes to the boxes, navigates to the one full of photos, and plops down on the floor without any qualms for dust and splinters.

I pull out the wooden chair. "You can sit, you know?"

She doesn't look up, lifting the lid and digging into the first stack of photos. "It's easier this way."

I don't like sitting in a chair while she sits on the floor, but I'm not a floor sitter. I like to keep my jeans clean, especially given the price tag they came with. Being a cowboy isn't implicit with being a southern boy. I don't like to get dirty or dusty. I like to be crisp and collected, pressed and polished. Even when I'm trying to look "natural" it's all been carefully cultivated.

Meanwhile, Eleanor's bohemian, bookish appearance seems to come naturally to an absurd degree.

I crack open the ledger and force myself not to be distracted by her. It's not just her beauty. It's the way she pays attention to each and every photo. It's like I have an inside look at what she does every day. I wonder what she's thinking as she sizes up each image. If she's cataloging them. Wondering if they'd look good in the museum's collection.

Eventually, though, I pull the book up in front of my face. I have to keep it close to read Bobby's scrawl. I page through. There's no method to the madness. On some pages, there are lists of expenses, on others there are phone numbers and birthdays.

I find the rhythm to the book eventually. This ledger was a catchall for everything as he went. I come across a list of acts in January. Not even in chronological order. Just a name next to a date. No wonder Kenny said Bobby did a shit job at taking care of The Lone Star.

Still though, while the acts aren't in chronological order, the months are. I have to be careful not to overlook the months as I page through detailed incident reports and event capacity notes.

"What was the date on the photo again?"

"May 26, 1993," Eleanor says, not missing a beat. She knows the photo like it's a piece of her.

Maybe it is.

I navigate toward a page where Bobby wrote in black marker, "May." Half the page is waterlogged, the writing having turned into inky splotches. "You've gotta be kidding me?"

"What? What is it?" Eleanor asks.

I turn the ledger around to her. "All the dates are gone. Just have names."

Eleanor crawls over to sit in front of me, her eyes scanning the pages. "Well, that's better than nothing! Instead of a needle in a haystack, it's a needle in a tumbleweed, huh?"

Her enthusiasm is contagious. "You're right about that."

"Here, you read all of them out and I'll type them into my phone. Even the band names. Who knows, she could have been a part of a group."

I flip the ledger back around and clear my throat before reading through the list. "Eve Miller. Rusty and Co.—that's an all-male band, don't write that down. Theo Quincy." I keep reading through the names, sometimes noting if I know the artist. If they're local. If they still perform. If they've passed. I pause on a familiar name. "Diane Bloom."

I bite my lower lip.

See, the thing is, I know more than I've been letting on to Eleanor. I've told her that the music of this city is my bread and butter. I know it like the back of my hand.

That doesn't mean I don't still have questions, though.

And seeing that name on this list. Knowing the face in the picture.

Each discovery only leads to more questions.

"Is that the end of the list?"

I lift my head, my mouth falling ajar. "Uh. No. Sorry."

I finish listing out the names on the page until we finish May. I go through the rest of the ledger for posterity's sake while Eleanor sorts through the pictures. She stacks them in three piles.

First, there's the not applicable pile—pictures that have nothing to do with the task at hand. Then there's the interesting pile—pictures that aren't relevant, but Eleanor sees as potentially interesting to the museum. I've offered to ask Bobby if she can take them as a donation.

The final pile only exists in theory because no pictures are stacked there by the time she's finished with the box. It's the helpful and relevant pile.

Not a single photo. Not a single further clue.

"That's it," Eleanor says with a sigh.

"A bust, huh?" I ask from my place in my chair.

She shrugs and picks up the short stack of interesting. "Not totally."

There's frustration in her voice. I can hear it. Annoyance that the mystery has not been solved. Guilt builds in pit of my stomach. I'm helping, but not as much as I could.

If I helped as much as I could, we wouldn't have gotten beyond that first conversation outside The Yellow Rose.

Perhaps I'm tempting fate, though. Perhaps we were never meant to. If I had just been honest . . .

"How are the treasure hunters?" a woman's voice flicks up through the hatch of the attic.

"Good, Mrs. Sutton," I say.

The ladder rungs creak as she climbs up. I stand and go to the edge of the alcove, rising on my tiptoes to try and spot her.

"Oh, please, Luke, you know to call me Mandy."

I can only spy the tight coils of hair at the top of her head.

"You've been up here a while in the heat. I'm sure you're hungry. Dinner is ready when you two are."

I glance back at Eleanor. She shrugs and then nods.

"Yeah, we've got what we needed Mandy. We'll be down once we can find our way out of this mess."

"Well, take your time. This double date isn't going anywhere!"

I freeze before I can wriggle myself through the tunnel out of the alcove. I don't dare look back at Eleanor for fear that she might have the same shocked look on her face as I do.

"Fried catfish, corn on the cob, red beans . . ." Bobby's wife starts to rattle off as if she hasn't just dropped an inconvenient bomb.

"Mandy, we're not—"

Eleanor places a hand on my arm. Sparks shoot through me. "Don't bother. It's fine. One double date won't kill us," she says in a playful tone.

11

ELEANOR

"No, sorry, that's not me," the bartender says, shaking her head so the unnaturally red curls piled on top of her head jiggle.

"You sure?" I press.

She smiles sympathetically. "Yes, I know it's surprising, but I can indeed recognize myself in a picture, hon."

I bite my lip. Of course she can. I glance down at the photo. If I'm honest with myself, even *I* can tell it's not her. It might have been nearly 30 years, but age doesn't change a person's entire bone structure.

Leaning on the bar, Luke says, "Well, thanks for indulging us, Susan."

"Anytime. I like reliving my glory days," she says with a toothy smile. "I played the spoons with the best of them, let me tell you."

My curiosity is piqued. "The spoons?"

"*Oh*, yeah. A rarefied skill. That's what Garth Brooks told me after he watched me play."

"You met Garth Brooks?"

She waggles her eyebrows. "*Met* is a way to put it."

"Wow. Okay. That's . . . I bet that's a great story."

"You want to hear the details?" she says, folding her hand on the bar and leaning toward me. "I've got time."

Of course she does.

It's the middle of the day on a weekend and her bar is empty, save a few flies discussing their game of darts in a darkened corner. It's a quintessential dive bar. It's comforting to know that no matter where you go, a dive bar will always be a dive bar. Sticky floors, vibrant neon signs advertising beers, and a jukebox that still takes quarters. I imagine that, late in the night, patrons are elbow to elbow in here. However, in the day, it's a ghost town.

A dive bar is as a dive bar does.

"Um . . ." How am I going to politely refuse this woman's kissing and telling?

Luke puts his hand on my back, a comforting touch. Almost as if he is saying, "I got this." My body relaxes immediately. "I think we're good. We've got somewhere we have to be, and I bet that story is too interesting to rush through."

"You got that right," she says with a point of her finger. "Well, if you ever need a bit of entertainment, I'm around. Not just for the spoons." She clicks her tongue and winks before waltzing off down the bar to attend to one of the dart throwers.

Luke and I look at each other. "Was she . . . propositioning you?" I ask.

His face sours. "No. At least, I don't think so."

"I think so," I say in a low voice.

Luke scoffs before ticking his head toward the door. "Let's get out of here. The smell of Schlitz is giving me a headache."

He urges me toward the door with a press of his hand before removing his touch all together. Disappointment courses through my body. I ignore it.

We emerge from the bar into Saturday sunshine.

"Well, another bust," I say sadly.

"Just a step closer to knowing the truth, right?" Luke says.

I grab my phone out of my bag and pull up the list of names. "Only one name left."

"Oh?"

"Yeah. Diane Bloom."

Luke scratches his hand back through his hair before tucking his hat onto his head, shade engulfing his features. "Let's head to the car. Need the AC."

We walk side by side toward his car. Luke and I have spent the last two weeks going through the names on the list we formulated from Bobby's ledger. We've called some people and others we've found on Google. It's been a true scavenger hunt through the who's who of Austin's music scene past. At first, it was fun. Nancy Drew and one of the Hardy Boys.

Except now, we're at the end of the list and no closer than we were when we started.

Luke walks faster than I do. It's not just the long legs this time, though. I've got my eyes plastered to my phone screen as I type in "Diane Bloom." I can't wait until I get to the car. I need to rip off the Band-Aid.

The webpage thinks for a moment before the results pop up. A PhD at UNC. Some LinkedIn profiles. A purveyor of crystals.

I return to the search bar and type in "Austin" after the name.

"Eleanor, come on, you're going to get a sunburn," Luke calls out.

"I'll be fine," I say before pressing search.

My heart falls at the sight of the first result.

Diane Bloom Obituary.

I stop in my tracks.

There was never a promise I would find whoever the woman in this picture was, let alone find her alive.

Still, though. It's heavy.

I tap the link and pull up the obit:

> *Diane Bloom, a devoted mother, musician, and animal lover, passed away peacefully after a courageous battle with breast cancer. Throughout her life, Diane's love for music was a guiding force, shaping her journey and leaving an indelible mark on those around her. Her guitar was never far out of reach, and she could always be caught humming a tune.*

> *Diane is survived by her loving daughter and her "pack." Diane's legacy lives on through the music she wrote and the love she gave to all the humans and animals around her.*

> *In lieu of flowers, the family requests that donations be made to Playing For Change to honor Diane's love for music and conservation.*

Below the paragraphs is a headshot of a woman holding a little girl with flaxen hair. One of those department store photo sessions.

It's her. The woman from the photo.

The screen blurs as tears fill my eyes.

"Hey."

I was so focused on reading I didn't notice Luke. He's standing in front of me, so close that his hat provides a little bit of shade for me. Blessed shade.

"She's dead," I say.

Luke is silent. I push my phone into his hand and head over to the car, knocking the tears off my cheeks with the back of my hand. I don't know why I'm crying. It's just a photo, a photo of a woman I've never met. So embarrassing. I grab the door handle and pull. It's locked. "Can you unlock it please?" I ask.

"Eleanor . . ."

"Luke, just unlock the car." I'm so tired. We've come this far. And she's not even alive.

His hand lands on my shoulder. Relief floods through me. "It's okay."

"It's not okay. This was . . . this was a waste of time," I say, my voice crimping higher and higher with each word.

Luke slides his hand across my back. "Was the point to find her alive?"

I sigh. "No, it's—" My voice locks in the back of my throat. I tighten my jaw to keep from a sob coming out of me. *Swallow it back. You're fine.* "I just didn't expect to get so attached. And I didn't expect she'd be gone."

It's my fault. Diane has never been only a woman in a picture. "She's real. You know? It's real life and I just wasn't prepared."

Luke smiles sympathetically. "C'mere."

I let him pull me into his chest. I don't care that it's hot as hell out here, and I don't care that I smell like sweat. The second I'm pressed to him, all my tears abate, and my body relaxes. I'm not sure why. Maybe the fact that he's one of the first friends I've made here in Austin. One of the first friends I've made as an adult. Something that's always been harder as I've grown older.

I don't know why he feels so compelled to be around me. Why he wants to comfort me as I cry.

But god am I thankful for it.

Luke's arms lock around my neck and his lips brush my scalp. Almost like a kiss. He whispers, "I know it's not what you hoped."

"I don't know what I hoped," I say tearfully. I wanted the truth. Wanted answers. Wanted a story. And after Jolene said a story might solidify my permanent place at the library, I've hung my hat on the idea that I could weave a beautiful tale of the woman in the picture.

Diane.

Who knows what her story really is? She isn't around to tell it.

I rip myself away from Luke and wipe the remainder of my tears away. "I'm sorry I dragged you into this."

Luke gives me a lopsided smile. "If I recall, I'm the one who invited myself along on this journey."

"Still. I get so obsessive and then . . ." I sigh heavily. "I don't know why I'm so disappointed."

Luke reaches his hand into my bag. I furrow my brow, but don't pull away, watching as he roots through all the contents.

"Jesus, does this thing belong to Mary Poppins? You've got everything in here," he remarks.

I manage a laugh, though tears still bud in my eyes.

Finally, he gets what he was looking for. The picture. He holds it up. And for the first time in a while, I get a good look at it again. Guitar case in hand. Arm up in the air. Celebrating. Smiling. Tousled dark hair.

"You found the truth out, didn't you?" he asks. "Found out who she was."

"Yes, but . . . I don't know, I thought there'd be more," I say, wincing at the truth. "Is that weird?"

Luke shakes his head. "No. I just think you're underestimating what a beautiful thing you've done."

I laugh humorlessly. "What's beautiful about some random person trying to track down—"

"The past few weeks, you've been celebrating someone who is no longer with us. You've been honoring her. And you didn't even know it."

I draw my eyes up to Luke's. I don't know how he manages to make his clear blue eyes feel so warm, but they feel like walking inside after a cold winter day in Chicago. The enveloping invitation of heat. "But now it's over," I say.

Luke's forehead wrinkles at the center. "What are you talking about? Just because she's not here doesn't mean her story doesn't live on."

"I guess." I take my phone from him. "There's probably a way to contact her daughter, but that feels invasive and inappropriate."

"Maybe."

My face is starting to hurt. Sinus pressure from crying.

"You know her name now, though. That might yield something new."

"The picture's not even an original," I grumble before taking it from him and stuffing it back in my bag, more harshly than I mean to. Guilt sifts through my blood. Just because it's not a real photo—just because she's not alive—doesn't mean the journey to get here is meaningless. "My heart hurts," I admit.

Luke hums thoughtfully. "Look at it this way. You spent the past few weeks learning Austin's music forwards and backwards. You discovered the city. That counts for something, right?"

The hopefulness laced in his voice kills me. "I don't want you to think I'm not grateful for all your help or the time we got to spend together."

"Don't do that," he chastises.

"Do what?"

"Talk about us like we're in past tense," Luke says.

My brows lift. "Well, I mean . . . I don't want you to feel obligated to spend more time with me."

"As if any of this has been an obligation? You know how much fun I have telling people about my city? About the best music in the world?" he asks, disbelief in his expression. "You seriously think I'm doing all of this because I feel obligated?"

"Southern hospitality, right?" I ask.

Luke's eyes pass over my face. His effervescent smile thins. He gives a subtle shake of his head. "Naw, you got me all wrong, Eleanor."

I swallow, praying it's not audible. "Well, you said it yourself. You're supposed to be kind."

"That doesn't mean I'm not genuine."

I chew on the inside of my cheek. I hope I haven't offended him.

"You think I'd spend three weeks carting you around Austin during my time off if I didn't enjoy being around you?" Luke asks, the smile returning.

Don't smile like a maniac. That's the nicest thing anyone has said to me in a long time. It feels nice to be enjoyed.

Luke bites down on his lower lip and sucks in through his teeth before giving a hard nod. "Yeah. Okay. I know what we're going to do."

He unlocks the car and opens the door for me as he always does. I resist a swoon as I always do. "What are we doing?"

Luke circles the car. "We gotta get your mind off things. I'm going to show you Austin. Not just because of a picture, but because I want to."

We stare at each other over the top of the car.

His tongue glides across his lower lip, eyelids hovering lower. "Got it?"

I nod like a dashboard bobblehead. "G-got it."

He grins. "Good."

12

LUKE

Eleanor walks down the aisle of cowboy boots, eyeing all the varieties. The store is filled with the delicious, intoxicating scent of leather. Boots, as far as the eye can see, line the wooden shelves. I'm sure Allens Boots is exactly what a northerner would picture when asked where they think we get all our gear.

"Like anything?" I ask.

"I'm just trying to take it all in," she says. "I didn't know there were so many kinds."

"Oh, yeah," I say. "We Texans love our boots."

Eleanor smirks over her shoulder, eyes falling to my own feet. "I can tell."

"What's that supposed to mean?"

She goes back to looking, settling on a black leather boot with a silver toe and a studded spur belt across the front. "I just don't think I've ever seen you wear the same shoes twice."

"I'll take that as a compliment," I say.

Eleanor lingers for only a moment before moving down the line. "I don't even want to picture your closet."

"Listen, it comes with the job."

She stops again in front of a cheetah print boot, fringe all down the back. She twiddles her fingers through the leather fringe. "These are . . . interesting."

"Not quite your taste?" I tease.

"The day I wear animal print is the day pigs fly," Eleanor says before moving to another pair. She places her hand on the toe of a traditional boot in a tan color with dark brown detailing. "These are most certainly more my speed."

I smile. "Try 'em on."

Eleanor considers for a moment, but she pulls her hand away as if the boot burned her. "No, I'm fine just looking."

I stop and put my hands on my hips. "Don't be ridiculous. I didn't bring you to Allens Boots just to browse. You gotta get the feel, cowgirl."

Eleanor adjusts her glasses. "Yeah, not sure I can own that title."

I ignore her. "What size are you?"

"Luke—"

"Just tell me your size, okay?"

Eleanor narrows her eyes. "What are you planning?"

I cock my head to the side. Eleanor loves to make things difficult. Fine with me. It's cute. She's been bristling against me all day since she found the obituary of Diane Bloom. "No, you don't have to do this," and "No, you don't have to do that." When will she get it through her head that I *want* to do nice things for her?

First, I took her to BBQ. Poor thing needed to eat something after she bawled her eyes out. And then, what's a good lunch without dessert? So, we went for ice cream. She tried to lay her credit card down for that, but I insisted. The day is on me. Screw it. If she thinks I'm being too forward, taking things away from friend territory, then let her think that. She'd be right.

I've questioned the boundary she set that day at the taco truck more and more each time I see her. I'd never cross it without her permission, but I can't shake the flirtations, the prolonged eye contact, and the way she smiles at me.

I want more of it. All the time.

So, when she started talking about us like we weren't going to at least be friends now that we've settled on the identity of the woman in the picture, I had to fix that right quick.

"You'll see," I finally say.

The standoff continues for just a few more seconds before Eleanor finally caves. "Seven and a half."

"Got it. Now . . ." I stride over to her, grab her shoulders, and spin her around. "You go find a place to sit and wait for me."

"Luke!" she exclaims as I push her forward a few feet.

She stops obstinately and I bump up against her, the whole front of my body pressed against the back of hers.

Shit. Couldn't avoid the way my groin bumped up against her full ass. Now I feel the blood rushing to my dick. That's going to make things really awkward if she doesn't listen to what I say as soon as possible. I lean my mouth down to her ear, pulling her curls out of the way gently. "Eleanor, would you let me take control one more time?"

Goosebumps rise on the back of her neck. I hold back a smile. Now I know for a fact I'm not the only one whose body betrays our "friendship."

Instead of pulling away like I expect her to, Eleanor lifts her chin and looks me in the eye. Our lips are inches apart. It's killing me not to grab a kiss from her mouth right now, but I am a gentleman through and through and until I get the word,

I will not cross the line. "You're impossible," she says, the air of the 'p' hitting my lips.

Gently, she shrugs my hands away before walking down the aisle away from me. I watch her hips swing side to side, khaki shorts doing wonders for the shape of her ass. Her sandals thwap against the wooden floorboards. And eventually she turns, out of sight.

But definitely not out of mind.

I pick out a few boots for her to try on. The tan pair she already pointed out, some black low-heeled ropers, and, because I think it might make her squirm, a pair of blue dress boots with a phoenix-like sunburst on the front.

I go to one of the salespeople, ask for a pair of each in her size, collect the big and unwieldy boxes, then go to find Eleanor.

She's sitting at the end of one of the aisles on a bench made for trying on shoes, the ones with the mirrors built into the bottoms of them. When she sees me, she rolls her eyes. "I knew you were going to do this . . ."

"Make you do a fashion show? Absolutely." I set the boxes down. "We'll start at the top and work our way to the bottom."

Eleanor makes no move to get up, settling her hands in her lap with an almost chastising smile. "*Luke.*"

"Eleanor."

She's got another thing coming if she thinks I'm backing down.

"I'm just trying to give you the *full* Austinite experience. Is this where you draw the line?" I taunt, placing my hands on my hips. "You can't be a local without boots."

She rolls her eyes, but her smile betrays her annoyance with me. She's playing it up, her resistance to me. Now it's a little game, a push and a pull. And I love it. "Fine, I guess

I'll do it." She opens the first box, the brown boot. "Do these boots come with a Texas twang?" she asks, holding up one boot into the light.

"Afraid not, but stick with me kid, and you can't fail," I reply.

Eleanor giggles.

That laugh. Oh, that laugh. I wish I could bottle it up and keep it for the times I'm apart from her. When I'm feeling down or troubled. So much better than the occasional text message or the mere memory. That laugh sustains me. It's always genuine and earned. Doesn't come from a place of obligation. Seems to take over her entire body each time it happens.

I need to appreciate it while I have her here. Lord knows if today is going to tip the scale whatsoever, I need to show Eleanor that the past few weeks haven't been a waste just because we've come to a sad conclusion in our search.

"Alright, come on, cowgirl," I say. "Put on a show for me, huh?"

Eleanor puts on the first pair of boots and gets to her feet. I take her seat so I can take her in and admire the curve of her olive toned legs as they dip into the boot's leather. She stands in front of a mirror and twists her feet side to side as she looks at all angles of the boots. "Looks kind of silly while I'm wearing shorts."

Silly would not be the word *I* would use. Sexy fits much better. "We wear cowboy boots all year round," I say. "They only look silly to you because you're—"

"I know, I know." She throws a narrow-eyed smile over her shoulder at me. "I'm a northerner."

I grin. "Now you're catching on."

"I don't know if I'll ever get used to wearing things like these, though."

I shrug. "You'll get used to it. Besides, if I have anything to do with it, you'll have plenty of opportunities to wear boots like that."

She admires the boots in the mirror a bit longer. "What's the price on these?"

"Don't worry about it," I say.

Eleanor frowns, meeting my gaze in the mirror. "Luke . . ."

I say nothing.

She turns, lunging for the box, but I pull it out of reach. Eleanor reaches across me to grab the box, resting her hand on my thigh. She doesn't even realize what she's doing to me. "Luke!"

"I said don't worry about it! My treat."

"This isn't lunch or drinks or ice cream, Luke!" She continues to fight to grab the box, but I keep up a barricade of my arm, wrapping one hand around her bicep so if she tried to come at me from a different direction, I could yank her back into place.

On my lap. In my arms. Where she should be.

"These are boots!"

"Yeah, and?"

Eleanor huffs in frustration, then drops onto the bench beside me. I don't get comfortable with her submission. I know she's the bait-and-switch type. I don't let down my guard while she glowers at me.

"Let me buy you a pair of boots, Eleanor," I say.

"That's ridiculous. They're expensive. Hundreds of dollars!" she exclaims, gesturing around to the various aisles. "I can't let you do that."

"What are friends for?" I say, making my own stomach twist at the mention of the word "friends."

"Luke, we've known each other three weeks," she says.

The knot in my gut tightens. "So?"

"So, dropping hundreds of dollars on a stranger is—"

"You're not a stranger! How many times do I have to tell you?" I say through a smile though my frustration is growing. Doesn't she realize the only distance between us is the one she insists on putting up?

Eleanor goes silent, looking into the long mirror across from us.

We look nice together. I'd say as much if it wouldn't freak her out. All her darker features, her hair and eyes, complement my light ones. And the way her body is settled in beside me looks effortless. Like a puzzle piece you thought you'd lost in a couch cushion, and when you slot it into the puzzle, relief floods through you.

I haven't spent much time looking for *the one*. I've always said I haven't *had* the time, but I'm starting to realize that's bullshit. I've been too scared. I kept women at arm's length so they didn't get in the way of my work, and I stopped going on dates because I didn't know how to be anything more than Luke Wyatt, music promoter.

Eleanor has seen me in a way not many people have.

I wish she understood that. "You like them, right?"

"I do," she admits. "But I have nowhere to wear cowboy boots."

I smile. "You're in Austin. You have everywhere to wear cowboy boots."

She looks up at me, her eyes weak at the corners, lips serious. "Luke, please don't do something you're going to regret, okay?"

Eleanor's talking about the boots, but she could be talking about so many other things. The desire I have to kiss her. The impulse inside me to pursue her to the ends of the earth. The way I want to beg her to never leave town, just stay, give me a chance.

Maybe she's right. Three weeks ain't much time. Not enough time to start thinking about all the ways our lives fit together.

Especially when we're "just" friends.

"I don't regret acts of kindness, Eleanor," I say with a tiny shrug. "Not in my blood."

Her seriousness melts into a smile. "Okay. Fine. Let's try on the others."

When all is said and done, Eleanor fights a battle with herself over the classic brown boots and the blue ones. She goes for brown, saying that it's better to go classic rather than jump in head-first. However, I make a mental note that for all of Eleanor's withholding—for all her reservation—there's a woman inside of her that wants to be wearing blue cowboy boots, strutting down the streets of Austin.

Who knew you could make a cowgirl out of a Chicagoan?

13

ELEANOR

I still have about two months of my tenure at the music library left, but a lot can change in two months. And from the brief glancing I've done at apartment listings, the rental market is just as competitive as Chicago. A little less expensive, thank the Lord. But my pay here reflects the difference in cost of living too.

I really shouldn't be using my slow Dell computer to look for apartments, especially not at work.

I can't help myself, though. It's a compulsion; it has been two weekends since Luke and I found the identity of my mystery woman. And he bought me my boots. Which I happen to be wearing right now.

His work schedule has been packed. I had apparently met him just before a slow couple of weeks. Now, however, he's not only working his butt off on his usual bookings, but he's also looking down the pike at Austin City Limits and bookings surrounding the festival.

For all his easy smiles and casual saunters, Luke is a hustler. Sometimes he's sending me text messages at 3:00 AM, after working late at the office or after a gig.

I'm grateful he's texting me at all. That he hasn't forgotten about me. Although this is the longest stretch of time we haven't seen each other—it's been 12 days.

Yes, I've counted.

Once I reach the listings I've already seen, I sigh heavily and glance at the clock. Still an hour until lunch, which means I should do some *actual* work. Time for a new stack of binders, so I head into one of the aisles and grab the next few.

Work has been less exciting since finding out the truth about the photo. I haven't had the heart to tell Jolene that I don't have some cool story that would fit into the exhibition. It's just a photocopied picture of a singer who has since passed away.

I've googled her further of course. But nothing comes up about her music. She still has a private Facebook profile. Her picture is so sweet though, her with a dog lapping at her face.

I would have liked to know her. In many ways, I feel like I do. Diane Bloom has spent so much time in my thoughts. I never had an opportunity to utter a single word to the woman and yet I feel like she's a part of me.

She's faded into the background of my life. Not gone. Not forgotten. Just a steady rhythm section to the high-flying melodies and guitar solos of any given moment.

When I return to my workstation, Jolene is peering down at my laptop with a furrowed brow. "Apartments?"

I flush. "Oh, yeah. Sorry. I know I shouldn't be doing that on the clock," I say, hurrying to my seat and shutting the window. "I can stay late, I didn't—"

"So, you think you're staying?" Jolene asks, a big, beaming smile on her face.

Weirdest boss ever. Best boss, but weirdest too. "Thinking about it."

Jolene pulls up a chair to sit beside me as I open the next binder. "Does this have anything to do with your 'friend?'"

I snort. "No," I say firmly, more for myself than her.

She leans back in her chair and kicks her high heels up on the edge of the table. "Uh-huh . . ."

"Jo," I scold.

"It's okay if it *is* because of him, by the way. I think that's kind of romantic."

I pull my glasses off and buff the lenses with the front of my shirt. A nervous habit. Gives me something to do with my hands when I'm uncomfortable. "It's not because of Luke. I like it here. And it'd be nice to stay."

"You should! I'd miss you if you left."

I throw Jolene a small smile. Luke's not my only friend in town. Jolene has also started integrating me into her friend group. I've gone out for happy hours with them and even a dinner party at her friend Meredith's house. "It's just a pipe dream, anyway. I don't have a job lined up. Would be foolish to stay if I don't even have a job."

"What's the status on that picture you were researching?" she asks.

I swallow. "The investigation is stalled." I've been trying to figure out how to regroup with the information I have now. Next steps would require me tracking down the family and, while I'm an insatiably curious person, I haven't yet gotten the courage to prod them for information on their dead relative. She was young when she passed. It's still fresh.

"You think you can get something together by the end of next week?" Jolene asks. "A proposal for the exhibit?"

I knead my lips together. "Is that the deadline?"

She smiles sadly.

I've pushed away the thought that the picture would help me secure a longer tenure at the museum. Not helpful to think about what could have been if only Diane Bloom hadn't had breast cancer. Or what could be if I was a little pushier or more assertive. "It's fine. I haven't given up yet. And if not, I still have time to figure out my plan to say here."

"Yeah. You've got a couple weeks probably until you really have to put your nose to the grindstone to find a place, but once you hit that month-out mark, you're going to be in a pool of sharks smelling blood."

"Jeez, it's that bad?"

Jolene shrugs. "For the good places."

I sigh. "And I have to think about that on top of finding a new job? Don't know how I'm going to manage all of that."

"You will. And besides, if worst comes to worst, I have a couch you can crash on."

I scoff. "I'm over thirty, Jo."

"So?"

"So, crashing on a couch is against my code of conduct at this point." I can't imagine the mortification I would feel if I had to live on her couch while I figured out my next steps.

Jolene twirls a finger through her blonde hair. She's so coquettish in the way she presents herself, but I've seen her in meetings. The woman pulls no punches when she doesn't like what's being said. I admire people who can be exactly who they are despite the world trying to put them into boxes. "I mean, you could stay with *Luke . . .*"

"Okay, conversation over," I say, attempting a joke, but betraying my uneasiness with the unsteadiness of my voice.

"You're not doing any favors for this 'nothing is going on' narrative you're trying to sell," Jolene says. She tucks her hands on her stomach and stares me down. Not backing down.

I swallow. There are a lot of reasons I'm trying to push away my attraction to Luke. For one, I'm not convinced his flirting with me is coming from a place of actually wanting me. Too many times, I've been a pastime for men to throw their energy at until the woman they actually want comes along. For another, I'm not ready for anything more than what we have. At least . . . I don't think I am.

Friendship requires a different kind of trust than dating someone, and dating someone requires a different trust than a full-blown relationship. I can trust a friend.

Can I trust someone who is more than that?

I'm not convinced I can quite yet . . .

"I tell you everything, Eleanor," Jolene says. And that's the truth. Every morning she walks in and tells me all the details of her life, from the dates she's going on to something as banal as clipping her toenails. "You don't owe me your life's story, but it's totally obvious that you have feelings for him that aren't just friendly because every time we talk about him—" Jolene lifts her hands and pinches them. "You clam up completely."

I chuckle.

My phone buzzes on the table between Jolene and me. We both peer down at it.

Luke's name is on my phone screen.

I feel Jolene look at me so hard I'm afraid her eyes could peel my skin off.

"He's texting you in the middle of the workday and nothing is going on?" she asks.

"People text people all the time," I argue.

"*Girl.*"

I force myself to look at Jolene. Her chin is tipped down and she's giving me that, "You're full of shit," look.

Neither of us speaks.

Jolene waits. And waits. The look growing more and more intense with each passing moment.

"Fine. I like him. Yes."

"I knew it! Ha!" She claps her hands excitedly.

"But nothing is happening! We're friends and—"

"Don't give me that 'we're just friends' BS. You seem like a sensible person, Eleanor, at least way more than me. I don't believe you'd be fawning over a guy who wasn't giving you the time of day, huh?"

I gnaw on my lower lips. She's right. It's not like Luke is pushing away my touch or trying to avoid spending time with me. In fact, he's initiated most of our touching. He's the one who has tried to draw out the time we spend together.

And I keep thinking about that moment at Allens when he stumbled into my back, and I felt him. I think I felt him.

Thick and hard at my back.

I've tried to push that thought away, but how can I? The thought of a pretty playboy getting all flustered like that over me is hard to comprehend.

It's not that I don't think I'm attractive. I just don't think I attract people like *him*.

"Fine. Yes. We flirt. But who is to say it's anything more than that?"

Jolene raises an eyebrow. "Do you *want* it to be more than that?"

I drop my head into my hands and groan. "Joleeeeeene."

"You do! You do, you do, you do!" She grabs my shoulders and shakes me with each word.

"I do!" I exclaim.

She pulls me into a hug. "You have a cruuuuuushhhh!"

I could argue that calling it that sounds childish. Except it feels so good to celebrate the excitement of *feeling* something like I would back in middle school. Why do we lose the freedom to celebrate? To be candidly childish?

"Yeah, okay, I do," I say, unable to keep from smiling. "I just don't know if he feels the same."

Jolene nudges my phone toward me. "Have you told him?"

My eyes widen. "Why on earth would I do that?"

"Oh my god, don't be a coward. Guys love it when you're forward."

I pick up my phone. The screen brightens again, reminding me of the unopened text from Luke. "I've never told a guy I was interested in him."

"Well, what a perfect time to start! Luke is a beautiful specimen. Might as well shoot your shot. Something tells me, based on everything I know you're probably not alone in it."

"Okay, I'll call him after—"

"You'll call him now. I insist. As your boss," she says with a wicked smile.

I shake my head. "You're ridiculous."

"You love me."

I nod. "I do." And I mean it. It's much easier to admit to adoring someone as a friend in a short time than as a potential romantic partner. Maybe that's my problem. I'm treating the two as entirely separate when the fact of the matter is, romance is just an upgrade of friendship, an upgrade you only get once in a blue moon. "Okay. Fine. I'll do it," I say, not believing my own gumption.

"Atta girl!"

"Will you stay?" I ask her. "I think I'll back out if I'm left alone."

Jolene presses a hand to her chest. "It would be my honor."

I smile and open the phone to our text message chain.

Luke's message picks up where we left off last night.

Remind me to never accept a challenge from a drummer when tequila is involved. I'm a dead man walking.

I smile to myself, then press on the bubble of his name at the top of the screen to navigate to his phone number. My thumb hovers over the number. "You're going to have to push my thumb down, I think," I say as nerves influx through my body.

Jolene is more than happy to oblige. She also pulls the phone up to my ear. "It's going to be fine," she says, rubbing my arm. "He likes you. Worst he can do is—"

"Say no!" I hiss.

The phone rings a couple times. And then—

"I swear, I'm not actually a dead man walking," Luke answers. "I'm just hungover as all hell."

"Oh good. I was worried these were your last moments," I say, flicking my gaze to Jolene.

She gives me an enthusiastic thumbs up.

"Tell my mother I love her," he says.

My mouth gets hot. "Of course. I better get your hat though."

"Which one?" he asks cheekily.

I roll my lips together to resist grinning like a madwoman. "Am I interrupting something?" I ask.

"Uh, no, but I have about thirty seconds before a meeting," he says.

My heart sinks. "Oh, sorry, sorry, I—"

"Don't apologize." A moment. "It's good to hear your voice."

I look at Jolene for help. I'm going to need resuscitation after this. "It's good to hear your voice too."

"Let's get dinner later this week."

Is that a date? "Yes."

"Or a drink more like it. My schedule is *packed*."

Guess not. "Totally. Just let me know. I'm . . . I'm free."

"I'll text you after my meeting. Thanks for checking in on me."

"Yeah. Any time."

Luke says goodbye and hangs up before I can reply. I lower the phone and stare at it blankly.

"What happened?" Jolene asks.

"He's busy. Really busy. It—" I roll my eyes, trying not to let tears fill my eyes. There's no reason to cry over something like this. It's fucking silly. Just a crush. "It wasn't a good time."

Jolene's concern is obvious on her face. She glances up at the clock. "Come on. Early lunch. Burgers and fries. A milkshake. You need it."

14

LUKE

The crowd is good for a Wednesday night especially for an up-and-coming Tejano rock band. Since the audience isn't super familiar with the music, it's not at all rowdy. A lot of listening, a lot of nodding along when a lyric hits them, a lot of leaning into their friends, whispering, "S'good."

I watch from the bar. The venue is small, no big backstage area for me to hide out, keep tabs from the wings. Instead, you could probably feel a performer spit on you all the way in the back of the venue. The big stages are my bread and butter, but the little ones are where all the soul lives.

I lock eyes with the band manager, an old-timer who's been on the Austin circuit for years. He gives me a nod of respect. I nod in return, trying to keep my composure. The manager used to be a titan with his big mustache and ten-gallon hat. Now, he's slowed down and lost some of his cred. But still slings himself around like he's cock of the walk.

Regardless of his current status, I respect my elders. They're the reason I'm here, and why the Austin music scene still blooms anew again and again. So, when I promised him that I'd have the venue full for his band, I meant it.

There's not an empty cabaret table, and standing room keeps filling up with passers-by.

Very good for a Wednesday night.

In fact, I ought to consider giving up my seat at the bar so someone can sit and stay a while. I look down the bar at all the patrons. At the very end is a man tapping his foot against his stool, considering the band thoughtfully through a pair of black-rimmed glasses. His completely white hair is cut stylishly, and his lips are pulled down like a trout, the quintessential expression of someone who likes what he's listening to.

Skip Baxter, the Beat Cowboy, is a local disc jockey who's been active since the '90s. Though he's at least sixty, he wears his age well. Radio hosts are pretty good at staying out of the fray. They get to be in the industry while avoiding the party scene as much or as little as they want.

I narrow my eyes. He's been around. Probably has a catalogue of all the acts that have waltzed through town.

I wonder . . .

No. It would be silly to ask about Diane.

Except I haven't shaken her since Eleanor found out her name. Sometimes it keeps me awake at night, which isn't good considering how busy this month is for me. I can't afford to lose any more sleep.

I tried to give up on the mystery. Tried to have Eleanor give up on it, too.

But I can't.

That picture from '93 still prompts so many questions.

She performed at The Lone Star. Played guitar. A solo act, if I'm to believe Bobby's notes are correct.

Would it be possible that Baxter might know something?

It's worth a shot. Besides, it would give me a reason to reach out to Eleanor that isn't just me trying to make conversation, so she doesn't forget about me.

I give the bartender a nod and point at the end of the bar. "Two of what he's having," I mouth.

She gives me a quick nod before pouring off two straight club sodas.

No wonder the guy looks good. He doesn't even drink.

Then again, he's over fifty and it *is* a Wednesday. Could take a note from his book.

I take the club sodas and head down to the end of the bar, posting up beside Baxter. He glances up at me and gives me a polite smile before returning his gaze to the band.

"They're good, huh?" I say.

"Yeah, smooth stuff."

"Thinking about running their tracks?" I ask.

He does a double take in my direction, realizing he's been recognized, then smiles sadly. "I'd like to. Would people listen?" He shrugs. "Radio ain't what it used to be."

"Hear that." I hold out the straight club soda to him. "Name's Wyatt. Grew up listening to you."

Skip appraises the club soda before taking it. "Nice to meet you, Wyatt. Working tonight?"

I smile, glancing at the band. The singer is a flamboyant woman with a flat-black Cordobés hat, a lacy top, and high-waisted pants that are embroidered with bright-colored flowers. She's a show woman and the people are eating her up. "You can tell?"

"A tailored suit in a club like this?" he says with a raised eyebrow.

I chuckle, looking down at the pinstripe blue I've chosen for tonight and carefully adjust the silver bolo around my neck. "Caught me."

"They're good," Skip says. "Too bad you can't get them on a bigger stage. She deserves it."

"I agree," I say. "You still accept demos like you did in the old days?"

Skip huffs out a disdainful laugh. "Not since everyone and their mother has access to SoundCloud."

I remember the calls on the then up-and-coming radio station. "Send us your wild and your weird! Send us your Austin!"

For a while, Skip's station was straight up Austin. Local only, unless out-of-towners were promoting a show. Now, it's modern alternative. Sneaks in something new to the ear every now and then, but it's not the same.

"But I have no doubt their manager will corner me after the show. As he is known to do . . ." Skip says, eyeing the manager as he takes a sip of club soda.

I take the opportunity to pull out my phone. "Could I ask you a question? Since you've been around for a while?"

"Watch it kid," Skip says wryly.

"I mean that with all due respect, sir," I correct.

The audience erupts in applause. I hadn't even realized they'd finished their last song. Skip leans back on the bar, focusing on the band as they shuffle around before the next song of their set, not bothering to clap. "What is it, Wyatt?" he finally asks.

I pull up the picture of Diane on my phone. I took it after my first encounter with Eleanor so that I could try and pick apart more details myself. How I have *poured* over this picture, trying to find out anything and everything about it. "You recognize this musician?"

Skip looks at my phone, squinting through his glasses. He leans in, pushing his glasses up on his forehead. He looks for a long time and then utters a quick, "Nope. Should I?"

"No, no. I'm just working with an archivist at the Reeder and she's trying to get more information since this image is going to be shown in an exhibition." No harm in a tiny fib, especially not when it's the kind used to manifest goodness for someone I care about.

"Mm. Well, I'm sorry I can't help you," he says.

I flick off the screen on my phone. "How about a name? Would you recognize a name?"

A soft, brushing beat begins on the drums, and the singer begins to hum into the mic.

"Depends. Heard a lot of names over the years."

All of these old-timers and their attempt at mystery. I don't let myself look annoyed, but I'm starting to get tired of it. "Diane Bloom. Know the name?"

Skip's mouth gets small, and he lets out a "Hm."

The muscles in my stomach tighten with anticipation as the name rolls around Skip's brain. If he comes up empty, I will fall apart.

"Think she probably sent a demo back in the day. I remember the last name. Bloom."

I hold back every impulse to explode with excitement. "Yeah? You remember listening to it?"

"No, not particularly," Skip says, nonplussed.

Well, that was anticlimactic. "So, you didn't play it on the radio."

"Not that I recall."

He goes silent as he watches the band. I can't take my eyes off Skip, begging him to say more.

"We keep all of them though," he says, enchanted by the Tejana singer helming the band. "They've been digitized, but likely she's in the catalog."

If only Eleanor was here to hear this. She'd be vibrating next to me. Maybe she'd grab my arm. I swoon at the thought. I'm down bad if all it takes is me *thinking* about her touch to send me into the stratosphere.

"I can look tomorrow for you if you like," Skip says. "Wouldn't be hard."

"Could you? That would be fantastic! You have no idea how much that would mean to me," I say. And I mean it. It would mean everything to Eleanor, but it would mean *everything* to me too. Not only would I have answers, but I'd also get to be Eleanor's hero.

Maybe that will set something off in her. Show her just how much I'm trying to show up for her. As a friend, sure, but I'd like to me much, much more.

I can imagine what my father would say. That I'm being a wuss about it, and I should just go after her. The worst she can say is no thanks. I've been rejected before. Hell, I'm rejected on a daily basis just by being in the line of work I'm in.

However, I fear a no from Eleanor would kill me. Would *brutalize* me.

Skip cracks a smile, one that seems a little bit friendly for once. "You know her or something?"

My stomach drops like I'm on a roller coaster. He doesn't even know that she's passed away. A beautiful myth to us all. "Yeah," I say. "Yeah, I did."

His eyebrows jump up. He catches my meaning. "Oh. I'm sorry."

I shake my head. "It's alright." I don't believe I have rightful claim to grieving Diane. And yet I ache over her loss.

Skip shifts in his seat. Looks to the band then back to me. Opens his mouth, closes it. Looks back at the band and then back at me again. "After the set, you busy?"

"N-no. Why?"

"Because we can go down to the station tonight if you want."

I put my hand on the bar beside me, fearing my legs might turn to jelly and give out. "Are you serious?"

Skip's smile grows. "Yeah, we'll go after the show."

Jack-fucking-pot.

Just wait until I tell Eleanor.

15

ELEANOR

I am awakened by a sharp, buzzing sound. I blink my eyes open; my phone is lit up on the dresser. Someone's calling me.

Must be urgent because I keep it on Do Not Disturb at night. I wonder how many times they've already tried to get through. My stomach coils in on itself. It could be an emergency. Or it could be . . . someone I don't want to hear from. The only people who would call repeatedly late at night are desperate and people's versions of desperate are so different.

I have half a mind to bury my head under the comforter and not deal with it until morning.

But I can't ignore the flame of curiosity flickering inside me.

I grab my phone off the dresser, wincing at the bright light filtering through the darkened room. Then, I screw my eyes together to be able to read the name.

The coil of my stomach releases, exchanged for butterflies when I see Luke's name on the screen. At least I think it's his name. To be sure, I fumble for my glasses, pulling them on as fast as I can.

Yep, that's Luke's name alright. Why would he be calling me so late? I can't be his go-to contact in an emergency. Maybe I've had him pegged right from the beginning. A ladies' man, who sneaks into your heart, makes you feel special, and then booty calls you when the time is right.

I press the accept button and pull the phone to my ear. "Hello?" I answer.

"Good! You're up!" Luke replies with a voice better suited for the first cup of coffee in the morning than the middle of the night.

I can't help but smile. "Yeah, thanks to you," I say.

"Ah, sorry, sorry, I knew it was probably past your bedtime."

I roll onto my back. "I don't have a bedtime."

"You're exactly the type of person to have a bedtime," he says, teasing lilt infusing his voice.

"Why are you calling me past my bedtime then, *Luke*?" Now I'm wide awake, wanting to know what he wants. Hoping I can keep him on the phone.

"Trust me, it will be worth the lost sleep," he says. "I ran into a radio host at my gig tonight who apparently has access to one of Diane's demos."

I sit straight up, each nerve in my body pulling me in a different direction. "He—what?!"

"I'm on the way to the radio station to take a listen as we speak." I hear the clicking of a turn signal in the background of the call. "Just turned onto your street to pick you up."

My mouth goes hot. I scramble over to the window that looks out on the street below, spreading the slats in the blinds to look through. Sure enough, there's Luke's car, slowing right in front of my building.

"You in?" he asks.

Joy washes over me. That he's here. He's thought of me. Gone out of his way to get me, knowing just how important all of this is to me.

I adore him. And for now, I'll allow myself to do so with reckless abandon.

"Give me two minutes."

* * *

The DJ, Skip, leads us into his booth. It's a rather drab interior compared to how exciting things sound on the radio. Gray equipment lining three of the white walls. The soundboard is intimidating enough on its own, let alone the man who operates it. Skip Baxter, who I met less than a minute ago, is a very reserved Ira Glass type. Hard to imagine him rocking out at one of the shows Austin puts on. Then again, I'm sure he's lived many lives in his time as a disc jockey.

Skip drops down into his chair and boots up his computer. "Give me a minute."

Luke and I are silent as we stand behind Skip, waiting with bated breath. I look askance at Luke, chewing my lip. As per usual, he's wearing an easy smile. Encouraging and safe.

I pull my cardigan tighter around me. It wasn't until I was under the fluorescent lights of the studio that I realized just how stupid my outfit looked. A baby tee, windbreaker pants, a duster cardigan, and Birkenstocks. Not to mention I had to pile all my curls on the top of my head like Carmen Miranda's hat of fruit since they were already mussed from sleep.

Standing with Luke, it's like *The Prince and the Pauper.* He's crisp and pressed, not a hair out of place.

I focus my eyes elsewhere so as not to start salivating over him.

Above Skip's head of silvery hair is a window that looks into the main area where hosts and guests are able to go at it across a table with state-of-the-art mics hanging on black arms in front of every seat. The only splash of color is the green velvet chairs.

I imagine Diane sitting at one of those mics, lips curled into a soft smile as she talks about her music. I imagine she liked to laugh. A smile like hers is that of a woman who feels comfortable enough to let her voice free. She's a musician after all, isn't she?

"Okay, here we go." Skip presses a few buttons. Each click puts me further and further on edge until he clicks play on the track pulled up on the computer screen. "S'called 'Hyacinth.'"

There's a bit of static before the strumming of an acoustic guitar. Plaintive chords, swooping and solemn.

"Bad opening track for a demo," Skip says, triangulating his fingers over his belly as he leans back in his chair.

I ignore him. I don't give a single fuck about what any critic might say about what I'm hearing. It's beautiful.

And then she sings.

"*I've got arms to hold you too tight / I've got words to keep you up all night . . .*" Her voice is a soulful rasp, unlocked from somewhere deep inside, the definition of artistry. She isn't pushing herself to sound pretty or good. It's authentic and *that* is the beauty of it.

"A bit . . . trite, the lyrics," Skip remarks.

I close my eyes and let the music be the only thing I hear, the only thing that deserves to have a voice right now.

"I might not be bad / But I know I'm not good . . ."

My forehead tightens as I take in each and every word, each chord change.

"What's here isn't meant to be understood."

Her lyrics aren't anything novel. But they're poetic in their honesty and their candor. Complemented by the quality of her voice and the work of her fingers on the guitar, the picture of someone weighed down by love. Someone who has wanted nothing more than to be loved and yet has to accept that to love is to live with pain.

That might be a lot to get from a song. But it's what I'm hearing.

Something is unlocked inside me.

I pull my hands up to my chest, intertwine my fingers together, and bend my head forward, in a type of prayer.

"I might not get you tomorrow / But at least I have you today / And when you see me tomorrow / That's exactly what I'll say."

She's still so alive. Not on this earth. But her music . . . she's right here in the room with me, so tangible it's hard to believe there is a reality where she doesn't exist.

I know I don't know her and never did. I don't have a reason to be giving myself over to her so completely. To be so curious. However, coming to Austin was a way to get away from my old life. Leave behind my old self.

Wherever you go, though, your past follows you. You carry it in your mind.

So, when I laid eyes on Diane . . . on a woman who seemed so free. I wanted to figure out how to be that.

I feel a hand on my back. "You okay?" Luke asks tenderly.

I blink my eyes open, and a few tears roll down. I smile up at him, wiping them away. "Yeah. I'm okay."

His tight lips pull up at the corner. He moves his hand across my back sweetly, then lets his hand creep around my shoulder and pulls me to his side.

I lean into him, pressing my face into his side, and sigh in relief as the music continues to waft through the air. I'm content. And safe. And, if only for a few moments, I'm not going to question whether where I am is exactly where I'm meant to be.

Here. Next to Luke. Being whatever I am to him.

The song rolls to a close with a repeating finish, suggesting that the desire for the love she sings of will be a Sisyphean task, an endless suffering.

I let out a big sigh.

"We found her," I say.

And all the uneasiness is gone.

16

LUKE

"We found her."

Eleanor's words echo in my ears.

I feel like the worst person alive.

Scratch that, I *am* the worst person alive.

I could have nipped this in the bud the first time I met her. The second I saw that photo I could have told her the truth.

See, I've known. From the beginning, I've known exactly who the woman in the picture was.

Diane Bloom isn't a stranger to me the way she is to Eleanor. Not at all.

At the time, I was caught off-guard to see her in the photo. To see the *year* on the photo. I needed time to process. And by the time I sat down with Eleanor at the Fried Polyester show, I decided to let the picture be a mystery to me, too.

It was selfish. I know. The actions of a guy who was thinking with his dick. Although, that's unfair to me. My feelings for Eleanor were never purely physical. It might sound a little naïve, but there was something about her, from the moment our eyes connected. Something I needed. So, when she offered up the photo, I saw the possibility of an adventure with a woman that my heart was calling for.

The truth . . . the truth is that Diane Bloom was Aunt Diane to me. A friend of my parents that us kids called "Aunt" simply because she came around a lot. I remember her long dark hair and her effervescent smile. She'd bring her guitar with her whenever she visited and we'd sit up late into the nightlistening to her play, laughing and singing along. We spent many beautiful summer nights out under a big Texas sky listening to Aunt Diane playing anything from Chicago blues to Greenwich Village folk. She had a particular love for Willie Nelson (who doesn't?), and she had a couple of Linda Ronstadt songs she would play on repeat.

Those nights are like pillars of my childhood. Something I thought would last forever until suddenly summer nights were quiet and Aunt Diane didn't come around anymore. I don't remember how old I was.

But I know by 1993, I'd seen Aunt Diane for the last time.

I've needed to know just as Eleanor has. More than, probably.

It's wrong of me to have led Eleanor along on this wild goose chase for so long. But once I stepped into the lie, I couldn't step out of it. Each day I was just digging myself deeper. I let her follow the trail, doing my best to support her at every turn, just as I am now with her tucked under my arm.

How would she have reacted if suddenly I just said, "I've known from the beginning who that woman was"? She wouldn't have let me keep coming around, I can tell you that much.

And now . . .

Now there's no way she can ever know. Because by admitting I lied, I'd lose her.

I can't lose her. I just can't.

She's become so special to me in the short time I've known her. Her pensive, thoughtful expressions, the way she speaks about and sees the world. Her softness. Her stillness. My little shutterbug.

I want to be a part of her world.

I've never been so scared to cross a line with a woman as I am with Eleanor. Because even as she leans into me, a part of me doesn't quite believe she'll take me seriously.

"Can we hear it again?" Eleanor asks once the recording fades out.

Skip turns in his seat and looks at me with a raised eyebrow.

I nod. "Yeah. Let's hear it again."

I'll do whatever I can to make Eleanor happy.

Even if the guilt kills me.

* * *

In the car, the exhaustion hits me. It's well past midnight and, though I'm a night owl by trade, nature is starting to catch up with me.

Eleanor sits alert in the seat beside me, bobbing along to another one of Diane's songs that plays through the speakers of my car.

It took some teeth pulling, but I got Skip to send over the MP3s. What good would they be doing just sitting on the computer with no one to listen to them?

"God, she's so good," Eleanor says, putting her hands on the sides of her head and leaning back in the passenger seat.

I laugh through closed lips and nod. I always thought the same. Children, of course, love the things they love without knowing the quality of it. As an adult, though, I can now say that objectively, she *is* good. A little rasp of Lucinda Williams with a tough of Emmylou Harris lightness.

"I can't believe she didn't get famous," Eleanor says, glancing out the window as the scenery rolls by.

"Music scene is tough," I say simply and readjust my fingers on the wheel.

"I know. I mean, all art is tough," Eleanor replies. "But this is really good! What's wrong with people?"

I chuckle. "You should start evangelizing the gospel of Diane Bloom."

"You're right, I could start a new religion."

I glance at Eleanor for a moment to capture an image of her. Corkscrew curls tumbling from the top of her head like a fountain, a serene smile on her lips, eyelids lolling low in that delicious hypnosis of good fucking music.

I could start a new religion too. "You think this discovery could help with the exhibit?"

Eleanor sighs heavily. "I mean, it certainly helps. But without an original photo, it feels like it might be a fool's errand."

"You should still try," I say, turning onto Eleanor's street.

"I will, don't worry."

My chest warms.

I pull the car in front of her apartment, and put it in park. Eleanor makes no move to go, and I'm grateful. I want to bask in her a little while longer.

"Sorry, just want to finish the song," she says.

"I'd never dream of interrupting that," I say.

Eleanor throws a smile in my direction, then lets her eyes close.

"*Something told me you were mine / But the world had a different plan . . .*"

The lyric hits my chest like a dart as I watch Eleanor listen. Something *is* telling me she's mine. Something deep in the core of my being. But gut feelings are often an excuse for people to act rashly. Maybe the world's plan doesn't align with the way I feel.

I'm breaking my own damn heart before I even give Eleanor a chance to.

Her eyes pop open. "I should have brought my camera."

"I'm shocked you didn't."

"Yeah, well I don't usually have guys calling me in the middle of the night to take me on adventures," she says with a smirk.

"You don't? I'm shocked," I say. And I mean it.

Eleanor laughs it off. "You're the first, Luke."

First. *Only.*

The song ends, and Eleanor still doesn't make a move to go.

I trace my thumb over the top of the steering wheel. What do we have to hold us together if not for the photo? "Well, I hope that the museum appreciates your research."

"Me too," she says in a soft voice. "I'd like to stay in Austin if I can."

I withhold a grin. "Austin would like you to stay in it too."

Eleanor giggles. "Sounds dirty."

Thank god it's dark in here. I know I'm blushing. "That came out wrong."

"I'm just giving you a hard time."

If only she knew how true the double entendre in that was. "Fun plans this weekend?"

Eleanor tilts her head from side to side. "No, not really. You've been my plans most weekends."

"Oh yeah?" I ask, leaning onto the center console subtly.

"Mhm. You have singlehandedly prevented me from being a hermit," she says. Her eyes fall to my arm on the console, then rise back to meet mine. "I think I'm overdue for a weekend where I rot alone in my pajamas all day."

I tense the muscles in my thighs. If only she knew how sexy that sounds. "Well, I think I have to uphold my tradition of making you leave the house."

She quirks her eyebrow. "You've got some ideas?"

Lots. All kinds. "Yeah, I've got one."

"I thought you were busy."

"I have Saturday night, shockingly," I say.

"Don't you need a night off?"

"Would rather spend it with you." Why dance around the truth?

Eleanor pauses. Her lips lift. "Okay, I'm listening."

I peer down at her feet. "Let me guess. You haven't worn your boots once yet."

"Hey! I'm working up the courage to!"

"*Eleanor*, it's your right as an Austinite to wear your boots!"

She crosses her arms over her chest and pulls a foot up to rest on the edge of her seat. "I'm not technically an Austinite."

"I'm an Austinite and I'm dubbing you an Austinite, alright? I'm making you shed your Chicagoan skin."

Eleanor's face squinches together. "Fine."

I laugh. "We'll hit a honkytonk this weekend. You'll break in your boots the best way I know how."

Eleanor's face falls. "Oh no . . ."

"Two-stepping!" I say with a cheerful smile.

"Please, god, don't make me dance," she says, putting her hand over her face.

"Eleanor, I'm not friends with people who don't have rhythm."

"That's not true, because I'm—"

"Nope. It's the truth. The universe wouldn't have allowed this to happen if you had bad rhythm." The universe wouldn't have allowed this to happen if I had been honest from the beginning either.

Eleanor laughs and shakes her head. "What am I going to do with you?"

I can think of a few things. I lean in a little closer. I'm not going to take the moment, but if *she* takes it, I won't say no. "Come dancing with me," I say in a low voice, one I save for those "Wanna get out of here?" moments at a bar.

Eleanor's teeth settle onto her lower lip. Does she have to do that? I'm a gentleman, but she's making it so hard not to just *kiss* her. "Fine," she says. "But you have to promise that if I'm bad you won't get mad at me."

"You won't be bad," I say. My eyes swoop across her mouth. So kissable.

Eleanor darts forward and, for a second, I think she's going to kiss me. *Finally*. But she misses my mouth and lands the kiss to my cheek. Polite. Not passionate. *Dammit*.

Still, her lips brushing against my stubbly cheek sends a shiver down my spine.

I'm head over heels for her and she doesn't even know it.

Eleanor draws back. Not far enough to make my heartbeat slow. "Thank you for everything."

All the guilt creeps back in. I swallow. "No thanks necessary."

"Don't do the modest southern boy thing," she says.

"You do the modest Midwestern thing all the time," I reply pointedly.

Eleanor scrunches her nose and pushes me away by my shoulder. "Oh, whatever."

I laugh and retreat back to my side of the car. "So, Saturday?"

"It's a date," she replies.

My stomach drops. "Is it?"

Eleanor shrugs one shoulder and pushes her door open. "It's a figure of speech."

Fucking Eleanor. "Right . . ."

Before she closes the door, Eleanor gives me a final smile. "Text me when you get home."

"I will. Night, Eleanor."

As soon as she makes it inside her apartment, I let out a breath I've been holding in since the moment we met. The lie. The closer Eleanor and I become, the heavier the weight. I don't know if I'll survive getting as close to her as I'd like.

But the image of her hearing Diane's song for the first time doesn't leave my mind. The whole ride home, I remember. The joy. The contentment.

Knowing I helped make it possible.

I'm so consumed by the image that I forget to text Eleanor until I'm in bed. I hope she's dead asleep by now.

I'm tempted to type out a lyric from Diane's song, one that stuck so clearly in my brain.

In the morning, please remember me.

Would be a leap. Would be . . . a little sappy. It's how I feel though. I'm consumed by her, and I can only hope she's at least thinking of me in the in between moments. I wouldn't wish the way I feel on anyone. Still, though . . . to be thought of.

Eleanor's got my head all in knots. I don't know how to be the man I've always been. I want to be the right one for her. And her lips still burn on my cheek.

Instead, all I write is, "*Home. Sleep well.*" Then put my phone aside, praying that I'll dream of her.

17

ELEANOR

"Did you know hyacinths represent regret?"

"You're stalling, Eleanor."

Of course, I'm stalling.

Standing outside a bar called the Broken Spoke in my cowboy boots, I feel like a fish in a fur coat. Every person who walks by seems to be giving me the once-over. It's like they can see the northerner in me just with a single glance.

From the outside, Broken Spoke looks like an old-timey saloon, painted brick red. It's clearly an *establishment*. The sign glows red, which might be an inviting beacon for some, but for me it is a harbinger of doom. Above the entrance, a wooden marquee displays upcoming events and live performances, its hand-painted lettering adding to the venue's nostalgic charm.

Each time the door swings open, I can hear the din of voices and music. I'm scared shitless as I prepare myself to go inside.

"I'm not lying," I say. I looked it up the second I got home from hearing Diane's song. It struck me all at once . . . there was no mention of hyacinths in the song. So, I searched the internet for the language of flowers. Lo and behold, hyacinths are the floral emblem of regret.

It fits. The lyrics, the keening tone of her voice.

Something about knowing the meaning, though, breaks my heart. What did Diane regret? There's so much about life that can be regrettable. Especially in love. What did love look like to her?

Luke smiles. "I know you're not lying."

"Do we have to do this?" I ask. "I look ridiculous."

"Then, you're gonna hate when I make you wear this." Luke swings his arm out from behind him and produces an honest-to-goodness cowboy hat. It's dark brown.

I glower up at him. "Luke . . ."

"Dress code!" he says defensively.

"First of all, you're supposed to stop buying me things."

"I never agreed to that."

I roll my eyes. "Second, I'm gonna look like an idiot."

"Oh, stop it, do I look like an idiot?"

Far from it, and I resent him making me look him over once again. Tonight, Luke has gone full cowboy. Plaid button-down, blue jeans, boots, and a cream-colored cowboy hat that bends up at the sides, almost like a seagull. He's even wearing a belt with a fancy buckle. Who knew cowboys could look so expensive?

The image of him, a sturdy and lanky cowboy, is one I won't be forgetting for a very long time. "Of course not. But you were like born for something like this."

"Eleanor, Eleanor, Eleanor . . ." Luke drawls. *Drawls.* Like he's been overcoming with some holy cowboy spirit. Maybe it's the outfit or the milieu. He's taking the role seriously. "Cowboys aren't born, honey. They're made."

He may as well have just dripped a little honey on my tongue, calling me that. I swallow, trying to push down the way that made me feel.

Luke places the hat on my head, and I oblige him, not trying to duck away. "There ya go . . ." he mutters. "Let's just . . ." He delicately arranges my curls so that the hat sits a bit better. I oblige him there too, because I always welcome when Luke interrupts the distance between us.

Luke lets out a whistle. "Look at you!"

I blush. "Stop that."

He does not, promenading around me and looking me up and down. While insistence is normally something I don't like in a man, I like it in Luke. He pushes me. Not in a bad way. He makes me get out of my comfort zone. And it feels good to go out of my comfort zone with him. He makes me feel . . . capable. Like all I need to do is reach out and take it rather than wait for something to claim me.

"She's a cowgirl," Luke remarks once he stops in front of me again.

My shoulders fall. "I still feel silly."

"Okay, well—" Luke runs his hand along my shoulder and places it against the nape of my neck. In control. I love it. "We'll take a shot of whiskey, get you on the dance floor, and then you'll forget you ever felt silly at all."

I groan, but I let him guide me inside.

The place is packed with people dancing. At the back of the room is a stage where a band is already in full swing. Fiddle and guitar, an upright bass. There's a sign overhead that reads vehemently, "No Line Dancing," which makes me laugh because I thought that's what I was in for.

The floor is large, but eventually transitions from wood to tile toward the bar area where the non-dancers and those taking a load off can congregate. There are also a few pool tables with people waiting in the wings to snatch them up as others finish their games. Neon signs advertising different beers line the walls.

As promised, Luke gets us shots. Two for me, at my request. The whiskey burns so good going down and I get that lightness in my head almost immediately. When Luke asks if I'm ready to take the floor, I know I'll never be ready, but I'm definitely more ready with two shots of whiskey in my system.

He takes me by the hand and leads us to an open patch of floor where the two of us can bob and linger until I get my bearings since stopping is expressly forbidden.

"Okay, you've got rhythm at least," he says.

"I've been to a few school dances. Bar Mitzvahs . . . weddings . . ." I say, watching a couple plodding past us with serious expressions.

"You know how to two-step?" he asks.

"I know both of those words!" I say with a smile.

Luke's lifts his chin and laughs, allowing me to see most of his face without the brim of his hat shadowing him. "Let me teach you."

Objectively, a two-step is easy. Subjectively though, not everyone is taught two-stepping by a guy they're totally obsessed with. The liquor in my system is a double-edged sword. It makes me less prone to self-consciousness but also makes me stupider, especially with one of his hands tucked under my shoulder blade.

I'm surprised that I am not the only one who might have two left feet. The floor is filled with people who *seriously* know what they're doing, sure, but there are also young, fresh-faced couples who don't know what to do with their gangling bodies and those who have the spirit but not the technique.

It makes it easier to enjoy the music and the man in front of me and just . . . give in.

After a spin around the floor, or more of a walk, Luke grins at me. "You ready for a spin?"

"Wha—" Before I get the question out, he whips my arm up and I have no choice but to follow the motion lest I want to sprain my elbow. I'm not nearly as graceful as some of the other women on the floor as they spin, but I manage not to fall on my ass.

Luke pulls me back toward him just in time for me to admonish him. "Luke!"

"Sorry, that wasn't very gentlemanly of me. Bad form," he says with a fake grimace.

We idle in our place rather than traversing the floor again. There is a pull inside me, inching me closer. No one warned me that the brim of a cowboy hat was kind of like a circle of safety. Who needs to leave room for Jesus when you're afraid you might knock your hat off if you're too close?

"Who taught you to dance?" I ask.

Luke looks away. "You won't laugh?"

I furrow my brow. "When have I ever?"

His blue eyes flicker back to me. My chest warms.

"My dad, he—" He laughs at himself before he continues. "He made me practice with my mom."

"*Made* you?"

"Yup," Luke answers, popping the 'p.' "No child of his was going to be a slouch on the dancefloor. Especially not his son. A woman can get away with anything if she has a good partner."

I narrow my eyes.

"On the dancefloor, that is," Luke adds with a half-laugh. "But if you're meant to lead, you have nothing to hide behind. And dancing *is* the language of love."

I blow a raspberry. "Yeah, maybe 50 years ago."

"Oh, please. You ever been dipped? That works every time."

"No, and I don't—"

Luke grips me tight, swings me one way, preparing to bend me backward. My body goes brittle, and I scream. Instead of dipping me, Luke makes me trip over my own feet, and I shriek. Still, he has me tight in his grip. To prevent me from falling, he pulls me flush to his chest, forcing the brim of my hat upward and sending it tumbling to the floor.

"You have to let yourself be dipped, Eleanor!" he says.

"I wasn't ready! I wasn't . . ." I trail off when I lift my face upward and realize how close I am to Luke. As close as two people can be. My chest to his.

Luke seems to have noticed this too, because he goes silent and serious. His eyes fall to my mouth.

My belly flips with terror.

A kiss from Luke sounds incredible.

But I'm not sure I can handle it.

I'm pulled out of the moment when I feel my hat forced back on my head from someone behind me, pushed so far down that it nearly reaches my eyebrows. "Don't lose your head, little lady!" a man's Texas accent warns.

"Thank you!" I call out over my shoulder, though I'm not sure which man I'm directing my thanks toward. I adjust the brim. "Um . . . maybe we can take a break."

Luke nods. "Sure, we should get out of the way anyway."

We head back to the bar area. Luke stops by an empty high-top and places his palm on it. "What do you want?"

"Whatever you're having," I say because I can't nearly think straight. My blood is still rushing from being pressed up against him, making my heart race, my head swirl, and the place between my legs swell with need.

"Got it," he says and then shuffles off to the bar.

I take a seat at the high top and watch him go. I had been so ready to ask him out the other day. Where did all that courage go?

Luke slinks up to the corner of the bar and leans onto his elbows, trying to get the attention of the bartender. His ass looks *so* good in those jeans. My hands ache to slide into those back pockets and squeeze.

Clearly the whiskey is going to my head.

As he waits, I watch as a woman sidles up to him. She's got auburn hair and wears the cowgirl look well. A native. Less anxious than me for sure.

I hold my breath when she gives his arm a squeeze. Luke turns to her and smiles. He knows her.

I wonder *how* he knows her. Same circles? Friends? Former lovers?

Current lovers?

I push that last one away. No way he'd be bringing me out in public all the time if he had a girlfriend. But maybe it's not a girlfriend. Maybe he just gets around. Maybe he's looking to add me to his roster. Just another girl.

I want to throw up. The past is too heavy on my shoulders. The feeling of being unwanted. It lingers in everything I do.

In a way, it's why I latched onto the picture of Diane. I couldn't bear to think of tossing it aside. What if that's me one day? Just a woman in a picture. Would someone try and learn my story if they saw me? Or would they cast me aside?

I'm not loud like Diane was. I don't sing. I don't stand up in front of people. I hide behind a camera. I avoid wearing things I think will make me stick out. I try not to draw attention to me.

And then I met Luke, and he *pursued* me. Wanted to be around me. Wants.

Except now the woman wraps her arm around his waist and looks at him with sparkling eyes and he doesn't push her away. He locks his arm around her neck.

I press my hands against the table. I need to get out of here. I need to go home and bury my head in the sand.

A drink thumps in front of me, the heavy bottom glass thumping loudly. The hand around it is not Luke's hand. Thicker, callused fingers. I follow the hand to a forearm covered in dark hair, to a shoulder, up to a face half covered by a formidable beard.

The man in front of me smiles. There's a drunkenness about his eyes. I've never seen him before in my life.

"You alone?" he asks in a deep voice.

"No, my friend is getting me a drink," I say.

"Well, she can join us when she comes back," he says, pulling out the other chair and sitting down. "The more the merrier."

Every muscle in my body locks up.

"What's your name?" he slurs.

"What's yours?"

He laughs and runs a hand through his beard. "Fair, fair. I'm Dave."

I blink.

"Your turn."

I glance over at the bar again, trying to see if I can flag Luke's attention. The woman who was hanging on him is gone, but now he's engaged with the bartender. Another woman. Looks vaguely familiar. Purple hair. She's leaning toward him with bedroom eyes. Or maybe I'm making it up. If he was looking at me, I might indulge the guy at least a little bit. Play the jealousy game.

But it's not worth it.

"Eleanor," I say. Fuck me, I should have come up with a fake name. For all I know, the guy is harmless, but it's always safer to assume the worst.

"Like Eleanor Roosevelt?" he asks with a finger gun in my direction.

"Sure. That works," I say.

Dave laughs at his own—I hesitate to call it a joke, but *joke*. He swigs the rest of the liquid in his glass back, leaving only ice. Then, he slams it back down in front of me. "What are you drinking?"

"My friend is—"

"No, I wanna buy you a drink. What are you drinking?" Dave presses, leaning toward me. His breath is sour.

"I only need one at a time," I say.

"Come on, don't be like that, Four Eyes," he says.

"Four Eyes? Good one," I say dryly.

Dave laughs again, harder this time. "Come on, I'm teasing you." He places a hand on my knee before I can jerk away. "I wanna get to know you. Let me buy you a drink."

This is so embarrassing. Of course, Luke is approached by women all more beautiful than me, ones that would look better next to him in an aesthetic Instagram photo, and I'm hit on by *Dave* the drunk. The kind of guy who won't go away when you ask nicely and will get butthurt if you *aren't* nice.

"Pick your poison, Eleanor Roosevelt," Dave says with a smile, his hand sliding around my knee to the back of my thigh.

18

LUKE

Fuck no.

I should have known better, leaving her alone for more than a moment. She might not believe it, but I know there are eyes on her all the time. Her otherworldliness draws people in. Their gazes. Now their hands.

My blood boils seeing this guy's hand on her knee. Then her thigh.

I shoot a look to Cressida. She picked up a shift here tonight and usually takes good care of me, but she's swamped, having to balance several drink orders at once. I'm at the bottom of that list because she knows I won't give her a hard time. All I asked for was two whiskey cokes. Broken Spoke isn't known for its cocktails. All I need is the well whiskey and a squirt of Coke in each glass.

Instead, I have to wait and watch Eleanor squirm in her seat while Cressida works her way through the drinks.

I look back at Eleanor and this guy. It burns my insides to have to look, but if I *don't* look, he might do something, and I wouldn't forgive myself if I stood idly by while that happened.

The man's hand shifts to the bottom of her seat between her legs, and he drags her closer to him. Eleanor laughs, however, her eyes are rolling away from him, wide through the lenses of her glasses, crying for help.

Fuck the drinks. We don't need them. Cressida and I can hash it out next time she's at Lonesome Rose.

I stalk over to the table, trying to rein in the fury I'd like to unleash. My father always said calm, cool, and collected is the best way to deal with assholes. And if that doesn't get rid of them, let out the fire and brimstone.

As I close in, my shadow drapes over the table.

Eleanor notices: her eyes shoot to me. The relief is visible through her eyes and body when she sees me.

"We got a problem here?" I ask.

The man glances back at me, then at Eleanor. Back to me again. "Shit, you didn't say your friend was a *guy*," he says through a laugh, still well-humored.

Eleanor says nothing. Her lips are sealed shut. Poor thing looks like she's been scared half to death.

"Yeah, *he* is," I say. I place my hand on the back of his chair. "And I think you're in my seat."

Dave lifts his hands. "Sorry, buddy, if I'd known she was yours—"

"She's not," I interrupt. Because she belongs to no one. As much as I wish she belonged to me, I've been too much of a coward to ask. And even so, it doesn't matter if she's got a guy or if she's on her own—discomfort is discomfort. No one deserves that. "And that shouldn't matter. I could tell from a mile away she wasn't interested. Shocked you couldn't."

Eleanor covers her mouth with her hand, resisting a laugh.

The guy gets up out of the chair, a little uneasy on his feet. "I got it, I got it. Have a . . . night," he says before stumbling off. Just a hapless dude who doesn't know his way around flirting. So many of them like that. They're harmless until they're not.

I watch him go, limping off to the next object of his desires. I lower myself into the seat across from Eleanor. "You okay?"

Eleanor nods. "Yeah, I'm fine." Her voice, while plain, is clearly veiling a well of emotions.

I wish she didn't feel she had to hide herself from me. "You sure? You want some water or—"

"Can we just—" Eleanor begins, but her breath is trapped in her throat.

I'd like to reach out and touch her. But the last thing I want to do is make anything worse.

"Can we just get some fresh air?" she manages to choke out.

Fuck the drinks, fuck the dancing. We need to get out of here. "Yeah, let's go out back."

Eleanor follows me through the crush of people in the bar back toward the patio at the back of the bar. I want nothing more than to reach back and take her hand, make sure I don't lose her in the throng. Let everyone know that *she is mine* because, fuck it, I'm done pretending she's not.

It might not be the right moment, but the second I get her alone, when the world softens around us, I'm letting it out. I can't hold it down anymore. Life is too goddamn short. I know well enough from losing my dad. If I lose her by being open, so be it.

It's gotten to a point where *this* hurts more. Pretending I'm not feeling everything I'm feeling.

The night air isn't necessarily cool, but it feels like menthol to my lungs. Although that might be the smoke of cigarettes pilling in the air.

Eleanor emerges next to me, her eyes glassy.

Luckily, the concrete patio is only peppered with people. There's the group of smokers in the corner and a couple whispering sweet nothings to one another, leaned up against a fence post. At the back of the patio, out from under the portcullis, is a fire pit surrounded by a few curved benches, all empty.

Eleanor and I share a fide-side bench. It's big enough to leave a gap between us, but the curve in the bench makes it impossible not to be angled toward one another. Fine for my purposes, but for Eleanor's, I'm not so sure.

We're silent for a bit. I'm not sure where to start or what to do. I remove my hat and lean my elbows on my knees, waiting for inspiration to strike.

"Thank you," Eleanor says in a soft voice.

I shake my head. "No, you shouldn't thank me. I shouldn't have left you alone."

"You couldn't have known."

"Of course, I could have," I say, looking into the fire. The flames waver, dancing together. A perfect image to encapsulate how I'm feeling inside. Chaotic burning threatening to incinerate me. "You're a beautiful woman and if guys see you alone at a bar—"

"Are you about to say, 'boys will be boys?' Because I'm not—"

I sit up with a scoff. "Of course not. That's not what I mean at all, I'm trying to . . ." The words are trapped inside me. My heart has so many things it would like to say, and I can't manage to string a couple of words together to get them to come out right. "You're a catch. That's all."

Eleanor smiles sadly. "You are too. Obviously." She grips the edge of the bench. "I mean, I see how women talk to you."

I frown. So, she's been watching? She notices? Is she jealous like I am?

"I mean, just at the bar you were like—"

"No, come on," I say, laughing at the ludicrousness of the situation.

Eleanor balks. "What do you mean 'come on?' You were talking to that woman and then the bartender—"

"I *work* with them, Eleanor. Cressida is a bartender I've known for years and—"

"You had your arm around the other woman," she says coldly.

So, she *is* jealous. "And Jen runs a venue on 6th. With her wife."

Eleanor is quiet before she lets out a singular, "Oh."

"Yeah. Oh," I huff. I dig the toe of my boot into the gravel circle surrounding the fire pit. "What's it matter to you anyway?" I don't ask it meanly. It's just a question. A question I would love an answer to.

Still quiet. I lift my eyes to look at her. *Break my heart. I fucking want you to. Put me out of my misery like Old Yeller.*

A strange smile appears on her face. "I can't tell if you're an idiot or a gentleman or both."

"What's that supposed to mean?"

Eleanor purses her lips, rubbing them together.

"Nor . . ." I slide a little closer. "Please tell me."

"I'm starting to think it's Option C," she murmurs, then shakes her head. With a deep inhale, she finally says it. "This is more than friends, right? What's happening between us?"

The elation inside me is so great I'm mute.

"I'm not good at this kind of thing. I don't like guessing because I don't want to be wrong, so just tell me so I don't—"

"Yeah," I say, though it's barely a word, more a breath. "Yeah, it's more than that."

Eleanor's eyes twinkle.

"You think I would have gone to a radio station at midnight for someone who was just my friend?" I ask.

She giggles. "You've been telling me that this is what friends do for each other! How am I supposed to know if it's southern hospitality or—you know, something more?"

"Let me make it incredibly clear, then," I say.

Eleanor's lips part, eyes widen. As much as I'd like to kiss her, I haven't gotten this far to ruin it with overenthusiasm. I grab one of her hands in mine and lift it to my mouth. With our eyes locked, to be sure there is no mistaking what I'm about to do for "friendship," although that would be a logical leap for anyone, I kiss the back of her hand.

God, it's only the back of her hand, but it makes my stomach swoop. My eyes flutter shut as I plant the kiss there like seeds that will bloom in springtime. Every part of her needs to know from this kiss what I've wanted from the moment I laid eyes on her.

I could remain there forever. I could kiss the length of her arm, all the way to her neck, up to her mouth, and taste every part of her.

Slow, Luke. Slow.

I tear my lips from her and push her hand up against my chest.

Eleanor's face is still painted with shock. "Well, you're not wrong. That was incredibly clear."

I chuckle, but I say nothing. With my free hand, I tilt the brim of her hat back, then pinch her chin between my fingers, angling her face perfectly toward mine. Her lips are either going to take me to heaven or pull me into hell. I welcome either outcome.

"Luke," Eleanor says. Though my name is a single syllable, her voice still trembles.

"Eleanor," I echo.

Her eyes flick across my face. Not the welcome expression of a person about to receive a kiss from someone they are presumably attracted to. She's scared. "We can't go back. If you do this, we can't go back."

I laugh, extend my hand against her cheek and drag my fingers through the curls. "Why would I want to go back?"

"Because you might change your mind."

"It's a kiss, Eleanor, not a contract."

Her cheeks flush: she turns her face out of my hand.

I make a fist of my empty hand and place it reluctantly in my lap. "Did I do something wrong?"

"No, I—no, it's not you. It's me. I'm—" Eleanor places her hand against her face and rubs at her eye. "I'm afraid to get hurt."

"Well, I can't promise anything, but that's the last thing I want to do, Nor." I hold tight to her hand against my chest so she can't pull that away too.

"If I tell you why I'm scared, I'm afraid you'll freak out."

"Nothing scares me."

She scrunches her nose with a smile. "Shut up."

"When it comes to you, nothing. I swear." Though I swear out loud, there's a pang in my heart knowing that there is *one* think I'm terrified of with her. My little white lie that's grown into a big fat one.

Ignore it.

"Swear," I repeat. "You hear me?"

Eleanor nods. "I hear you."

The fire crackles.

"My ex-boyfriend cheated on me. For, like, months," she says and then has the gall to laugh at herself.

"Oh, god Nor, I'm sorry." I've been pretty damn lucky not to come up against that even though most people I know have dealt with cheating in one form or another. Because of that, I've never worried about infidelity. But I can only imagine how hard it would be to let someone in if you're scared that they'll hurt you like that again.

She shakes her head, looking away. "It's stupid now."

"Not stupid. *At all.*"

"He's kind of why I left Chicago," Eleanor says. "We were living together."

"No, *Eleanor.*" As if it could get worse.

She laughs, no doubt to stave off the pain she's had to unwind from. "Yeah, I went home from work with a migraine and walked in on them."

Apparently, it could get much worse. "Fuck, I'm so sorry."

Eleanor stares into the fire, warmth dancing across her face. She hasn't taken off the hat which I take as a good sign it's growing on her. It's an appendage, a new vestigial organ. Her profile is elegant. Like a marble statue in a museum. Long luscious lashes. Full lips. Pretty nose. You know you're down bad for someone when you're admiring their nose.

"I think it's going to be okay," she says. "I think I'm going to be . . ." Eleanor returns her gaze to mine. "I think I'm okay."

I've done things I'm not proud of, but it doesn't compare to infidelity, right? It was a lie to bring us closer, not push us farther apart. In a few years, I can tell her, and we'll laugh about

146

it. Assuming we have a few years together. Is it crazy that I hope we do?

"I'd never do that to you," I say. "I'd never betray you like that." That is the truth. A solid fact.

Eleanor's lips perk up at the corners.

"You've . . . since the moment I saw you, you've had every bit of my attention." Also the truth. I have more truths than lies. They should weigh more at the end of the day. I'll choose to believe that or else I'm not going to make it through this next moment. "Your ex is a total dumbass."

She laughs. My laugh is trapped in my chest. My rib cage is squeezing around my heart. I'm aching.

If she turns away from me now, I think I'll absolutely die.

19

ELEANOR

For once, Luke does not know the next right thing to do. At least he's not pretending he knows. He's staring at me, waiting for me, beholden to me.

An idiotic gentleman.

Fuck it. Fuck my ex and fuck Chicago and fuck the past.

Now, it's Luke. And it's Austin. And it's *now*.

"You should probably thank him," I say softly.

Luke's eyebrows lift.

"Otherwise, I wouldn't be sitting here with you."

Luke lifts his chin and smiles. "You know what? You're right. I owe him."

I grab the edge of the bench behind us, a subtle movement to get closer to Luke. I let my eyes fall to his mouth, and then lift back to his dreamy blue eyes. He's like a fucking Ken doll. A hotter, cowboy version of Ken.

"Eleanor?"

"Yes, Luke." I say it like an answer to the unasked question. I feel it, the connective energy between us, urging us closer together. I'm not saying no anymore. Not when I've captivated his attention from the moment he saw me.

In an instant, every self-conscious thought I've had about our differences washes away. So what if he's the pretty boy and I'm the bookish girl? This isn't high school. It's real life. And in real life, we feel without reason. Without plan.

God, do I feel for him.

As Luke takes my hand and flattens it against his chest, I can feel his heart pounding against my palm. Mine beats at the same pace if not faster. Both our hearts hot and furious with us. *Get on with it,* they say.

With both his hands free, he cups my cheeks in his hands. His thumb coasts along my cheekbone tenderly.

Aw fuck it. Idiotic gentlemen don't hurry moments, but fake cowgirls do. I close the small gap between our lips and in a split second, we're kissing.

We're *kissing*.

Luke's lips are insistent, pressing against mine with a need that has been building for a long time. I can only imagine I'm kissing him with the same intensity. I've never had a kiss this explosive and chaste at once. Tongues aren't rolling, we're not tangled up in bed, and yet I feel hot all over. Pretty sure it's not just the fire doing that.

Luke's lips part from mine, but he remains in my space, breathing into my mouth. "You're full of surprises, Eleanor."

Enough talking. I've been talking and thinking for ages now. Give me more.

I loop my arms around his neck and kiss him again, this time delving my tongue between his lips. Luke inhales sharply through his nose in surprise, but he doesn't dare draw away. As I thread my fingers through his soft locks, he slides a hand around my waist, pulling me as close as the bench will allow without us making a complete scene.

He grabs my hat off my head and tosses it aside, then fingers my curls intensely, palm stretching out against the back of my head.

I'm flushed everywhere. And though I have wanted him for his kindness and charm for weeks now, I first wanted him with my body.

The throbbing between my legs is not going to let me forget about that any time soon.

"Woo! That's right!" someone cheers and I realize when they "Woo!" again, they're directing their cheering at us.

I draw away first, blinking my eyes open and realizing my glasses are fogged up.

Luke might not have glasses, but his gaze is fogged over too. I don't think he even noticed that someone was flinging jeering in our direction.

Once I clear off my lenses, I look in the direction of the patio.

There's Dave. Rooting us on, holding another glass of whatever he's been drinking.

I shake my head. What a weirdo.

"Should we go?" Luke asks low in my ear.

I snatch another short kiss from him. "Yeah, let's go."

* * *

The drive back to my apartment is quiet except for the radio. We've been in this car so many times, but the air has never been this charged. The potential has always lingered, but now it is mutually agreed upon. The stage has been set. What comes next is up to both of us to create.

My heart pounds as Luke pulls the car over and he murmurs, "Let me walk you to the door." I've done this song and dance before. Sure, he can walk me up to the door and then walk me in the door, then into my apartment, then into my bedroom . . .

I don't usually move so fast with someone, but hell, we've built a relationship. It's not like we're strangers who met tonight and are going to go down in a blaze of glory.

It will mean something.

Luke opens my door for me, takes my hand to help me out, and doesn't let go. We cross the street hand in hand, up the stairs to my door, and then . . .

"You're right, dancing was fun," I say as I root through my bag for my keys.

"Oh, I'm glad it wasn't too torturous for you."

I glance at him. Luke is leaned up against the door frame. Quintessential cowboy.

"Where are my keys?" I ask myself aloud, feeling self-conscious he's standing there watching me.

Suddenly, he pushes me up against the door, right next to the call box. Body on body. There is hunger in his eyes. A hunger I would like to sate.

Luke drags his thumb along my jaw to my chin. "Man, you're beautiful."

"Oh. Thanks," I say. What an idiotic thing to say.

"You're welcome," he says with a kindly nod. Southern fucking hospitality at its finest. Then he kisses me.

I grab his sides as tight as I can, inspired by primal need. I'd fall if he weren't pressed so hard against me. And speaking of hard, I'm not sure if his belt buckle is digging into my belly or something else. I'd welcome the latter.

Before I can sneak my tongue into his mouth again, Luke withdraws and kisses the corner of my mouth, then my cheek, then the hinge of my jaw. He stops at my ear. So close that I can hear the saliva move in his mouth as he decides what to do. "I want—" he stops short of finishing his sentence.

"I want" hovers in the air. We are both wanting. That much is clear.

Luke gulps as he lets out a breath. "I want you so bad, but I'm not coming up tonight."

My tingling nerves screech to a halt, an eighteen-car pile-up of senses.

"Not to assume you'd invite me up, but . . ." Luke says, resting one arm over my head, his free hand on my waist.

"No, that was on my mind."

For a man who was just whispering how badly he wanted me, he looks remarkably calm. "I don't want to rush it. Don't want you to think that's all I'm after. Cause trust me, I'm after a whole lot more."

How can I resist smiling at that?

"How's that for southern hospitality?"

I thwack him in the chest. "Rude."

Luke laughs and pulls me into his arms though I'm trying to squirm away. Trying and very purposefully failing. "I'm teasing you."

"And I hate how much I love it," I grumble.

Luke leans down for another kiss, and I rise to meet him on my tiptoes, his arms wrapped around my shoulders as close as two people can be. I imagine we resemble two characters in an old movie. Kissing with an unearthly amount of passion.

"Can I see you again?" Luke whispers against my mouth.

"Obviously."

He grins, then kisses my forehead. "Goodnight, Eleanor."

I sigh mournfully, gripping the front of his shirt. "Goodnight, Luke."

He gives me one more kiss before he releases me. The second I am no longer surrounded by the vise of his arms, my body wilts.

I try not to watch him go, or else I might be tempted to run after him. I reach into my bag and find my keys immediately. Guess I should thank them for being a pain in the ass earlier, bought me some extra time with him.

I unlock the front door and glance back at Luke's car. He's standing by the front door waiting for me to get inside.

He has the nerve to tip the brim of his hat down, a smirk on his lips. I'm reminded of the throbbing pulse in my core.

Fucking cowboys.

20

LUKE

I lean against the back wall as the band I'm working tonight, Orson Dwells, goes through their soundcheck, playing covers of Spoon songs. They'd be pretty faithful covers too if not for the fact they're an acid jazz band with a lead singer that raps half the time.

It sounds like it doesn't work, but trust me, it works.

It's one of the rare gigs where everything is going as planned. The band is easygoing, Lonesome Rose is running like clockwork, and my team is all on their best behavior.

I catch Randy's eyes at the soundboard. He's been doing some last-minute checks for me. I lift my hand and mimic drinking while mouthing, "Coffee?"

He gives me a thumbs up, which is good enough for me. I slip out of the venue and onto 6th. There's a stream of people walking the streets as per usual under the smeary twilight sky. The sky reminds me of Eleanor. We met under a sky just like this not that long ago. Feels a lot longer, though, the way she's rooted herself inside me.

I pull out my phone as I walk to pick up my coffee and open my text exchange with Eleanor.

We haven't spoken today. The last messages sent were that I was outside her apartment, and she was coming down to meet me.

I should have texted her first thing this morning, but I couldn't find the right thing to say. At first, I was going to say, "good morning" with a little smiling emoji, but I waited too long. So I thought I'd tell her she left her hat in my car, but that didn't feel quite romantic enough. As I vacillated on what to say, time ticked by and now it's nighttime.

It should be simple. Just ask her out on a date. Easy. I've done that plenty of times before.

Except I've never asked *Eleanor* out and that's a whole other can of worms.

She hasn't texted me either, to be fair, but that's not a good excuse at all. I might be as modern-minded as they come in Austin, but I still like some things traditional. I should ask her out, plan the date, pay for it, and take the fucking lead.

I'm stunted. Remembering the sheen of her eyes as she told me her fears fireside.

I replay the conversation in my head as I stand in line. How her ex betrayed her. How scared she is to trust.

It's apples and oranges what he did and what I did. Right?

That's the question that has me going in circles. Should I tell her now? Give her all the information so she can make an informed decision about me? Or do I keep it close to my chest and hope that enough time passes that it's a story we can laugh about in the future?

The truth will eat at me any time she brings up Diane. I know she won't be leaving our conversations any time soon, especially if Eleanor's able to cobble something together for the exhibit at Reeder.

And I . . . can't get Diane out of my head either. If my dad was alive, I'd have no qualms asking about where Aunt Diane went. Why we never talk about her. But I can't ask Mom. Talking about the past is too hard for her right now.

I order two red eyes for Randy and me and head back to the Lonesome Rose, somewhat in a daze while my thoughts cloud together.

Wanting Eleanor. Wondering if I'm as good for her as I've felt. Not wanting to hurt her or be hurt. Because while I've had my fair share of flings I walked away from, I've never been this head over heels for someone.

I focus on the head of the woman walking in front of me. Curly hair, loose-fitting dress.

I've seen that dress and that hair before.

She stops and steps out of the way of oncoming traffic, reaches into the slouchy bag at her side. Produces a camera.

No fucking way.

I walk up beside her, subtly peering at her face. "Nor?"

Eleanor's head jerks away from the viewfinder of her camera. She pulls her glasses back down over her eyes and blinks at me. A ginormous smile appears on her face. "Oh, hey!"

"What are you doing out here?" I ask.

"Well, I . . ." she flushes. "I actually came out here to see you."

I arch my eyebrows. "Oh?"

"I mean, that's what I *was* doing. Until I got to the Lonesome Rose and realized it would be creepy of me to show up where you were working when you only mentioned offhandedly to me where you'd be tonight, like, two weeks ago."

I tighten my lips, suppressing a smile. It'd be creepy if it were anyone else. Not when it's the exact woman I want to see though.

"So, I thought I'd spend some time taking some pictures. Didn't want to waste a trip out here."

"You should have texted me. I would have come out to see you."

Eleanor narrows her eyes. "Yeah, you could have texted me too."

I gulp down my nerves. "I . . ."

"Then again you said you weren't going to rush things. I guess I should have expected it would take you a few business days to reach out to me."

I laugh. "No, I wanted to reach out to you today. In fact, I was going to."

"But?"

My mouth is so hot, and my palms are sweating so bad. Why didn't I get iced coffee? "I got nervous too."

"I never said I was nervous," she says with a smug smile.

What a far cry from the hesitant and tender-footed woman I met weeks ago. She's coming out of her shell and making herself at home in Austin. In my heart too. Damn her. "Fine, you weren't nervous. But I was."

Eleanor laughs. "I find it hard to believe that *you* get nervous."

"What?! I absolutely do. Especially around you."

Her eyes widen. "That's silly."

"No, it's not. Not at all. I want to get it right with you."

"There's nothing to get right."

"Uh, yeah there is."

We both go quiet. The swell of 6th Street speaks for us. Life goes on. It moves. The music plays.

We only have so much time on this earth. If there's anything I've learned from losing my dad, it's that. And Diane too.

Being nervous, being scared is a waste of it.

I wish I had a free fucking hand to gesticulate or nervously scratch my jaw. Instead, I'm stuck with all this coffee. "Okay, Eleanor."

"Yes, Luke."

I pinch my lips together in a smile. She's so cute and sassy. "I'd like to take you on a date."

She crosses her arms over her chest, tilting her head to the side.

"Would you . . . let me?" It's coming out all stilted and weird, but at least it's coming out.

"Yes, *obviously*," Eleanor answers without hesitation.

Every organ in my body somersaults with excitement. I don't want to taint this, so I resolve to keep the dishonesty down. It won't be hard if I know what I might lose. "Okay, well, that's good."

"When?" she asks.

"Wednesday?" I offer.

"Deal."

"*Deal?*"

"Yeah! It's a deal."

"It's not a deal, it's a date."

"Whatever."

I bite my lower lip. I look forward to more of this rapport on Wednesday. I know conversation can be easy with Eleanor, but colored by explicit romance is uncharted territory. Gotta up my game. "Okay, well, I'll pick you up."

"Of course you will. Southern gentleman."

"Obviously."

"Obviously."

The anticipation is already killing me. I don't know how I'm going to make it until Wednesday. However, I've got a job to do and a crew that's probably wondering why I've been gone longer than ten minutes.

"You should probably get back to work," she says as if reading my mind.

"Yeah, probably. I'm glad you decided to be a creep."

She gapes at me. "Hey! I wasn't actually a creep, I changed my—"

Before she can finish her sentence, I press my mouth to hers in a solid, simple kiss. How I wish I could fill my hands with her instead of these damn cups of coffee.

Eleanor gasps into my mouth and leans into me almost immediately, welcoming the kiss.

Just one kiss with her is dangerous. I'd like to throw the coffee down, pull her into my arms, and take her all the way home. Fuck the show. I have something much more important to do.

Eleanor rips away first, much stronger than I am, pushing her hands lightly against my chest. "You should go before I don't let you."

A shiver runs down my spine. "That gives me lots of ideas," I say, backing up a few steps.

"Get out of here, Wyatt," she says, grinning after me.

The swarm of 6th Street starts to engulf her as the space between us grows and eventually, I am resigned to leaving her behind.

Wednesday, I'll have her all to myself. No distractions or interruptions. Wednesday will be like seeing her for the first time. Something between us has finally been born.

I want so badly to get it right.

21

ELEANOR

"I know it's not a *Great* lake," Luke says. "But it *is* a lake."

It might not be as endless as Lake Michigan, but Lake Travis is stunning in its own right. Especially from right *on* the lake. The view from our pontoon is stunning. We're surrounded by panoramic vistas that stretch for miles. The lush water is streaked with the setting sunlight. There's a shocking amount of greenery since I've always pictured Texas as a desert. And though there are plenty of other people at the lake, it feels so peaceful to be out here to take in the moment alone with Luke.

"I love it," I say softly.

From his place in the captain's chair, Luke throws me a soft smile. I never thought I'd say it but a man who can navigate a boat, even if it's just a pontoon, is sexy. So, we've added cowboys *and* boat captains to the list of guys who are my type.

Hell, I might as well just write Luke's name on the list in all caps.

The night has been an ideal first date. Luke picked me up at my place with flowers at the ready. We had a beautiful dinner through which conversation was giggly and a little bit awkward in the best first date kind of way. And then Luke brought me out here for a boat ride. It's all been . . . too much. No one has ever treated me like this. It's always been dinner or drinks. Usually, we'd split the bill.

I haven't had to lift a finger tonight and I have to say, I'm loving it.

Luke scans our surroundings, calls it good, and drops the anchor. Once we're locked in place, he starts to put the canopy down which he's informed me is called a Bimini. "Can I help?" I ask.

"No," he says, remaining focused on pulling the top down. A lock of hair falls onto his forehead, his white dress shirt rumples. Rumpled to the point of looking delectable. "You just sit there and look pretty," he says, then gives me a devilish smile.

I scoff at him, but play my part, drawing my legs up onto the bench and straighten out the legs of my black jumpsuit. A loan from Jolene. When she heard the date was happening, she insisted I buy a new dress for the occasion and when I told her that there was simply not money for a new dress, she offered one of her own.

"It will look better on you anyways," she said when she brought it into work this morning.

It *does* look good on me. I won't argue with her on that. The spaghetti straps and keyhole cutout right at my sternum between my breasts show off my best assets. And I'm inclined to say Luke agrees, not only because he was eager to tell me how beautiful I looked tonight, but also from the way his eyes kept traveling the length of my body whenever he got a moment.

If we'd just met, I'd be uneasy. But it's Luke. He's proven ten times over that he's not just in it for my body. Case in point, his refusal to come up the other night and sleep with me, which, while disappointing, has had me swooning since.

Once the Bimini is down, the sky is open above us, soft purple and twilight blue.

"Okay, now . . ." Luke takes a seat next to me on the bench, extending his arms over the back of the bench, grazing me ever so gently. "Where were we?"

I laugh and tentatively slide my arm over his, resting my hand against his bicep. I resist squeezing to feel the firmness of the muscles. Quietly, I toy with a lock of my hair and keep my eyes away from him. I'm playing coy. Interested to see where he takes this next.

Luke reaches across my lap and places his hand on my thigh, pulling on me until I twist my leg over his lap. "You're too far away."

I giggle, relishing the way his hand slides up and down my calf.

"Am I moving too fast?" he asks softly.

I shake my head. "No, this is perfect."

Luke's eyes drop to the keyhole cutout on my chest, then lift to meet my gaze.

"I know you're looking at my boobs."

He winces, head dropping back. "Sorry, I'm really trying not to."

"I'm just giving you a hard time," I say, shimmying closer. "I don't mind."

Luke turns his head toward me, continues rubbing my leg.

162

"In fact, I like it. I've been wanting you to look at me like that for over a month, so—"

"So, the truth comes out!" he says through a laugh.

"Oh, come on, it wasn't that much of a leap. We knew this."

"I knew nothing. I thought you were way too smart for me."

I lift an eyebrow. "I mean, if you're worried about not being able to pull your pretty boy antics on me—"

"No, no, nothing like that," he says. "What even are 'pretty boy antics?'"

I flush and gaze out at the water. "I mean, you know how you carry yourself. You're attractive and you know it and I'm sure you've broken a few hearts in your day."

"I bet you have to."

I shake my head. "No, actually. I'm the one who ends up heartbroken."

Luke frowns with puppyish concern.

"No, don't feel bad for me. I don't want to feel pathetic."

"I don't think you're pathetic. I think that anyone who would break your heart is a complete idiot and if I ever met them, I'd have a few choice words."

I observe Luke for a moment. He's so at peace sitting here next to me. Blue eyes open and vulnerable, his lips poised and ready for whether I speak or go in for a kiss. He's shaved today, his cheeks clean from stubble. And his golden hair is tousled and begging for my fingers to tousle them some more.

He's beautiful.

I'm still terrified, though. My ex, Vic, screwed me up in the head. How can someone love you to your face and go against all of that the second your back is turned? And I had known Vic for years by the time we dated.

Luke I've known months. I know a first date isn't a promise of a future, but the way Luke looks at me, speaks to me . . . I have to wonder what he sees in the next week, next month, next year. "You barely know me," I say.

Luke sits up suddenly. "That's not true."

"I mean, it kind of is. You've known me for, like, a month," I say objectively. "For all you know, I could actually be crazy."

"Now, you know that's a ridiculous thing to say."

It is. "I could be awful to be around after a while."

"I highly doubt that," he says.

I twist my lips. "I could be terrible in bed!"

"I highly doubt that too," he says, his eyelids lowering with lust.

I sigh.

He repositions his arm on the back of the bench, sliding himself closer. "Do you not want me to like you?"

"No," I say.

Luke's brow hardens. "You're trying not to hurt my feelings?"

"No," I say even more firmly. "Of course not. I wouldn't be out here in a boat with you if I didn't like you . . . a lot."

"Then what's going on in that pretty head of yours?" he asks, then presses a kiss to my temple. "Tell me. I want to know."

I lean into his kiss. "I might have to leave."

Luke adjusts some of my curls out of my face. "You mean because of your job?"

I nod. "If I don't get an extension at Reeder, I'll need to find a new job. And that might not be in Austin. And I'm not trying to get ahead of myself; I know this is—shit —this is our first date, and we're not talking marriage or anything, but—"

Oh my god, Eleanor, just shut up.

Thankfully, Luke isn't pulling away or looking for an exit plan. "I don't think it's fair to either of our feelings to act like the past month we've spent together hasn't informed at least some of our feelings. Right?"

"It's so irrational," I say. "To already be thinking long-term when—"

"When something's right, it's right . . . right?" Luke asks.

His blue eyes are almost pleading with me to agree. Let him know he's not alone in this.

"What happened to not *rushing*?" I ask with a half-laugh.

Luke lifts his head and laughs. It echoes across the water. "Okay, fair point. But *you* were the one who brought it up."

"I know I did. I'm just trying to sort out . . ." I place my forehead in my palm. "I care about you. So much. And I'm scared."

"Nor, look at me," he says, grabbing my wrist gingerly.

I do so though it's hard because I know my body has a mind of its own when Luke crowds my vision. All common sense goes out the window. Logical steps become hurried and desperate actions. And my heart fucking *aches*.

"I want to date you. And keep dating you. And hopefully, date you even a little longer than that."

I laugh, pressing my lips into a smile.

"If you want to stay in Austin, then I'm determined to keep you here. And if you want to go, you go. Even though that will probably kill me."

"Stop that."

"It will, I'm sure of it," he says, then gives me a playful smirk. "We don't have to know everything all at once."

I huff. "I like knowing everything all at once."

"I *know* you do, that much is clear," Luke says. "Too bad life doesn't go to Eleanor's plan all the time."

I fall into him, resting my head on his chest and looking up at the streaky sky. "It would be a lot easier if it did."

"I know, baby, I know."

The word "baby" singes my insides. Leaves a mark I'm not going to forget.

Luke trails his fingers through my hair and, for a long time, we're quiet, watching the changing sky. The boat sways, gently rocking us into a comfortable state of bliss.

I want to stay in Austin. I want a life here. But I want a life with *him* too. And if I can't divorce Austin from Luke, I'm going to make a bad decision. I can't live my life for a man. I did that before. Stuck to what I was used to so that everything made sense, to keep my relationship in line.

Luke starts to hum.

I recognize the tune almost immediately. "Hyacinth." It settles my insides.

I don't want to have regrets. Especially not in love.

For now, I'm here in Austin. And I don't' have to be anywhere else.

I lift my head off Luke's chest and kiss his neck softly. Then a bit harder, my teeth nipping at his skin.

"Nor . . ." Luke breathes.

Placing my hand against his cheek, I direct his mouth toward mine until we're kissing. We've already got the first kisses out of the way and while it's the first date, I have abandoned propriety and sense at the door for want, impulse, and the *nowness* of it all.

With our lips locked in kiss after kiss after kiss, I take hold of each of Luke's hands and place them against my belly. Slowly, I guide them up, up, up until they're pressed against my ribs, right beneath my breasts.

Luke breaks away from me, panting. "You don't have to—"

"I want to," I say before he can finish. "I want you to touch me."

A soft groan tumbles out of the back of Luke's throat.

I move his hands up to cup my breasts. He tightens his grip on me, and I sigh in ecstasy. Just to be held. To be wanted. By him, like this, out under a big and beautiful sky.

Luke jerks his hands away from my chest, drops them to my waist, and yanks me into his lap, peppering kisses down my neck. I squeal in laughter.

"You're trying to rush me, Eleanor," he growls in my ear like I've been bad, his twang coming out.

My body sings.

"And we might not know how much time we have, but goddammit, I am taking my time with you."

22

LUKE

A month. A month of Eleanor. The way I've wanted her from the beginning.

I have been on my best behavior. I've been a gentleman. And every time she's tried to push me over the edge to go faster than I'd like, I've held firm.

It's not that I don't want to sleep with her. Of course, I do. But my father always told me when you *know*, you don't rush things.

And I just know that what's between Eleanor and me is more than her three months in Austin. Which is why, now that she only has a month left of her job, I've been on the hunt to find her an apartment so she can focus on the job search. She doesn't know this, hasn't asked me to do it, but I want to.

Because I need her here.

The museum hasn't yet extended her contract, though they've happily taken her work to include in their exhibition. Jackasses. If they knew how she put her heart and soul into figuring out the truth behind that picture, surely, they'd reconsider.

Maybe they don't care.

I'm scrolling through Zillow for the third time this morning. I'm in the office today, and I should be doing any number of tasks on my to-do lists. I've got a full inbox, a list of people I need to call, and the barrel of the shotgun that is Austin City Limits pointing right at my forehead.

Needless to say, Zillow shouldn't be on that to-do list. However, it's my priority.

I'm an inch away from calling her my girlfriend in every conversation I have about her. I want to shout it from the rooftops. But I know until her plans are settled, Eleanor is going to resist that shift.

"Moving?"

I jolt in my chair and spin around to find Randy hovering behind my desk. "Jesus, dude, you scared me."

"Sorry," he says, then takes a big bite of the banana he's holding. "But are you moving?" he asks with a mouthful.

"No." I own my place. It's a bit out of the way. Market prices are hellish. When I bought, I thought it might settle me down. Three years at the house and it's still barely decorated.

"Then why are you looking at apartments?" Randy asks.

I tap the arms of my chair. "Um . . ."

"Is it your girlfriend?"

"Not girlfriend. Not yet," I say. This isn't the first time Randy has caught me distracted on the job over something to do with Eleanor. On more than one occasion, he's caught me smiling like a dope as I read a text from her.

Randy rolls his eyes. "Okay. Fine."

There aren't consequences for me being distracted, at least not in a managerial way. This is my business. What I say goes. But that also means when I'm not working, work doesn't get done. My team needs me at my best. It's still a grassroots effort every fucking day.

"Her contract is ending at the end of the month, which means she's looking for a new job and a new apartment."

"Mm. The double whammy."

"Right."

Randy polishes off the last of his banana and throws the peel in my wastebasket.

"Gross," I say.

He gives me an impish grin. Love the guy and hate the guy. "Listen, my brother is a . . ." He looks both ways and tucks his hand over his mouth to whisper, "Landlord."

"Are we not allowed to say land—"

"Uh bup bup!" Randy cries out before I can finish the word. "I don't like to talk about it. I went the arts route, and he went the business route. We work through it."

I furrow my brow. "Where are you going with this?"

"Well, he was complaining to me last night about how he's just taken over an old property, and there are a couple of tenants still there so he can't do a full gut and remodel. So, there are a few spots there."

My heart flutters.

"A little out of the way, but you know, it's got a roof and electricity and all that."

Barebones. A little out of the way. But who cares. It's an option.

"Basically, it's gonna be pricier than it's worth, but I know he just wants the units filled. If you tell him I sent you, you might be able to haggle."

"Give me his number," I say, too anxious to modulate the insistence in my voice.

The rest of my to-do list can wait. Keeping Eleanor in Austin is my priority. Plain and simple.

* * *

I pace the lobby of the Reeder Music Library. I've been here to pick Eleanor up from work many times over the past two months, but never have I been *this* anxious.

"You want to sit?" the young woman at the reception desk offers in a chipper voice, gesturing toward a wooden bench along the wall.

"I'm good," I say.

She smiles haplessly. I can tell she's worried I'm driving away customers, but it's the middle of the day on a weekday, and the lobby is absolutely silent. "Eleanor is helping with the final touches on an exhibition; it might be a while until she can step away."

"It's fine," I say. "I've got time."

"I'll try the archive extension again," the woman says, lifting the phone to her ear.

"Please."

She doesn't get an answer. I've sent Eleanor a few text messages already. When I left the office, when I got in my car, and when I arrived here. She'll know when she knows, and I'll be here when she does.

A few minutes later, Eleanor emerges from the exhibition hall. I want to run to her with all my bursting excitement, but it's her place of work, and I've already made enough of a scene. Plus, her forced smile and dull eyes give me pause.

"Luke, what are you doing here?" she asks, her phone in one hand, drawn up to our text conversation.

I close in on her so as not to be overheard. "Hey, I needed to talk to you about something."

There's obvious annoyance in her expression. "Now?"

"Yeah, it's important," I say. Randy's brother gave me until the end of the day to accept the offer or else he'd be raising the price and putting it up for rent online tomorrow. It's now or never.

Jolene appears behind Eleanor. "Well, hi, Luke," she says with a smile.

"Hi, Jolene." We've met a couple of times now through my visits to the archive.

"Jo, can I have a couple minutes?" Eleanor asks. I hope the edge in her voice will be alleviated once she knows why I've come.

"Of course, I'd never dream of keeping you from your cowboy," Jolene teases.

Eleanor flushes cherry red. She's so damned cute when she's flustered.

"In fact, why don't you go show him the exhibit? A sneak peek?"

With a large sigh, Eleanor agrees. As she leads me into the exhibition hall, I mouth a "thank you" to Jolene who gives me a big thumbs up. It's always helpful to have an ally on the inside.

Eleanor leads me into a room off the main gallery. There are photographs lining the walls, memorabilia in cases, and music is already wafting through the speakers. A few other people work around the room, discussing things in hushed voices or carefully adhering lettering to walls, all of them blank except one at the very back.

I follow Eleanor in silence through the exhibition hall, not wanting to draw attention to us. We stop in front of the covered wall which I realize is a blown-up image of 6th Street, blurred and edited to serve as a backdrop to the other framed images and memorabilia.

"Is that . . ." I begin.

"Yeah, it's mine," she says with a proud smile, her arms crossing in front of her.

I can't draw my eyes away from the photo.

"I took it the night we met. Cool, huh?"

I laugh in disbelief. "Cool? It's beyond cool."

Eleanor merely smiles.

I grab her by the shoulder and pull her to my side. "You're way too humble, Nor."

Her cheeks turn red. She pulls off her glasses and distracts herself polishing them with the front of her shirt. "Would have been better if I'd found the original photo of Diane. Could have used her recordings and everything." She gestures with her glasses, across the room, then sticks them back on her nose. "There's a Skip Baxter portrait over there that I took, though."

"You took it?!"

"Oh, yeah, I tracked him down for the radio section. We didn't have any new portraits of him on file. There are also a couple pictures of The Lone Star through the years that I worked on restoring."

I shove my hands in my pockets. "I had no idea this is what you've been working on."

"I thought it would be a big surprise once it all was finished. You know, I'd have this awesome exhibit and the museum would love me so much they'd want to keep me, and—" she stops short of finishing her sentence. "They're not going to."

The record scratches. "What?"

173

"Jolene told me today. They can't afford to keep me on in the archive," she says. "They love the display though, so that's good." Her smile is conciliatory at best.

No wonder she looked so dower when I first saw her. "Nor, I'm so sorry," I say.

"It's okay. I assumed by this point."

But I know she hoped. With all her heart. I did too. A reason to stay would have made this all so much easier.

"What do you need to talk to me about?" Eleanor prods.

"Right, right, well . . . bad news, good news, I guess." I ruffle my hand through my hair. "I have an apartment for you."

Eleanor's head whips toward me in shock. "What?"

"I found a lead on an apartment and, if you want it, it's yours."

Eleanor blinks her big amber eyes, the news still sinking in.

"It's, um, a bit of a fixer upper from what I hear, but I got a deal because I know the guy who owns it." A loose interpretation, but true enough. "And if you want it, it's yours."

She remains silent. I shove my hands in my pockets. I didn't know what kind of reaction I expected, but after the month we've had, I thought there would be some semblance of excitement even if the fear is present.

"I probably should have asked you first if that's what you wanted, but I know you've been busy with work and I . . ." For a tall guy, I feel so small right now.

Eleanor shakes off her silence with a flick of her head. "No, that was really nice of you, Luke."

I can practically see the wall she's just put up between us. "You're not planning on staying, are you?"

Her lips twist to the side. "I was going to tell you tonight. I don't know how I can without a job."

"You can find a job."

She shrugs. "Maybe."

The defeat in her body is so unlike her. I am used to an Eleanor who pushes to the extreme, pounds the pavement until she gets what she wants. The one who follows dead end after dead end. "Nor . . ."

"Look, I really need to get back to work. Can we talk later?" she says.

"I've got a show tonight."

Her head ticks with the memory, curl falling out of place onto her forehead. "Right, I forgot. Tomorrow then." She forces a smile before turning on her heel and heading out of the exhibit.

I follow her, walking in exact step beside her. "Let me walk with you."

"Luke, could we not do this here?" she asks.

It's not fair to her, but I can't just let this go until tomorrow. Hell, even until tonight. "You love it here."

"I do."

We emerge from the exhibition hall, back into the main lobby. The woman at the reception desk watches us intently as we cross toward a door that requires keycard entry. "So why not stay? It's not like you have a job anywhere else."

"I know more people in Chicago. My network is bigger."

It's a knife to the chest that I know she didn't intend, but hurts, nonetheless. "You have a network here."

Eleanor scans her badge and opens the door. "I have you," she says with half a laugh. "And Jolene I guess, but that fell through."

"Is that not good enough?" My annoyance comes through despite my best intentions.

Her eyes avoid mine. "That's not what I was trying to say."

I follow her through the door and down the staircase. The air is so cold it bites at my skin. "You'd be making a mistake deciding to leave now."

"I have to get back to work," she says, hurrying down the stairs.

"Hey." I reach out and grab her arm. "Just stop for a second."

Eleanor whips around, yanking her arm out of my grip. "Don't *grab* me."

I swallow. "Sorry, I didn't mean to, I just . . . please listen for a second."

"I have been listening and I *told* you—" Her eyes waver across my face. "I need to go back to work."

"Then you're not *hearing* me. Nor, *hear* me." I delicately place my hands on her shoulders and smooth them down her arms, thankful she's not drawing away. "You should stay. I want you to stay."

Eleanor's eyes flutter shut. "*Luke* . . ."

"Don't you want to stay? And see what happens?" I told her a month ago that we'd enjoy each other to the fullest. For now. Until she had to decide. But I didn't want her to make up her mind like this. "With us?"

Eleanor's head drops forward. "Yes, but it's not that simple."

For me, it's simple. For me, it's her. She's all I want. It's so crystal clear to me. But it's not for her. And telling her would terrify her even more, I'm sure. "You have until the end of the day to get the apartment," I say. "Then the deal's off. So, if you change your mind, you have to let me know. Soon." My desperate expression reflects off her glasses.

Eleanor nods. "Okay."

I'm not sure if I've just been broken up with, but lord help me if I'm going to give in so easily. "It's going to be okay. Whatever it is, okay?"

She nods again.

Though my heart's starting to crack, I pull her into my arms and hug her tight, pressing a kiss to the crown of her head. I'm here. I'm not going anywhere.

She grips the front of my shirt, presses her face into my chest. How can someone hold me like this and not want to stay?

If I'm here any longer, I'm going to cry. I release her. "I'll send you the guy's phone number. You can call him if you think you want to stay. Promise me you'll think about it, Nor."

"I will," she says in a slight voice. "Promise." She steps away and then stops. "Thank you for looking out for me."

"Of course."

Her purses her lips. That's the face of a woman who knows she's breaking a heart. At least it looks like it hurts her too. "I just need to think about it."

"I get it, Nor. It's okay."

The walk up the stairs, out of the museum, and back to my car is as close to a zombie as I'll get. I don't know what more I could have done to do right by her. Other than being fully honest about Diane. Maybe if I'd been upfront, she'd have something for the museum right when she got there and could have been in their graces in a flash. Maybe they would find the money to keep her.

But would I have known her the way I do now if I'd been honest?

Did I doom us from the start?

23

ELEANOR

I descend the stairs to the archive in a haze. On one hand, I should be grateful Luke is looking out for me. On the other, I'm overwhelmed. He looked without telling me. Planned for my remaining in Austin without telling me. I should be swooning that he's so invested.

Instead, I'm terrified.

"What was *that* all about?" Jolene asks as soon as my foot lands on the bottom step.

I freeze and glare at her. "You were listening?"

Jolene shrugs from her place leaned up against the wall. "Voices echo in the stairs. Couldn't help but overhear."

I roll my eyes and blow past her toward the archive door. I don't have time to indulge her antics today.

"From the sounds of it," she says, trailing after me, "he really wants you to stay in Austin."

"Yeah, that was kind of the whole crux of the conversation," I mutter. *Which you should know since you were listening.*

We enter the archive. I'm hoping Jolene will read the fucking room and leave me alone to get back to the work I was doing before we popped up to the exhibition hall, but *noooo*, of course she doesn't.

Before I can even plop down in my chair, she's pulled a chair out for herself to sit across from me at the table. Maybe I can ignore her into leaving me alone.

"Look, I know that wasn't what you wanted to hear from the museum, but what you did isn't a small feat! There are plenty of establishments that would want someone like you on their permanent team."

I ignore her, pulling open my old, slow laptop.

"And Luke wants you to stay, I mean, that feels like an easy decision to me."

It's not.

"Don't ignore me!" she snaps.

"It's *not* an easy decision!" I reply. "I'm not going to stay in Austin just for some man."

"*Some* man," she scoffs. "Please. He's a babe."

"Babe or not, he's a man. And men do stupid things. Like search for apartments without asking you."

Jolene's eyes widen. "Is that what he did?"

"Yup."

She's quiet for a moment, then twists her lips into a smile. "That's pretty romantic."

"Jolene! That is not romantic! It's presumptuous! It's stupid! It's—"

"Don't act as if you haven't spent nearly every moment of your free time with him for the past two months!" she quips.

I seal my mouth shut. Damn her for being right.

"Unless you were just trying to pass the time, which doesn't seem to be the way you do things, I'd say that's something to consider."

Since our first date, Luke and I have spent all of his free time together. *His* being the operative word because he's the one always working. I have my nine-to-five and he has his whenever to whenever the fuck. Sometimes it's only a day a week, but other times it's several.

And he's been driving me crazy in the best way possible. Holding out on sleeping with me as if to prove his restraint, which only makes me more feral.

However, it's not just the sexual component. It's so easy to be around him. From the very beginning, he's helped me find my footing here. Helped me embrace Austin with open arms and vice versa. He's treated me like a queen, even when we weren't involved romantically. He's a good fucking man.

So why do I feel like running away?

"Eleanor, what are you afraid of?"

I bite on the inside of my cheek. Chew for a few moments. "I don't like taking risks."

"Okay, well I could have told you that," Jolene says.

"So, why'd you ask?"

"I mean with *Luke*. What are you afraid of? He seems like a great guy, so unless there's something you haven't told me—"

I can't let her finish that sentence. "He *is* a great guy."

Jolene smiles in her sweet way when she thinks she knows better than me. "So? Are you *not* attracted to him?"

"Of course, I'm attracted to him! You've seen him."

"Just asking! Pretty isn't everyone's type," Jolene says, holding her hands up.

"True, just look at the guy *you're* dating."

She kicks me under the table. "Tom is cute!"

"So is his wallet."

Snickering, she flushes. "Yeah, fair. And speaking of, Luke's no slouch in that department either."

"Oh my god."

"I'm just saying. Pays for most everything, right?"

I sigh. "True."

"Are you thinking what I'm thinking?"

I eye her. "What?"

"You're the problem, Eleanor!"

I gape at her, unable to keep from laughing though she's cut me down at the knees. "Wow! Thanks!"

"I'm just saying, you've got a sexy man with at least some amount of money who is totally obsessed with you to the point of trying to make your life easier by finding you an apartment and *you're* turning your nose up at him. You have to ask yourself why."

"Because I'm terrified it won't work out and I'll be stuck here in Austin because of some guy!" I cry out. "There. That's it."

"Oh, honey, from the sounds of it, I don't think Luke is just some guy."

He hasn't been. Not for a long time.

"You've been all out of sorts about him for a while now, and the second he looks like he's *actually* yours, you're running the other way."

I sigh. "People change, Jo."

"Sure. Fine. Let's say something changes and he becomes a total shit. You break up. Now you have a lease in Austin. Is that so bad?"

Is it so bad?

"It's not like you're going to give up on looking for a job."

"True."

"Not like I'm going to leave you alone," she says.

I laugh. The levity is much needed. "True."

"So, you have friends. You have a goal. The worst that can happen is a year in a city I think you like, right?"

Love. I love Austin. Fell in love with it through Luke's eyes. Though the weather is less than to be desired for a Chicagoan like me, I love it here. I like the people. Like the culture. *Love* the music and the history.

It's only been two months, but it feels like home.

I can settle into that. Accept that. But there's another truth. Something I have only whispered to myself in the dark of night. Alone. Where no ears can hear but my own.

"I don't want him to break my heart," I say. "I like him *so* much."

Jolene reaches across the table and grabs my hands. "Honey, love is such a bitch sometimes."

I laugh though tears fill my eyes.

"You can't predict it. It's kind of like a period."

"Oh my god, Jo."

"What! I'm being honest. It's natural, sometimes it hurts, and it can be annoying, but—" She pauses. "Okay, I guess the upsides are limited. But you have permission to eat lots of chocolate. That's the best."

"So, if I follow your logic—"

"Never said it was logic."

I grab Jolene's hands tighter. "Love is like a period. It makes you bleed out, and it hurts, but you get chocolate out of it."

"Eleanor. Fuck my stupid metaphor. Love is natural. Love is supposed to happen. And sometimes it hurts. But that's what makes it love. It wouldn't be anything if we didn't know we could lose it."

Her words hit me like a gust of wind.

"As long as it's not toxic, and as long as everyone is doing their best, that's just what love does. So, you can run back to Chicago and avoid the possibility that things will work out, or you can fucking run right into the fire."

"So, now love is a fire?"

She throws her hands up in frustration. "Okay, this is the last time I help you!"

"I'm joking! I'm joking!"

Jolene leans back in her seat, arms crossed over her chest, eyeing me. "So? What are you going to do?"

My phone buzzes in my pocket. I pull it out to find a text from Luke. The phone number for the owner of the building he told me about.

Something washes over me. Contentment.

It's all aligning. This is what's supposed to be. Fear shouldn't pull me away.

"I'm going to stay."

Jolene woops in delight.

I tap the number and put my phone against my ear.

24

LUKE

The venue is packed. I've been relegated to the backstage space where I sit on a road case, feet tucked onto the edge, my arms resting on my knees.

I'm a shell of myself. Going through the motions. Everyone knows something is going on with me, but every time they ask if I'm okay, I just tell them I'm fine. Not convincingly, mind you. But that seems to keep them at bay.

If Eleanor leaves Austin, I don't know what I'm going to do. I've been in the moment as much as I can be, but I haven't been able to keep my mind from drifting. All the things we could do together. The plans. The things people do when they share a life.

I've never been like this with someone. Not since I've gotten my shit together, and I'm not some bumbling twenty-something, trying to get by with no brain and a buck. I know in my gut that my connection with Eleanor is *right*. I'm not just trying to fill a void because I'm lonely. She answers something in me. Something I've been missing.

I'll go back to being the old me if she leaves. And I don't want to be him anymore.

But it's her prerogative. Her life.

If she doesn't want me in it, though, I'll be devastated.

The band tonight isn't really holding my attention. They're a regional favorite, clearly on the up and up as far as labels go, right on that tipping point between living for the fans and living for the business. I couldn't care less. Just want the job to be over. For today to be over.

I pull out my phone to distract myself, but there's no fucking service back here. It's like the universe is telling me that I have to sit in it.

Fuck the universe.

Through the fuzz of guitar and triplets on the drums, I hear the metallic clank of the stage flying open. One of the security guards on the circuit, Alan, gives me a nod. I'm needed. Thank god, because I need something to take my mind off things. Even if it is some rabid backstage drama.

I push myself up off the road case, straighten out my jacket, and head over to Alan. "What's up?"

"Someone's asking for you."

I frown. "What?"

"Thought she was a disgruntled fan, but she's asking for you. Maybe she's a disgruntled fan of *yours*?"

The muscles across my torso tighten. "What's she look like?"

"Glasses. Curly hair."

I push past Alan to the door, rip it open, and find Eleanor flanked by two other security guards who are inches away from grabbing her and dragging her down the alley.

"I swear, I'm not a creep or anything, I'm just trying to see—"

"Guys, it's fine," I call off the guards.

Eleanor's gaze shoots to me.

My brain can't decide if I'm happy to see her. I want to be overjoyed, bouncing off the walls. But I've already started grieving what feels like an inevitability. So, I don't smile. And I don't glare. I just look at her.

"She's with me," I say. "Thanks."

"She isn't on the list," Alan says from over my shoulder.

"Yeah, I forgot. I'm sorry."

All the guys exchange a look, clearly peeved with me. Whatever. Add it to the list of grievances I have with the world.

I go toward Eleanor while the three of them post back up near the door.

"Can we talk?" she asks.

I push my tongue into my cheek and nod. Talking will be too painful until I know where she's going with this.

Eleanor's brow laces together. "I'm sorry about earlier."

"'S'okay," I manage. "You were just . . . feeling how you felt." I cross my arms over my chest to prevent my heart from falling to the fucking ground. "You should have warned me that you were coming, though."

"I texted," she says haplessly.

I remember there's no service backstage, but I say nothing.

"The last thing I want to do is hurt you, Luke," she says.

Here it comes. The letdown. I brace for it.

"I'm scared. We know this. Seems to be a baseline for me," she says with a half-smile. "But that's not a good excuse to not go for what I want."

I ignore the flutter of hope in my belly. What's she talking about?

She reaches into her bag of magic tricks and fishes out a set of keys, a set I know not to be hers.

"What are those?" I ask. I can't get excited until I know. I won't be let down again.

"Keys to my new place."

My lips part. What do I say? What do I even do?

"I signed the lease after work."

Say it. Please just say it.

Eleanor's eyes twinkle in mine. "I'm staying."

The dam holding back the possible joy breaks. I wrap my arms around her, lift her into the air, and spin her around.

Eleanor lets out a gleeful laugh, throwing her arms around my neck, holding on for dear life.

"Tell me you're not kidding," I say urgently. "Tell me this isn't a fucking dream."

Eleanor frames my face in her hands. The cool metal of the keys brushes my skin.

No dream could feel this real.

"I'm staying, Luke."

I brush a hand through her hair. I don't know what to say. I'm overwhelmed with a torrent of hopes and dreams, of memories, of fears. Every pent-up feeling I had when I considered her leaving Austin happens all at once. "Oh, Nor . . ." I don't have anything good to say, so I kiss her. Deep and unfettered. The way I imagined I might earlier today when I thought I might be her hero. Better late than never.

Eleanor sighs into me, her beautiful body sinking into mine. Her lips split from mine. "I take it you're happy?"

"Was that not obvious?" I ask.

We both laugh, unwilling to draw away even an inch.

"Are *you* happy?"

Eleanor is quiet for a few moments, then nods. "Yeah. I'm really, really happy."

"Good. Good, that's what matters."

I finally set her back down on the ground, but I keep my arms around her. If I let her go, I'm afraid she might run back to whatever future she thought about in Chicago.

"I'm sorry, I know you're working—"

"Don't be sorry, I'm glad you came. I'm so fucking glad you came. You have no idea."

Eleanor grips my sides. "I'm so sorry about earlier, I—"

"Don't be sorry. No time for sorry. Not anymore."

She's beaming, a smile that goes ear to ear. There's no doubt in my mind she's made the right choice. *For her*.

"When do you move in?" I ask.

Eleanor rolls her eyes. "The lease starts *tomorrow*."

"But the apartment with the museum—"

"I know, but to lock it down I had to start as soon as possible."

Randy was right about landlords. Of course he switched the deal on Eleanor. "Well, I'll cover the rent until you move out of the—"

"You will fucking not do that, Luke Wyatt," she says, smacking me in the chest. "This is my choice. My apartment. I'm doing this."

I'm prone to argue against the woman paying for anything, but I'll support whatever she wants. "Fine. As much as I hate it . . . fine." I take her head in my hands and kiss her forehead. Sweet, sweet Eleanor. "Look, I've got to get back to the gig. You can stay if you want."

"I'd like that," she says.

"And after we can go out or get something to eat or—"

"I have a better idea," she interrupts, a mischievous look in her eye.

I raise an eyebrow.

Eleanor lifts her keys in the air and jangles them.

25

ELEANOR

The door sticks a little. I push it open with my shoulder and let it swing into the empty apartment.

The wooden floors creak and echo through the empty living room, or what I would assume to be the living room. It's nothing fancy, but it's mine. A living room, kitchen, and bedroom, with white walls and big windows that will let in gorgeous sunlight during the day. The living room might even be big enough for me to cordon off a bit of it for a studio, and I can use that light to my advantage.

My fingers itch for my camera.

In the dark, though, there is a pulsing potential. The quiet. The stillness. There's room for me here.

That's what I was searching for when I left Chicago. Room. I didn't even have room in my relationship after I had been cheated on, and the city carried that angst with it. I didn't feel at home on the streets I'd known for over a decade. I felt like all the midwestern smiles and nods were of pity and concern rather than the usual sweetness.

I've been hesitant to accept that Austin has made room for me from the beginning. Because my job was only a stint, because I was a stranger being given the southern hospitality routine, because, well, why should I fit in when the place I called home didn't feel like home anymore?

It was too easy. Too good to be true.

But I can romanticize a life in this apartment. In Austin.

And not just because of Luke. Although, he definitely helps.

Luke's arms wrap around my shoulders, and he tucks his chin on my head. I lean back into him, hooking my hands over his forearm.

"Welcome home, baby."

I sigh happily, and let my eyes flutter shut.

"Of course, it will feel more like home when you actually have furniture, but . . ."

"Isn't that picking nits? All I'd need is a sleeping bag and—"

"Okay, wise guy," he says. He reaches into my bag, hanging off my shoulder, and pulls out a bottle of champagne he snagged from the venue before we left. "In all the excitement, I forgot we don't have cups."

I step away to face him and shrug my shoulders. "What the hey, we'll drink from the bottle."

"Who are you and what have you done with Eleanor?" Luke says.

I giggle and fish my camera out of my bag before tossing it on the floor.

Luke strips the champagne bottle of its foil and cage with his long fingers, and I get a funny feeling in my belly, wishing his fingers were tangled up in my panties rather than the metal wrapped around the cork.

I shake it off and frame the shot.

Luke lifts his eyes. It's dark in here, the room only lit by the streetlight outside the windows. But my eyes have adjusted enough to be able to be struck by his baby blues as I always am.

I snap the shot. He smiles and drops his head bashfully. "You don't like having your photo taken?" I ask, glancing down at the small screen to check out the photo. For a tall guy, he looks so small in the empty room. His hand is wrapped around the neck of the bottle so tenderly it makes my insides melt.

"I'm not used to it. Not since I was a kid. Plus, I'm a behind-the-scenes kind of guy."

"Says the guy who hasn't worn the same hat twice the entire time I've known him."

He guffaws, the noise echoing off the bare walls. "That's not true."

"Admit it, you like the attention."

Luke shakes his head and smiles the kind of smile that looks like it could drip from one side of his face. "I like *your* attention, Nor."

My mouth gets hot.

Luke wraps his hand around the cork of the bottle and twists until the effervescent pop erupts, his hand following the trajectory of the pressure.

"Damn, you're good at that."

"The cork can sense fear," he says, holding the bottle out to me. "You get the first swig."

"Ah, what a gentleman."

"Southern hospitality."

I laugh and swipe the bottle from him before taking a big gulp of champagne. I haven't done something like this since college. Drinking directly from a bottle, standing in an under-furnished apartment. All that's missing is loud music that I don't know the words to and the smell of sweat and saliva.

The champagne pops and burns down my throat, invigorating and delicious.

"That my girl," he says.

I wipe my mouth off with the back of my hand, and hand him the bottle. I like being his girl.

Luke swigs the bottle too, then takes in the size of the room. "Couch can go here," he says, gesturing to the spot where he stands. "You'll need a credenza. You a television person?"

"I like watching some television from time to time."

"Okay, well that could go against that wall. A couple of chairs . . . you'll need some good lighting, none of that overhead shit."

His excitement is palpable. Totally adorable.

"And we'll get you some nice art. I know some people."

I cross my arms over my chest. "Is this my apartment or yours?"

Luke stops, then laughs at himself. "Sorry, I'm excited."

I sidle up to him and take the bottle. "You're allowed to be excited."

His eyes stay on mine as I take another drink of champagne. Once I've swallowed, he asks, "Do you promise this is what you want?"

I thrust the bottle back into his hand. "I promise, Luke."

"Not just because I coerced you or something," he says, scratching the back of his head.

"You didn't coerce me. I thought about it. Granted, I only had until the end of the day, but I've been thinking about it for a while." I go to the window, lean on the frame, and look down at the street outside. "I'm not staying for you," I say.

Luke clears his throat. "Right, of course you're not."

"Let me finish," I go on, glancing back at him. "I'm not staying for you, but I'm not *not staying for you*. Does that make sense?"

Luke places the bottle of champagne down by my bag and takes a few steps closer to me. "I think so."

"I want a career. I want to have a good job, and I don't *just* want to be someone's . . . someone."

"You'd never be 'just' that," he says.

I remain silent as Luke leans his body over mine, putting his forearm against the wall above my head. Damn, I love feeling small in his shadow. Protected and special.

"I trust you," I say, touching the lapel of his jacket.

"Yeah?"

"I'm terrified, but I trust you."

Luke tilts his head to one side, eyes softening. "You have no idea what that means to me."

"You have to be careful with me."

"I'd never dream of being any other way with you."

"Tender, you know?"

Luke runs his thumb down my jaw. "Always."

Though the moment between us is long and languid, my insides are spiraling out of control. I want him. I've wanted him and I'm ready for him to shuck off the gentleman and give me the full man he can be.

"I can't make any promises," I say. "About forever, or—"

"I'm not asking for that."

I grab his jacket harder. "But I can promise to try my best to make it so."

Luke's lips part. His breath is shallow and strained.

"I can promise to try for forever," I say. Maybe it's too much. And if it is, it's best we walk away right now. But I can't deny how I'm feeling. The longer I spend with Luke, the more I can see him in my life for a long, long time.

Longer than long, maybe.

"If you walked out of my life right now," Luke says, his voice gravelly and low, "the time we've had together would be more than I deserve."

I fist his jacket and pull him closer to me. "You deserve everything, Luke." I tip my head back, inclining my lips toward his. I want him to take what I'm giving without me having to ask. I know he can. "You deserve everything I have to give."

The spark goes off in the depths of Luke's growing pupils. He kisses me, finally. And as our tongues twine together, I push his jacket down his arms. The message should be clear by now. I want him. In every way a person can want someone.

The jacket falls to our feet, and once my hands are available again, I cup his cheeks and bend my body, pouring my weight into him so he feels every part of me.

"Jesus, Eleanor," he rasps against my lips.

I kiss him again before we can get lost in words. Luke gets the hint, lets his hands stray from my back to my ass. He pulls my hips flush to him and rubs against me.

I moan into his mouth. It feels so good, the throbbing between my legs, even better when Luke's the cause.

One hand tangled in my curls, Luke pulls back. "There's not even a bed."

"So?"

His eyebrows lift. "Okay, I—"

"I mean, do you need one?" I ask.

"No, you just didn't strike me as the type to be—"

"Luke, haven't you learned by now that I'm full of surprises?"

Luke laughs. "Trust me, Eleanor, not a day goes by where you don't—"

I shut him up with my lips, throwing myself onto him, wrapping my arms around his neck. If I could speak, I'd say, "Take me, take me, take me," but I'll have to let my body do the talking.

Luke's hands rush up the fabric of my skirt until he's able to tuck them around my ass cheeks. He groans, squeezes, fondles, and then his fingers are looping around my panties. Playing with them. Not rushing.

I respond in kind, grabbing his belt buckle, undoing it the best I can with my eyes closed, tangled in kiss after kiss after kiss. Once the belt is off, I grab a handful of him through his pants.

He grunts. "Fuck, Eleanor."

I rub, looking up at him with my lowered eyelids. Ever since I met him, he has been composed and coiffed Luke Wyatt. The most clean-cut cowboy in Texas. I want to see him lose control. All because of me.

"You're teasing me."

"No, if I was teasing you, I'd do this . . ."

I spin out of his grip and grab the skirt of my dress, inching it up my thighs.

Luke watches, smiling mouth ajar, his hand dropping to his crotch where his cock presses angrily through the front of his pants.

I finally raise the skirt up enough so he can see my underwear.

His eyes roll back, and he shakes his head. "Fuck it, I'm not patient enough for this."

Luke drops to his knees in front of me and before I can react, he pulls my panties aside and buries his face between my legs.

"Luke!" I choke out, placing my hand on his shoulder for balance.

His stubble scrapes the inside of my thighs, and his tongue, god his tongue, laps at my slit, circling my clit. "God, you're so wet," he says against me before going in for another lick.

"I'm . . . oh god." Every part of me wants to liquify.

Luke grabs my dress and tugs. "Off. Take it off."

I do so, which is a hard task when my muscles are trembling and I can't hold onto anything, but I manage it. I look down the front of my exposed body and find Luke staring up at me, his mouth pressed against me.

I rake my fingers through his hair, relishing how his eyes flutter shut.

Luke pulls my leg over his shoulder, forcing me to give into him, pressing my folds tighter to his face. He burrows his nose against my clit, making my body balk in surprise, a whimper stuttering out of my mouth.

Luke moans against me, the vibrations trembling through me. I'm so hot, hotter than if I was baking in the midday Austin summer sun.

"What the fuck . . . what the *fuck*," I squeak. I didn't take Luke for an asshole who refuses to eat women out, but I had no idea he would do it with such enthusiasm.

The way he's working me, I'm not sure I can last. And he knows it; he can feel the way my thighs are clenching and unclenching around his face.

"Fuck my face, baby," he says breathlessly. "Come for me."

I didn't realize I was bucking my hips against him until he said that. But I am absolutely grinding against his face, my clit swimming with impending ecstasy. "Luke, oh my god, Luke." I wrap my hand around the nape of his neck to steady myself, because once I come, I won't have a leg to stand on . . . *literally*.

He groans into me and snaps his lips around my tender bud of nerves like it's a delicacy.

A shock runs through me. I shudder. And with a few more undulations of my hips, I'm coming. I tell him as much, though it comes out strained and squeaky between a tremulous moan.

Luke's hands, which were gripped around the backs of my thighs, turn soft and tender, allowing me to sink down into his lap. He immediately kisses me, allowing me to taste how I've coated his lips and chin. A heavenly taste, made even better by the way it mingles with the natural taste of his mouth that I've come to know and love.

I've never been with someone this long and not had sex with them.

When our lips part, time slows.

I begin to undo the buttons of his shirt. One by one. No rush. I glance up to meet Luke's gaze. Something about him seems shy, which is surprising considering he was just devouring me like I was his last meal.

I smile. He smiles.

Once the shirt is undone, I trace the muscles of his torso. He's not overly built, but they're there. He takes care of himself. I press my palms to his pecs. Feeling his warmth, his thrumming heartbeat, and his soft swaths of chest hair. "God, you're sexy," I say.

Luke chuckles almost like he doesn't believe me. "I'm glad you think so."

"No thinking about it," I say. "It's a fact."

He shrugs off his shirt, then reaches around to undo my bra. "Fair is fair."

I blush. Unresistant of course. I want him to see me.

The way his eyes pin to my breasts once they're exposed could make me come again. Luke licks his lips and leans into lap at my pebbling nipples, but I stop him, grabbing his chin. "Luke?"

"What?"

I graze my lips against his, not quite a kiss. A taunt. "I want you inside me."

Luke's breath stills.

"I don't want to wait anymore."

He swallows. "Who am I to deny a woman what she wants?"

I laugh, long and hard. "Once a gentleman . . ."

We work Luke's pants down, then his boxer briefs. When his erection emerges, I can't keep myself from gaping.

"Too big?" he asks.

I push him on the shoulder. "Shut up!"

Luke laughs hard, falling onto his elbows as I pull his briefs off, followed by my panties, leaving us both naked on the floor of my new, unfurnished apartment.

I lick my lips. If I wasn't so desperate to have him inside, I'd take him into my mouth. Taste the bead of precum that's appeared on the head, delight in the salty strangeness of his taste.

"Condom in my wallet," he says, cotton-mouthed, anticipation racking every one of his words.

I reach into his pants pocket, grab the wallet, and fish out the golden package. "You would be a condom-in-the-wallet type of guy."

"Trust me, it's been a while since I've had to replace it," he says, holding out his hand for me to give it to him.

I ignore his hand and rip it open myself. "Can I put it on you?"

"Uh, fuck yes."

I place the condom at the tip of him and roll it down, watching how his face contorts with my merest touch.

"Eleanor . . ." he sighs, head falling back.

I say nothing, straddle his hips, and place the head of him against my opening. My nerves are already perking with pleasure, excited to have him again. Deeper this time.

Luke grabs one of my hips. "Take it slow, okay? I don't want to . . . too fast."

I smile at him. Luke Wyatt, ladies' man, scared to come too fast. Wanting me to go slow. "If you did, I'd be flattered."

"Eleanor, if I really didn't give a shit, I would have fucking lost it when you pulled off your dress, that's the kind of situation we're dealing with here."

"Just look at me," I say.

Luke's eyes meet mine. And I sink down onto him, just the tip at first because it's clear that it is a total shock to his senses. His hand tightens on my hip, a curse puffs out of his lips, and his expression is distressed.

Distressed over want of me, is a look I didn't know I liked on a man until now.

I follow his instruction and go slow, taking him inch by inch. For me too. He's big and I need to stretch. It doesn't take long for my body to adjust though, for the discomfort to turn into a numbness beyond which I know is exquisite pleasure.

Once I have enough of him, I start to ride, up and down. Taking my time.

"Fuck, look at you," he sighs. "Gorgeous."

I take off my glasses.

"Lean forward for me," Luke says.

I do so until his hand cups one of my breasts and he brings it to his mouth. I gasp. His tongue strikes against my nipple, and circles it like he did my clit, all the while massaging my breast. My body relaxes more around him. I brace myself against his chest as I ride.

Luke starts to move with me, withdrawing as I do, thrusting while I slide. He groans around my nipple and lets it pop out of his mouth to utter a singular "Goddamn" before moving to the other one.

I move my hands up his body to his shoulders.

We lock into a rhythm, the pace increasing without either of us thinking or deciding. It just happens. Breaths and moans fill the empty apartment, each one cascading into the corners and echoing back at us just how good we feel.

Luke takes his mouth off my breast and grabs me by the back of the neck, dragging me into a kiss. His other hand grips my thigh, and suddenly I'm not in control at all. It's all him. Fucking me hard and fast, driving up into me.

I drag my lips off his and cry out his name.

"Yeah, baby? You feel good," he grunts.

"So good, Luke, oh my god, you're going to make me—"

"*Again?!*" he asks, breathlessly.

Which makes him work even harder.

It's a different kind of orgasm, though. He's able to reach an untouched part of me, one that is wanton, warm, and willing.

I cling to him with everything I have in me, every muscle contracting to hold on.

Luke puts his mouth to my ear. "You have no idea how badly I've wanted to fuck you since the moment I saw you."

And then I'm falling off the edge of a cliff.

I can't see the bottom and don't know when the earth will strike, so I enjoy the thrill of falling, the euphoria coursing through me. I press my mouth to his neck and scream out, knowing that if I let it free and wild, it would ping against the walls of the apartment and make a strange first impression on my neighbors.

"God, you're tight, you're so tight, I'm coming," he husks with a few final thrusts until he gives into the way I'm pulsing around him. An unrepentant groan explodes from his mouth, but he does not pay any mind to decorum. He lets it free. Wild. So that I know exactly how badly he's wanted this.

Together, slick with sweat, we try to catch our breath. I couldn't get off of him even if I wanted to. Luke has his hands clasped around my lower back, keeping me tight to him, right there, afraid he might lose me if he were to let go.

I kiss a line up his shoulder to his neck, across his jaw and chin, and land at his mouth. He squeezes me tighter if that were possible. And though the kiss is chaste, it's the deepest kiss we've ever shared.

When my lips part from his, Luke smiles and nuzzles his nose against mine. "Welcome home, baby."

26

LUKE

By a stroke of genius, I remember I have a blanket in the trunk of my car. Part of my mother's idea of an emergency kit, and what kind of a good southern boy am I if I don't try to appease my mother?

Eleanor and I sleep in fits and starts thanks to the hardwood. And another kind of wood. Now that I've had Eleanor, I don't know how I'm going to stop having her. Lying naked on the floor of her new place, it's impossible to keep my hands off her. So, I don't. An hour of sleep here, a quick dip into her personal brand of heaven there . . .

It's paradise.

I didn't plan well enough ahead, so I only had one condom. But after the first time and a confirmation of her being on the pill, we both threw caution to the wind.

Because there are no curtains on the windows, we're up at first light. Earlier than early. So early that Eleanor hasn't even put her glasses on yet. Her curls are a rat's nest, pointing in every direction. And she's already grabbed her camera, pointing it at the way light is draping across the wall.

"My room . . ." she says, then turns the camera on me, grinning. "With a view."

I'm covered in all the places I'd need to be to avoid a scandal, but I'm still a bit camera-shy. "Someone should be taking pictures of you, not me."

Eleanor is quiet. She twists the lens. I don't claim to know what she's doing, but from the looks of it, she's a master. Her lips tense in focus and so does her forehead.

I remain perfectly still, marveling. Because she's sitting there, crisscross on the floor, blanket over her lap, and her torso bare. She's so focused that she's not trying to suck in her stomach the way most women do. Two perfect rolls of silk skin. I'd like to lean over and kiss them raw.

She snaps the photo and then checks the screen. Smiles to herself, pleased.

I'm glad I please her. In all ways.

Eleanor grabs her glasses off the floor and thrusts them on one-handed to get a better look at me. "I find more satisfaction with keeping a record of the world through my eyes."

My heart flutters. "And what does that look like?"

"Really fucking sexy," she says.

I laugh and grab her, rolling onto my back so she is splayed across my chest. "Shut up."

"Like a Calvin Klein ad."

"That's laying it on a little thick."

Eleanor traces her finger from my collarbone down to my belly, letting it loop and curve like a bumblebee. "Not thick at all. Except . . ." Her hand dips below the blanket toward my dick, which has been sporting a semi since we woke up.

I jerk away before she can touch me. "Don't touch me unless you're ready to get flipped on your belly and totally railed, Eleanor Hayes."

She withdraws her hand, which is for the best since we're enjoying a languorous early morning, but I can't help feeling a touch disappointed. With a scan of the apartment, she sighs. "Bigger in the daylight."

"You sound sad about that," I say, twisting my fingers through her curls.

"I could have hacked it in a studio for less, maybe. Or got some roommates," she says.

"Baby, if you're worried about the money—"

Eleanor's doing everything not to look me in the eye. "I'm not worried . . . yet."

"Hey. I've got your back. I'm not letting you fall flat on your face. Not that you ever would."

"Ha! You have too much confidence in me."

I shake my head. "I don't. And if you keep talking shit about my girlfriend, I'll have to square up."

Eleanor laughs. "I'd like to see that."

I flip her onto her back, pinning her down by her wrists. "I can show you a few moves."

She laughs more. "Let me go, let me go!"

"Yeah, I knew you'd give up easy," I say as I roll off her. If I don't get off, I'm going to take her again, and I don't think the conversation is over.

We lay there for a while, Eleanor on her back, me on my side, smoothing my fingers across her bare chest. Making sure I've touched every part of her. How many men have touched *every* part of her? And how many have done it because of sheer wonder and awe?

"What about taking photos? Why can't you do that?"

Eleanor snorts. "Like being an event photographer? I'll pass."

"You'd make good money."

"Soulless."

I kiss her shoulder and tuck my chin against her. "Concert photography. I know someone who could get you some gigs."

A smile perks onto her lips. "Oh, really? Are you suggesting nepotism?"

"More than nepotism because there's kissing involved."

She grins. "I mean, I wouldn't say no, but it would take me a while to get good at it."

"I've got people I can introduce you to. They'll show you the ropes."

Eleanor's smile fades. "I hate being a beginner. I've been a beginner so many times."

"Just because you're not a kid anymore, it doesn't mean you aren't going to have to begin again. And again. And again."

"How do you have it all worked out? How are you so wise, huh?"

I hesitate. I just haven't had a lot of bumps in the road. The biggest bump I've had recently was Eleanor, and what a lovely bump that was. That's a fun kind of beginning. Terrifying, but thrilling. No grunt work, no hustling, no grinding. "I'm not wise," I say. "I just haven't taken as many risks as you have."

"I find that hard to believe."

I shrug one shoulder. "Believe what you want, but it's true. The biggest risk I've taken is you."

And lying about the photograph.

Fuck. I push the thought away and exchange it for a new one. "Maybe you should sell your photographs. The world through Eleanor's eyes."

Her eyes roll back. I know it's not intended to sting, but it does.

"I know I don't know the industry, and I know it's harder than that, but—"

"Really, Luke, it's not easy to make people give a shit about what you see."

I tap my fingers one at a time against her stomach until my hand is splayed against her. "How many pictures have you taken since you've been here? Hundreds? Thousands?"

"I don't know, but—"

"Why not just try? We can rent you gallery space and have a show. Just one night. You never know what could—"

"Luke."

Her voice is insistent and pained.

I bite down on my lower lip.

She shakes her head. "I'm not ready for that."

I know she's ready for that. And I'll remain knowing until she's ready to see that. I'll be right here when she wakes up. Doesn't she get that yet? I squeeze her waist. "Okay, honey."

"Mm." Her eyes flutter shut. "I love when you call me names." Her eyes pop back open. "Nice names, not—"

I laugh. "I get your meaning, baby . . ." I drop a kiss to her clavicle. "Honey . . ." and to the inside of one breast. "Darlin' . . ." and to the inside of the other.

Her whole body jolts, a shock of excited laughter shooting out of her mouth. "Oh, darlin', fuck you with your little accent."

I chuckle against her, dragging my teeth along her skin. "I'm not even close to done, sweetheart."

We play this game until we're tangled together and I'm rocking into her. We are both tired. Our movements are soft and unhurried. Eleanor locked around me like a koala bear.

No room for me to pull out, not that I want to. I never want to leave. I've made a new home within her.

Eleanor whimpers into my neck, "Luke . . ."

Like she needs me. She can act like she doesn't, but I'll be here when she realizes she does need me. It's a reciprocal need.

Eleanor's body stutters and squeezes around me. I come with her, pressing a grunt into her hair. Her core is silken heat, gripping me, sending spasms of pleasure through every nerve and skein of muscles.

We can't go back now, and I'll do everything I can to keep us moving forward.

27

ELEANOR

I'm nesting in a big way.

No, there are no baby carriages involved, and there aren't wedding bells either. More like dog beds and kibble.

Since I moved into my new place, I've had heart-eyes at all my neighbors and their canine friends.

I'm closing in on the end of the job at the archive, a mere week left. And while I haven't found a permanent position, I've got some small gigs lined up thanks to Luke. Those will tide me over.

But still, I'm looking at having lots of time on my hands. And what better way to spend it than taking care of my own little fur baby?

"I'm all for it," Luke says as he sprinkles a pinch of salt into the pot of boiling deliciousness on the stove. The man is literally perfect. "If you're ready that is."

"Then you wouldn't have to worry about me spending the night here alone."

Luke's eyebrows quirk as he stirs. "What are you talking about?"

I sidle up behind him and wrap my arms around his waist. "Baby, you've spent almost every night here since I moved in."

"Because I'm obsessed with you, obviously."

I laugh. "To your detriment, Luke. Be honest."

He smacks the spoon on the side of the pot and places it on the spoon rest. "How could it be to my detriment when I—"

"There!" I point at his eyes. "The bags. You didn't used to have those."

"It's busy season," he says.

"When isn't it?"

"Fair point."

Luke turns and crosses his arms over his chest. He looks sexy all the time, even when he's bedraggled, but I know he's been sacrificing his own wellbeing for the sake of spending time with me. If I were him, after a late-night gig, I'd want to go home to my own bed. It's a different kind of rest.

"I was living alone before," I say. "I am a big girl."

He smiles sadly, grabs one of my curls, and tucks it behind my ear. "I know you are. I'm just . . . trying to help you make this place a home."

My insides warm in an all-encompassing way. The kind that sometimes thinks about the future and knows it shouldn't. "I can make a home here on my own," I say, which is true. But there is something romantic about the notion of my boyfriend caring about making a home with me, a home he isn't even supposed to be living in.

Luke looks down with a sigh. "If you want me to give you more space—"

"Slow down, cowboy. Did I say that?"

210

"No," he says, unable to hide the boyish smile that comes along with that. He turns back to the stove to futz with the dinner he's whipping up.

I sigh and lean against the counter, looking up at him. "I know you want to take care of me."

"I do."

And damn if it isn't the sexiest thing in the world. "But you need to take care of you, too."

His shoulders fall. I know he's been pushing himself too hard to make things right for me.

"Wouldn't it make you feel better if I wasn't here alone?" I ask. "With a dog. And you can come over and play with it? That's supposed to lower cortisol levels."

Luke's blue eyes flick over to me, twinkling. "I know of other ways to lower cortisol levels . . ."

"You dirty, dirty man," I say.

He dips the spoon into the pot and blows on it. "Open."

Luke guides the spoon to my lips, and I carefully taste the rich, tomato-based whatever the fuck he's making. "Mm. So good."

Luke wipes the underside of my lip with his thumb.

"Well, I'm going to get a dog."

"That's fine. It's your choice. You don't need my permission."

"I know, but . . ." It's not permission I want. It's . . . something else. "Just tell me it's not crazy."

"Oh, honey, you don't need me for that."

I shuck a hand through my hair. "I don't know, everything I've done the past few months feels a little—"

"Not crazy, Nor. Maybe you're just . . ." Luke turns toward me and runs his hand down my arms. "Maybe it's all just moving fast because you were looking for things to make sense, and now they do."

My heart expands. "Yeah. You're right. It all just makes sense."

I run my hand over his cheek, loving the way the stubble bristles against my skin.

"God, I can't believe my girlfriend is going to become a mother, and I'm not going to have anything to do with it."

I scoff, though a deep fire in my belly is stoked. "You can come with!"

Luke shakes his head. "No, it's your thing, baby. You live your truth, and I'll be here ready to be a part of it."

* * *

I drive way out of the city to the Harmony Hounds Animal Sanctuary. It's situated on a big plot of land where all the animals can live out their days free and happy if they never get a chance to find their forever home. It breaks my heart even thinking about it, but when the caretaker, Claire, leads me to a field of dogs living their best life, I see that it isn't that bad. "Here they come!" Claire says with a cheerful smile.

We are engulfed by dogs of all ages and sizes.

"I think I can die happy now!" I cry out, getting licked and sniffed from all sides.

I give so many head pats and scratches that my heart is pulled in all directions. Do I want a little cairn terrier with missing teeth or a hefty Pitbull who gives the sweetest kisses and is scared of the chihuahua a fraction of his size?

"So, for apartment living, I'd definitely put a restriction on the bigger dog breeds," Claire says. "I hate when people try to force big dogs into small spaces."

"Totally, I wouldn't dream of stuffing this guy into my shoebox," I say as I pat the side of a ginormous dog that looks like it must be part Great Dane.

Claire pats his head. "Sorry, buddy. Next time."

He looks up at her and woofs once before rushing off to go play.

"This place is amazing," I say.

We exchange a smile, then stare off at the dogs as if they're children on the playground. It's beautiful out here. My heart will always be in the city, but sometimes taking a big old gulp of fresh air is necessary. The sky is so big and blue with clouds that Bob Ross could have painted.

Out of the corner of my eye, I see a shorthaired blonde dog skulking by the fence, sniffing the perimeter. He's lanky with perky ears that fold up at the top. He hasn't come up to say hi. "Who's this?"

Claire glances at the dog, her golden ponytail whipping in the wake of a stiff breeze. She smiles solemnly. "That's one of our new guys. I've been calling him Shortbread, but I think he hates it because he barely even wants to give me a sniff. That is common with dogs found in his circumstances."

I don't know if I want to know, for fear my heart may break, but I keep listening.

"He was dumped on the side of the road, nearly starved to death. He's a few years old so I'm sure he had an owner, and then . . ."

"Didn't?"

Claire nods.

"Poor baby."

"We've just been able to introduce him to the pack. He was too skittish at first. Trust issues. I hope he wasn't hurt

213

in his previous home, but . . . it's good to assume the worst when it comes to these guys."

I look up at the sky, trying to keep my eyes from welling up. "Oh my god, how do you do this every day?"

Claire laughs. "Been doing it since I can remember. My mom opened this place when I was just a baby. Comes with the territory." She claps her hands. "Shortbread!"

Shortbread lifts his head in our direction, then goes back to sniffing.

"He's trying to find a way to escape," Claire mutters.

"Aw, poor guy doesn't know how good he's got it."

"Just like humans. We accept the love we think we deserve."

We return our gaze to Shortbread.

"Give me your bag; I'll let him sniff it," Claire continues.

I hand over my satchel and watch her approach Shortbread cautiously, making sure he can see her.

"Hey, Shortie. Got a treat." Claire crouches down and holds the treat out in front of the bag.

Shortbread perks up. Even a boy who's been hurt can't refuse a treat. He goes over and nibbles at her fingers, big pink tongue flicking out. Then, he sticks his head right into my bag. I wonder for a second if I left a half-eaten protein bar in there or something.

Shortbread comes up for air and rounds Claire, giving her a sniff. And then he looks at me.

And something just locks into place.

He bounds over and stops short, a few paces from me. I look at Claire.

"Get on his level if you can," she says in half a whisper so as not to scare him.

I crouch down. "Okay, buddy. Hey there."

Shortbread is still and his dark eyes are wary of me.

I kneel in front of him.

"Hold out a hand," Claire encourages.

I do so, close to my body so he can see it and doesn't feel threatened.

Shortbread noses his way closer. Sniff, sniff, sniff. When he's inches from my hand, he stops and then decidedly licks a stripe up my palm.

In an instant, the shy dog bursts to life, nudging his snout up against my neck, sniffing and looking for any bare plot of skin to lick.

I laugh and run my hands over his head. His ears are as soft as velvet. "Hey Shortbread. Hey."

He calms enough so we can look into each other's eyes.

I scritch my fingers over his scalp, tilting my head to the side and smiling. "I'm not so bad, huh?"

"I'll be damned," Claire says, getting back to her feet. "I can't even get him to come when I call."

Shortbread plops his bottom down, his long pink tongue lolling out of his mouth. When his eyes catch me again, he leans his head toward my neck.

"More pets? Of course," I say, giving him all the scratches he's so desperately needed.

"Love at first sight," Claire says.

My eyes cloud with tears. "Yeah, I think so."

Paris might be the "City of Love," but I have a strong argument that Austin might take the crown.

28

LUKE

I daydream about Eleanor quite a bit, but I have to admit, I dream about her a whole lot more often since we've started sleeping together. How can a man not when he's got *the* perfect woman for a girlfriend?

Today's fantasy is taking her on a road trip. Not in my car, in my dad's old pickup. It's just been sitting in the driveway at the house, unattended to. It probably needs a lot of maintenance at this point, but it would be worth it. I'm imagining hours on the open road with Eleanor, playing all the greatest hits on the radio, enjoying the tranquil scenery. We could go all the way out to the Grand Canyon if she could hack it that long. Seventeen hours ain't but a two day's drive if we're being generous.

And boy, I'd like to be generous. Hit all the stops in between here and there. Tourist traps and natural wonders. Take it slow and easy.

We could even go camping. I've never asked Eleanor if she's the camping type, and I'd hazard a guess, but she is a constant surprise.

That's where my fantasy deviates to something more untoward and *much* more distracting. Having Eleanor under the stars while camping. *Fuck.*

That's heaven.

Of course, she'll probably want to bring the dog. That will put a cramp in my style, but I'll make do.

"Wyatt."

I snap out of my fantasy and find myself face to face with Jen, the owner of the venue where I'm working. From below the brim of her baseball cap, she eyes me with a raised brow. "You good?"

I push off the stack of amps I've been leaning on. "Oh, yeah. I'm fine."

"You were in la-la land for a bit there," she says, swirling her hand in the air a little too close to my face.

"Naw. Me? La-la land?" I pshaw and wave my hand before straightening my suspenders.

Jen grabs one of the suspenders and snaps it against my chest. "Haven't seen you in these in a while."

I don't tend to wear them a lot after I had some out-of-towners claim that I was trying to bring hipster back— as if it ever left Austin. Usually, I can't be swayed by those who don't know what the fuck they're talking about. But the thought of being compared to memes of dudes with handlebar mustaches, bowler hats, and a "Shhh . . ." tattoo on their finger was enough to scare me out of wearing suspenders. There is *one* reason to break them out again, though.

"Uh, yeah, my girlfriend thinks they're cute," I say, again straightening out the suspenders since Jen so unceremoniously put them out of place.

"Oooo," she cajoles. "Your *girlfriend*. Did you hear that, Whit?"

Jen's wife perks her head up from behind the soundboard, light glinting off her septum piercing. "What?"

"Wyatt's got a girlfriend." Jen reaches up and ruffles my hair.

"Careful!" I exclaim, ducking away from her. Jen and I go way back. She caught me sneaking into her bar when I was nineteen to see an impromptu Roky Erickson gig. She's one of the only people who won't lose a hand for messing up my hair.

Jen grins, putting her hands on her hips. "No wonder you're all starry-eyed. You're in love."

"Not—ha! No, not—" My face is getting hot.

"Wyatt's in love!" Whit calls, cupping her hands around her face.

The few guys I have on this job all start snickering. They've been privy to my lovesickness for a while now and it always tickles them when people point it out.

"Not in love. Let's not get ahead of ourselves."

Jen snaps at Randy who is in the middle of coiling an unused cord. "Randy?"

Randy smiles. "Very much in love."

"Fuck off, Randy," I grumble.

Jen and Whit's bar is an easy venue. Unfussy. Bar, folding tables and chairs, a stage. Nothing much, but homey as hell. Jen and Whit are always working on something, which sometimes does more harm than good. Gotta be careful about zoning out, or else Whit futzes too much with the balance on the soundboard, and Jen gets overly chatty with the artists.

Tonight is an old country stalwart on the scene who gets a little ornery if you mess with his preshow routine of drinking malt whiskey at the bar while reading from the same book of Edna St. Vincent Millay poems that he's had since the '80s.

Artists, man.

"Bring her tonight," Jen says with a forceful shake of my arm.

"Oh, she's all the way in the burbs, I don't think she'll want to—"

"We have to give her the fourth degree!" Jen says.

"Third. The *third* degree," Whit corrects.

I scoff. "There will be zero degrees tonight, but thank you both for making it such a welcoming environment for any potential ladies in my life."

Jen and Whit are both silent, before exchanging a look. The look that means they're communicating telepathically. Dammit.

"You're protective," Jen says.

"And?"

"You're never protective," Whit says. "In fact, you never have girlfriends, you only have—"

"*Girls.*"

"You two are killing me," I say and run a hand through my hair, hoping it resettles the damage Jen has done. "I've gotta work."

They giggle with each other. I ignore the whispering and head over to the door crew to make sure everything is handled since Jen and Whit's venue, The Maverick, can get a little rowdy with a weak door crew.

If I keep busy, I won't be distracted. I won't get thrown off course. I won't get lost in "la-la land" as Jen puts it.

Except for the second I'm done with the door crew, a text comes through from Eleanor and I'm down so bad that I can't ignore it.

And fuck, it's a photo. I'm dead, done for, toast.

It's Eleanor sitting out in a field, the afternoon sun shining down on her, with a dog a little too big for her lap trying his best to make a spot for himself. His tongue is blurry, midlick.

The text that follows is:

I think I'm in love.

Same, Nor. Same.

I text back as quickly as I can, so as not to be caught.

So, what you're saying is that he's replacing me tonight?

Eleanor texts back fast.

If all goes to plan!

I grab my heart as if I've been stabbed. It's a joke, but I'm a bit jealous of a dog edging me out in Eleanor's heart.

Another text follows.

I'll ask him if we can make room. Bring treats.

I smile to myself and I'm about to text back, "Can do," when hands wrap around both of my biceps. I am framed by Whit and Jen.

"Who are you texting?"

I try to click off the screen. Too little too late. Whit wrestles the phone from my hand and announces, "*Eleanor!*"

Jen bats at my arm. "See! I knew you were in la-la land."

"I was just texting her to let her know—"

Whit holds up my phone and shows off the photo. "Oh my god, she's gorgeous. Is this her dog?"

"Not yet," I say carefully.

"Text her to come tonight!" Jen says.

"No, y'all, please don't—"

Whit flips the phone back around and squints her eyes. "Hold him in place. I'm taking a photo so she can see the suspenders."

"Seriously! Do not—"

Jen's hands tighten on my arms. "Got him. Take it before he starts flopping like a fish."

I roll my eyes. "This is the worst."

"Got it! And send."

I cover my face. "Augh!"

"You look adorably resigned," Whit says and tosses the phone back to me.

I fumble it, but keep it from dropping. "You guys are going to kill me." I glance at the screen. "Oh god, I look aw—"

"Adorable!" Jen interrupts, patting my arm. "And she'll think as much, too."

I don't want to be adorable. I want to be handsome. Sexy. Irresistible. Not *adorable*. Whit has followed the photo up with a text.

Come to the Maverick tonight.

No question. No suggestion. A demand.

The three dots appear. Then disappear. Appear again. Then—

"She's killing me," Jen groans.

I huff. "Tell me about it."

Finally, her message pops up.

Is that what you're wearing? Sign me up.

She follows it up with a string of emojis, including the salute and the hot one with its tongue out.

"That seems like a yes to me," Jen says with a waggle of her eyebrows.

I shove my phone back into my pocket and hold up my hands, announcing to the bar, "Can we get back to work?"

"Says the guy who has a one-way ticket to la-la land," Whit mutters.

They both laugh.

Jen claps me on the back. "Can't hide her from us forever, Wyatt."

I suddenly feel like I've swallowed a bunch of rocks. Any mention of hiding or secrets has me on red alert these days. The guilt hasn't disappeared. It mounts the closer Eleanor and I become.

Our relationship has been built entirely on a lie. A little white one of my telling.

And this kind of thinking, this isn't la-la land.

This is nightmare fuel.

One last text comes through.

Were the suspenders for me?

My response is quick and unflinching.

All for you, baby.

Maybe if I can make her believe it, the day she knows the truth she'll understand I've never done anything to hurt her.

29

ELEANOR

"I need to keep Shortie here for a couple more weeks. He's already been fixed, but he needs to be vaccinated. It also gives us a chance to observe his behavior and make sure he's ready for a new environment," Claire says as she leads me into the main building of Harmony Hounds. It's a beautiful wooden cabin on the outside that's been upgraded on the inside to house all the animals in their kennels on two separate floors. Big windows let in lots of natural light and there are more than a few cats wandering freely, lying on the windowsills and enjoying their lives as they've always deserved.

Claire is greeted by a mammoth wolfhound and a tiny, scraggly mutt; a funny pair I could imagine a children's movie being written about. The massive wolfhound, ironically called Whisper, strides up without hurrying while the smaller dog hurls her body toward Claire until she runs smack into Claire's shins.

"Easy, Janis—" Claire coos, scooping the dog into the crook of her arm.

"That's a cute name for a dog," I say.

"She was my mom's. Named after Janis Joplin," Claire says with a laugh that feels distant and yet deeply rooted in her chest. "Anyway . . ."

I say nothing more as Claire takes me into an office. Whisper sidles up to me like he's my spirit guide or something. He's humongous, comes almost all the way up to my armpit, and yet so utterly unthreatening.

Claire's office isn't updated like the rest of the building. The walls are made of the cabin's original wood. The cedar smell is distant yet intoxicating.

The walls are covered in framed photographs of various animals that must have had their home here.

Whisper goes directly into the corner to his bed that matches him proportionally, while Claire keeps Janis on her lap when she plops behind the desk and begins to tap around on her ancient-looking computer. "What we can do today, is get you in the system with your application to adopt," Claire explains, beginning to type. "If you're interested in adoption, that is."

I sit in the chair across from Claire's desk. "Yes, absolutely."

Claire smiles to herself as she taps on the keyboard. "I didn't think he'd find a home so fast since he's so standoffish, but when it's right, it's right."

"That's kind of been my life the past few months," I say with a wistful glance out Claire's window that looks out at the pasture of dogs rumbling around. Shortbread has left his searching at the fence and is letting a puppy gnaw on his ear.

"Must be nice," Claire says. She means it. "Nice when everything aligns, and you don't have to wonder if you're doing the right thing or if you should be doing something else."

I nod. "Tell me about it."

She makes a couple of clicks, and then the printer on a pedestal in the corner wakes up and starts to churn out a few inked pages. "So, we'll work on getting his shots, and make sure he's in good shape for his new home. I know you live in an apartment, so I need you to provide me with some proof of access to a dog park, or a backyard, or—"

"I can definitely do that," I say. I've already mapped out my neighborhood, all the parks we can go to, the walks we can take. Not to mention that Luke has a whole house. We could visit him and give Shortbread space to run around in a fenced-in yard.

I mean, I've never been to Luke's house, so I don't know if he *has* a fenced in yard, but . . . a girl can dream.

It's odd that I've never been to his house. But it's out of the way, and he's been so focused on getting me settled at my own place, that he's never even suggested we spend the night at his place. It makes me a little uneasy, like he doesn't want memories in his house on the off-chance things don't work out. He doesn't want to be haunted the way I would be.

Although things are going so well, there's no reason for me to believe either of us will be haunted any time soon.

I shake off the feeling, and focus on the excitement of today, and the swelling of love in my chest. It's a love close to pride. I'm proud of making a life here and proud of the woman I've become in such a short time when I was so scared, so nervous to leave footprints or lay down roots.

"I'll work on crate training him," Claire says, then pushes her chair away from the desk. It rolls over to the printer. Janis scrambles in Claire's lap, looking over each arm of the chair nervously. Claire's hold on the dog is the same as it's been the whole time—steady and unconcerned. I'm sure she's had a lot of practice from working with animals. "And usually, our animals are pretty good about being housetrained because they have so much access to the outside."

As she's fetching the paper from the printer, I notice three photographs above the printer aren't of animals, but people. The first one, directly above the printer, is of Claire and a woman sitting on a swinging bench that I noticed on the front porch of the main building. The woman is thin to a degree that seems to suggest something is wrong. Her beauty is still apparent, but her cheeks are sallow, and her arms lack the usual amount of sinew, even for an older woman. Her head is wrapped in an elegant scarf. Claire has her arms around the woman, her head tipped onto her shoulder.

That must be her mother. Claire has only made past-tense references to her mother.

Above that is a portrait picture of the same woman and Claire, I'm assuming, when she was a little girl. It's one of those department store photos with a gray, swirly background. Claire is wearing a dress scattered with watermelons and a floppy hat like Blossom might wear. She's leaning back into her mother's arms, arms that are full of life and strength.

It must be difficult to watch someone go like that. I think about Luke's father. How he was gone all at once. Would he rather have watched him go bit by bit?

The woman's face catches me off-guard. Her hair is long and almost black. And her face . . .

I know that face.

Claire rolls back to me and starts to slide the paperwork toward me, but my eyes travel up to the top picture.

My jaw drops.

I catalog every detail. Dark shoulder-length shag haircut, big grin, flannel draped over a dress, a guitar case in her hand.

The Lone Star.

"So, all you have to do is sign and date. There's no obligation, financial or otherwise, this is just so we have it on file that Shortbread—"

"Is your mom's name Diane?" I ask, my mouth growing hot.

Claire's eyebrows jump up. She follows my gaze to the wall as if trying to figure out how I got that information just from the photos. "Um, yeah. How did you know that?"

I get to my feet. I can't help myself. I need to see it up close, to know if this is real. "I've seen this picture before," I say, pointing at the top photo.

Up close, nothing changes.

It's the exact same picture.

Maybe even the original.

"You have?" Claire's tone is skeptical. I'm probably scaring her.

I place my hand to my chest, gesturing toward the photo with the other one. "I've been working at the Reeder Music Library in the archives, and I came across a copy of this photo. My boyfriend and I were trying to figure out who the woman was and—and—" I smile. "She's your mom!"

Claire stops looking at me like a crazy person and starts to smile too.

"We found her obituary and then my boyfriend—he's in the music industry—he was able to find her demos. Have you ever heard her music?"

Claire's brows jump. "No, I mean, she played, but I never knew she recorded anything."

"She did!" I exclaim. My heart is starting to race. There's a reason I stayed in Austin. I mean, there are plenty of reasons, but this one feels the most incredible. If I had walked away, if I hadn't decided I was going to make Austin my home, I never would have thought about getting a dog here, I never would have come to Harmony Hounds, I never would have met Claire, and I never would have— "In fact, I wanted to get your mom's photo featured in an exhibit we're having at the library, but, because I didn't have the original, they wouldn't let me. But if you'd be willing to loan it to me, maybe I could feature her."

Claire gets up, plopping Janis in her chair before coming over to meet me in front of the photos. "As long as I would get it back—"

"Of course, of course." I adjust my glasses. "I will bring you the copy as collateral."

"Okay. I can do that."

Claire's blue eyes are glistening. "And the music. Please, could you bring her music?"

"Yes, absolutely, I'll load it onto a flash drive and bring it the next time I come up."

She inhales, a smile spreading across her face. "Thank you. That would be . . . thank you."

We both look at the photo. This is why I love photography. It's just a piece of paper, but it's a moment in time that can unite strangers in an instant.

I clap my hands at my chest. "Could I see it? Out of the frame."

Claire laughs. "Is this a photography thing?"

"There's nothing like an original photograph."

Claire takes the photo down from the wall and begins to undo the frame. "I've always loved this photo of her."

"Me too. I mean—" I'm rambling like a madwoman. "When I came across it in our archives, I was immediately intrigued. She is just magnetic."

Claire smiles proudly, her eyes pinching hard to keep from crying. "She was."

When she removes the backing of the frame, I pause. There's writing on the back.

Love, Frank

Obviously, on the copy, there wasn't anything on the back.

"Who's Frank?" I ask.

Claire frowns. "I don't know, I never . . . I've never opened the frame."

Frank must be the person who took this photo. And whoever Frank is had some love for Diane. Whether that's friendly love or romantic, I'm not sure. But I have a feeling.

You can tell what a photographer is seeing from the quality of their images. And whoever was holding this camera saw Diane for the supernova she was.

They saw her beauty. They saw her magic.

They loved her.

And now I have even more questions.

30

LUKE

When I see Eleanor's car pull up, it takes everything in me not to run over. Still, after all this time together, I count down the minutes until I can see her again.

I stride over to her car once it's stopped and grab her door handle before she can step out.

Eleanor leaps out of the car and into my arms.

"Hey!" I say through a laugh.

She embraces me tight, tighter, tightest.

"Okay, anaconda, I can't breathe!" I choke out.

Eleanor releases me, her head flying back with laughter. Ever since she's decided to stay in Austin, she is so much more at ease. And it's a beautiful thing. I love her poise and how she lifts that veil for me.

Before I can catch my breath, she pops upward to snatch my mouth into a kiss. When our lips part, she finally says, "Hi."

"Hi . . ." I say, scooping her up by the waist, trying to hold as much of her as possible. "How was your day?"

"Good. Amazing. Fantastic." Her hands slide down to my chest, fingers tracing the suspenders. "Better now that I'm seeing these in person."

I laugh. "Okay, down girl. Tell me about your day before you get all hot and bothered over the suspenders."

Hand in hand, we walk into The Maverick where the set is just starting. We sneak up to the bar where Whit and Jen are waiting eagerly to meet Eleanor. Her stories will have to wait. Introductions are whispered and friendly words are exchanged. Whit and Jen don't give her the third degree they promised, instead remarking what a cute couple we are and how she's different than the women I usually go for. I don't love the mention of my past dating exploits, but I have to take the wins where I can.

Eleanor, is, of course, perfect. As always. Again, at ease, rather than on edge.

Whit and Jen finally leave us alone to go enjoy the stylings of Eddie Black, fingerpicking extraordinaire.

Over two Shiner Bocks, because she's an Austinite now, Eleanor regales me with the story of her day.

"So, Claire—that's the woman who owns the place—said that Shortbread needs a couple more weeks to get his shots before he'll be available for adoption," Eleanor says.

"Sounds like it was meant to be," I say.

Eleanor leans toward me. "Yeah, that's what I'd say too."

Our lips brush in a chaste kiss. Just because it's chaste doesn't mean it doesn't light my body on fire. I have visions of taking her home tonight and giving her the ride of her life, watching her curls tumble around her face and the look of ease transforming into pleasure.

"But that's not even the craziest thing that happened," Eleanor says.

"Oh?"

She clamps her teeth down on her lower lip, smiling. "You are not going to believe this—Claire is Diane's daughter."

It takes me a second to add up all the words she's said into a sentence that makes sense. "Diane?"

"Like *the* Diane."

My pulse skips.

"Diane Bloom? The woman in the photo that brought us together?"

Don't remind me. I knew I wouldn't be able to keep the guilt at bay forever. I knew that one day it would all catch up with me. I prayed it wouldn't, that I would luck out and Diane would become just a plot point in our love story, not a recurring theme. I should have known I wouldn't be so lucky. "Yeah, I'm sorry, I'm just confused. How did you—"

"The picture. The *original*. It was on the wall of Claire's office."

"And Claire is Diane's daughter?" I ask, trying to add up the pieces. Aunt Diane had a child? Assumedly, a husband too, and a whole life beyond her life I was a part of. I guess that's the self-possession we all have as children. When we are little, we believe that the road rises to meet us. That the world is conjured for our benefit, rather than us existing amongst stories that are already being told.

"Yes! Diane apparently started the sanctuary, and when she died her daughter took it over. Claire didn't even know about her mother's recordings. Isn't that crazy? I told her that she should come to the library and check out the exhibit as my guest. I mean, think about it. All the ways we can fill in the story."

I nod slowly. Life is moving around me like water. The bounding fingerpicking of Eddie Black is sludgy, and the soft conversations and clinking of glasses are like echoes in a cavern.

"And! Oh my god, this is the best part!"

"Oh, there's something better?" I say, trying to laugh. It squeaks out from the back of my throat. I hope Eleanor can't tell how panic is strangling me.

"There was a note on the back of the original photo," she says in a clandestine whisper.

"A note?"

She takes a big swig of her beer. "Yes, a note."

"What kind of note?"

Eleanor smiles. She's enjoying this so much I don't think she's even clocking my reactions, thank god. "Two words. That's it."

I wait with bated breath. I don't even have a guess. I have no idea what kind of note it could be, especially one that's only two words.

"Love. Frank."

The slowness of the water turns into the rigidness of ice.

Love, Frank

"That's crazy," I say, though my voice doesn't feel like my own.

"I know! Like, who is Frank? And were they in love or was he just a friend or—"

I'm going to be sick.

Eleanor continues to posit her theories and guesses without any help from me. "I mean, I think based on the photos, that's the photograph a lover would take. You know something I would take of you." She elbows me in the ribs, then turns on her bar seat to watch the musician play. "I wonder if Frank is alive. I wonder if we can find him."

No. We can't.

"Because I wonder what kind of stories he might have. God, wouldn't that be cool?"

"Yeah, it would be," I say.

Eleanor's smile is proud and triumphant.

My insides are withering. Dying.

She swigs her beer again and slides the empty bottle onto the bar. "You going to have another?"

"Yeah," I say. I push myself up to my feet. "You order us another round. I gotta hit the bathroom."

I don't wait for her answer. I just let my feet do the work for me. I am on autopilot, wading through the crowd until I make it into the red lit hall with signatures peppering the walls around the restroom doors.

I shoulder my way into one of the restrooms and lock the door behind me.

My stomach heaves upward, threatening to expel everything inside it. I grab onto the edge of the sink and try to steady myself.

This wasn't how it was supposed to go.

She wasn't supposed to find out more. The story was supposed to be finished. I could have lived with that guilt and shame.

Now, she's exposed another thread. A thread that is just a curiosity to her, an exciting new path to follow.

Eleanor doesn't know what pulling this thread will cost me.

Because, Frank . . .

My stomach heaves again. I gag, but nothing comes up. I turn on the water, the rusty faucet handles squeaking angrily. I splash the cold water onto my face. The shock to my system steadies me enough to get a grip.

Water drips from the front of my hair into the sink.

I don't know how long I've been standing here, muscling the sink, my temples pounding.

Time is not relevant.

When I finally get the gumption to lift my head, my eyes meet my reflection. Blue eyes. Exact copies of my father's.

"Fuck," I say, although it's more like an exhale.

Frank isn't just a name. Not just Diane's friend or lover or some new piece to the puzzle that Eleanor wants to find in order to make the picture as clear as possible.

Frank is my father.

I guess I can't be completely sure that it's the same Frank. But the questions I had about Diane's disappearance from my life have opened pockets of memories that I haven't ever reached into. How Diane's disappearance was also marked by Dad's absence. His late nights at work and business trips. His empty chair at the dinner table. Mom's caginess, and when pressured, her short temper.

One memory comes forward, the clearest of them all.

I wake up in the middle of the night at the sound of my father coming home. He lumbers into the kitchen as I tiptoe down, hoping he'd take pity on my sleeplessness and make us midnight snacks that we could share together in front of the television. He stands in the doorway to the kitchen, humming.

Oh, my fucking god.

It was the song.

"Hyacinth."

I wipe my hands over my face, wicking away the water. "What the fuck, Dad?!" I mutter.

What did he do? What did *they* do?

Do I want to know the answer?

Though I have more questions than answers, I know one thing for sure.

235

I can't keep up the lie. I have to tell Eleanor that I've known about Diane from the very beginning, and that I've harbored this lie since the inception of us.

And I have no one to blame but myself if the truth causes everything to collapse.

31

ELEANOR

My face is warm, my brain buzzing, and my body is like gelatin in the best way possible. I know I might be paying for it in the morning, but for now, I'm enjoying the lighter than air feeling.

I lean on the door frame and watch as Luke finagles my keys into the lock. He's so handsome. That golden hair, those blue eyes, his long and lanky frame.

Mmmm . . .

I never thought a guy like him would go for a girl like me. I know I'm pretty, but he's just the conventionally pretty type, and I'm the . . . well, I thought I was the unconventionally pretty type. Maybe I should start reevaluating that.

As soon as he opens the door, he pushes it open for me. "After you."

Instead of going through the door, I swoon into his arms, trapping him in a messy kiss. Luke balks. "What are you doing?" he asks though my lips muffle his.

I grab at his suspenders. So grabbable. And I answer him with another kiss, yanking him into my apartment.

Luke trips after me. "Eleanor—"

"These suspenders are so damn sexy," I say into his mouth, then I snatch another kiss. I taste beer, but I don't know if that's his mouth or mine. Though the apartment is silent, I still hear the twanging guitar in the background, revving me up and setting the scene.

I grip the bottom half of his shirt and untuck it, kissing and kissing and kissing him. I don't think I'll ever get tired of his mouth.

Luke's hands drop to my shoulders. Prodding. Away? Pushing? "Eleanor, slow down, I—"

"I know we've been drinking, but I'm consenting. I'm totally consenting," I reassure him, then plant sloppy kisses on his jaw. "Okay? It's fine."

"That's not—"

I don't give him a chance to finish his sentence. I shove him down onto my couch and plop down onto his lap.

"*Eleanor.*" His insistence eggs me on. The syllables of my name on his tongue with his accent—*fuck.*

I've never felt this way for a man before. In every part of my life. It's cosmic. It's destined. It's *perfect.*

Maybe because we started as friends, started with our minds, though our hearts were all tangled up from the very beginning, too. It's only gotten better; every moment I have with Luke paints a bigger, more beautiful picture of us together. Like I can take a snapshot of the future—it's glorious.

This is what people mean when they say when it happens, you'll know.

Because I know.

I run my fingers through his hair, moving my hips against him.

Luke places his hands softly on my hips. Not grabbing. His hips aren't moving against me.

In fact, he's not even hard.

That's fine. Whiskey dick. Maybe. That happens. Doesn't mean we can't kiss and have a little fun. Penetration isn't *everything*.

I pull his suspenders over his shoulders and lower my mouth to his neck. "You're so sexy when you're working," I say.

"Eleanor, stop."

That gets my attention. Oh my god, was that what he was trying to say this whole time? Trying to ask me to stop? And I just kept going. I lift my head and cover my mouth.

"I'm so sorry," I mutter. I push myself up from the couch, stumbling back a bit, but thankfully catching myself. "I'm so sorry, did I hurt you?"

Luke pulls his suspenders back up. "No, Nor, no. Not—"

I fist my hands and bounce them against my forehead. "I'm so sorry, oh my god."

"It's fine, it's not—"

"The last thing I want to do is push your boundaries or make you feel like I'm taking advantage of you, oh my god, was I taking advantage of you?" I clutch my chest. Is this a panic attack?

"*Eleanor!*"

The room snaps with . . . is that anger? Is he mad at me?

I look back at him. Luke's eyes seem to be sizing up a task he thinks might be insurmountable, his jaw tight and mouth pursed.

"Just *stop* for a second," he says, spreading his hands up.

Oh, I'm stopped alright. Frozen in place. Waiting to know what the hell he's thinking. Or what I did wrong.

Fuck, did I screw everything up?

Luke puts his hands on his thighs and rubs them up and down. "Could you sit?"

"What's going on?"

"Eleanor, just sit. Over there." He nods toward the armchair across from the couch.

I sit in the wingback chair. The back is too straight for how I'm feeling. I'd like to slouch and curl my legs up under me to protect myself like a hermit crab.

"I need to tell you something," he says.

He has another girlfriend. He's married. He has kids. Oh my god, he's going to die. He's leaving Austin. He thinks this has all been a mistake.

My mind rushes through possibilities all at once, not able to land on anything except *bad*.

This is *bad*.

"Okay," I squeak.

Luke's tense expression softens. He leans toward me, elbows on his knees. "I want to preface and say that the last thing I've ever wanted to do is hurt you."

He's totally married.

"I never wanted to do anything to hurt you."

I am now incredibly sober. Viciously sober. I could walk a straight line, touch my nose, and say the date with flying colors. "Luke, what's going on?"

Luke gnashes on his lower lip and his eyes shift. Fear. "Stay with me, okay?"

Does he mean in this moment? Or in the broader sense?

"I knew Diane."

The words rest over us and float downward. The closer they get, the more I understand. "You *knew* Diane?"

Luke nods.

I narrow my eyes. "What does that mean?"

"I mean that I knew her. I mean I . . ." He swallows and his eyes fall from mine. "I recognized her. In the picture."

I frown. "So, I showed you the picture and you knew who she was?"

Luke nods.

I laugh. It's unexpected. "Is this a weird joke?"

He shakes his head.

I'm not sure how I'm feeling. The web is still too tangled. "So, I showed you the picture and you already knew. So . . . you lied?"

"Yeah, that's what I'm getting at."

Fuck the chair. I pull my legs up under me and let my shoulders slump. "How did you know her?" That's not the first question most people would likely ask. "Why?" should have been the first. But maybe I'm holding out hope that if I understand the what, then I'll get to the why. And he won't have to grovel. And I won't feel this hollowness in my chest.

"She was friends with my parents. Kind of like a part of the family. We called her Aunt Diane."

I wince. *Aunt.* That's closer than close.

"I have a lot of awesome memories from my childhood with her around. She'd bring her guitar around, and we'd have singalongs out in the backyard, and . . . then she just disappeared. I never knew what happened to her."

"But she was here the whole time."

"Apparently. My parents never gave me a straight answer. My dad—" Luke stops short, then shakes his head, throwing his golden locks out of place. "I never got an answer."

I stare at him, waiting for more.

The silence is vast. And it extends for a while. Luke scratches his cheek and leans back on the couch. His eyes are flicking back and forth trying to figure out the next thing to say.

"Why didn't you just tell me?" It's not fair that I have to prompt him, but I can't sit here on pins and needles any longer.

"The date," he croaks. If he cries, that won't be fair to me. I won't be comforting him. I'm the one who deserves a cry right now. "The date was after the last time I saw her. I think. I can't be too sure, but I—"

"You should have just told me."

Luke sighs. "I know. You're right. It took me off-guard. I didn't know what to say about it. We were strangers."

I scoff. "So, you decided to lie to a stranger instead? It's not like you didn't have plenty of opportunities to tell the truth, Luke. You could have told me after we met, it would have been less weird than this."

Weird is an understatement, but it's the only word that comes to mind at the moment.

"I know. I know I should have just—but then it was too late, and then—"

"I've known you for months, Luke! I've—I thought—" There are worse things he could have said. So many worse. But I feel like a whole part of our history has been betrayed. "Why didn't you just—"

"I wanted to keep seeing you," he says. "And I had already lied the first time, so it just felt easier to follow the trail with you. And to be fair, I didn't know what Diane had been up to. I didn't know that after—"

"You knew her name! We went to bars and houses and made phone calls to people to figure out who she was!"

Luke shuts his eyes tight. "I know, I know. I just didn't think you'd want to keep seeing me afterward. You barely wanted me to get involved at first. I thought if I let you go before you understood who I really was, you know, not just some playboy because I *know* that's what you thought. I know it was, then I would—"

"I feel like a fucking child who was taken on a scavenger hunt. Oh my god." I cover my face. "Oh my *god*, I feel so stupid."

"You couldn't have known."

I snap. "Obviously!"

Luke is smaller than he's ever been before me. As he fucking should be. "You tried to push me away at every turn. You tried to—"

"So instead, you controlled my reactions. You manipulated me into thinking—"

"I didn't manipulate you!"

"Yes, *you did*!"

Luke's face darkens. "I wish I regretted it, but I don't think I can. I don't think we would have gotten here if I hadn't lied to you."

Maybe he's right. Maybe I wouldn't have let myself be enjoyed by him. I probably would have gotten in my own way.

"You would never have seen Austin, and you'd never have fallen in love with it. With me."

I let out a shaky breath.

"And you love me, Eleanor," he says, desperation creeping into his voice. "You love me, right? Because I love you. I love you so much. And I'm telling you now because . . . because . . ."

"Of course, I love you. That's why I'm so fucking angry at you."

243

The corner of Luke's mouth perks up and I understand why.

I have not felt this hollowness since I walked in on my ex fucking another woman in our home. This wrong shouldn't feel comparable, and yet it does. "You know why cheating hurts?" I ask.

"*Nor*, I would never—"

"Listen to me."

Luke's nostrils flare, but he clamps his mouth shut.

"You'd think it's because you don't feel like you're enough. Your partner needed something else from someone else. You'd think that would be the worst part of it." My lower lip trembles. I'm not going to cry. Not over this. Not again. "But it's not. The worst part is having to look back at the past however much time, and having to reconcile that the safety and security you thought you had, wasn't there at all. That they had an entirely alternate history in the making that they tried to hide from you."

We stare at each other.

I lick my lower lip. "This. What you've done. It's not that different."

Luke's head drops forward. "Fuck," he says. Then his body jerks up straight. "Fuck!"

The violence in the word hurts my ears. "You should go," I say.

Luke, in his cute suspenders, pushes himself up from the couch, clinging to the arm of it like he might collapse if he lets go. "So, what does this mean? For us?"

"I don't know. I just need to be alone right now, okay?"

I want to look away, but his gaze is on me, bidding me to look toward him. And when I do, the tears begin to lay siege on my eyes.

He hangs off his own body—a broken man in adorable suspenders. Screw him for still looking so good, even when he's bereft. "Please, just don't—" His voice catches, and he touches his chest. "Please don't decide we're done. Not yet."

"Luke . . ." If I say anything else, I'll start to sob.

"Just don't decide right now," he says, backing away to the door. "Okay?"

I can't take looking at him anymore. I drop my head, trying to pull my legs up closer to my chest.

"I love you," he says.

He doesn't wait for me to say it back.

Once the door is shut, I cry.

Though he's gone, I'm haunted by him the entire night.

32

LUKE

Seeing my mom on the front porch takes the edge off my heartbreak a bit.

Just a bit, though.

She looks as beautiful as ever. Her silvery blonde hair is coiffed in a Mary Tyler Moore bob, and she's wearing a blue skirt and a white blouse. I know even if I wasn't coming to visit, this is the outfit she'd choose.

I woke up this morning with the biggest emotional hangover of my life. I'm shocked I was able to sleep at all without Eleanor next to me, knowing that she holds the future of our relationship in her hands. That she could break it.

It would be her right.

Even if it would totally gut me.

So, I decided to head down to see my mom. I don't know how or if I'll broach the topic of the photo of Aunt Diane. Mom's always been strong, even in the wake of losing Dad so unexpectedly, but that strength is a tenuous, thin film overtop the grief.

I don't want to break it.

She meets me on the front steps, wrapping her arms around me from a step above so I'm at her height. It makes me feel like a little boy again.

Mom kisses the top of my head. "You need a haircut."

I laugh and breathe in her perfume. She's always worn Elizabeth Arden Red Door. I have my own bottle for when I get homesick.

Life has gotten to be too much. Working too hard, loving too hard. And now the picture. I don't realize I'm crying until my mom chides me softly. "Now, why on earth are you crying?"

We go inside, and I tell her everything—well, regarding Eleanor. I'm not going to mention Dad. That would kill her. Giving her something to focus on outside herself has been invaluable to her grieving. Which is why she's always having her friends over and going to book club and church functions. Consoling a crying thirty-five-year-old son fits the bill too, I suppose.

"You've fallen in love, and this is the first I'm hearing about it?" she asks. "Tsk, tsk. *Luke.*"

I laugh, rubbing my sleeve over my face to clear away the tears. "It's still new."

"Well, who cares if it's new? Goodness gracious," she says, then sips her cup of coffee. "What's her name?"

"Eleanor."

"Mm. And what did you do to make her mad?"

I hesitate. "I don't . . . I told her a lie, and I thought it was, you know, a lie that would help and not hurt."

"Mm . . . I know a man like that."

Dad. How much *does* she know?

"You know, honesty is always the best policy, honey."

I roll my eyes. "Yes, Mom."

She giggles and pats her hand over mine. "You know I love my adages."

"Yeah . . ." I sigh heavily. "I'm afraid she's not going to give me a chance to make up for it."

"Have you talked to her today?"

I shake my head. To my chagrin, she hasn't reached out to me. Which isn't shocking. And though I wanted to text her this morning, I thought giving her space would be the best Idea. I don't want to look desperate, but that seems like an impossible task when I've laid myself at her feet over and over again.

"Give her time. She'll come back around," Mom says.

"But what if she doesn't?"

She sighs, then grabs a cube of sugar and drops it into my coffee. "I wish your father were here to give you better advice. I can give you the woman's perspective, but what to actually *do* about it . . ."

"What would you want Dad to do then?" I ask.

She looks at me. There's a flash of something in the back of her gray eyes, a strike of lightning. She's silent for a moment, then says, "Grovel."

"I can do that."

We both laugh. And once that's off my chest, I let her talk my ear off for a while. There's a lot to catch up on since I've been so busy with work and women. Time always passes so quickly that I'm shocked when I come back home and realize how long it's been.

"So, did you come all the way out here just to cry about a girl?" she asks after she's had her fill of chatting.

Not entirely. In fact, I didn't even know that was going to come up. "I wanted to see if you were ready to go through Dad's stuff."

Her body jerks. "Oh, heavens, you should have warned me about that before you came."

I try not to be sheepish. Boxes of Dad's stuff sit in the attic. His clothes still hang in the closets. The way the house looks, you'd think he's going to walk through the backdoor any minute, sweating his ass off from mowing the lawn. He'd chase her around the kitchen trying to give her a kiss, and she'd whack him with an oven mitt to get his sweaty face away from her.

Ah, the good old days.

"You would have told me no," I say.

"I would have said 'no, but come down anyway,'" she grumbles. Mom tinkles her manicured nails on her coffee cup. "I'm not ready for that, baby. I know you think I'm crazy, but—"

"Not crazy at all." I think about the way I'll have to mourn Eleanor if she walks away from me, and that's only been a few months. How do you mourn a whole lifetime with someone?

However, I'm not leaving here without learning something about Diane and Dad.

"Could I poke around? Just find some things maybe to . . . to remember him by."

Mom's mouth turns from a hesitant smile into a full one. "Well, that's a great idea."

* * *

I go to the boxes in the back. The ones hidden and buried.

Because if there's any evidence to what I think might be there, it's hidden and buried.

I sort through boxes of newspaper clippings, old books, albums of people I don't recognize, tchotchkes and other memories. Each item I touch feels charged with a memory of my father. Nothing specific, no images. Just him.

I miss him. I miss him so much.

And I'm afraid that when all is said and done, I'm going to be mad at him.

Eventually, I start coughing. The attic is a haven for allergies. It gets to the point I'm coughing more often than I'm not. I know I'll need to stop soon.

One more box. One more box.

I keep saying that to myself. Just one more box.

And finally, one more box pays off.

This box is mostly packing material. Old newspaper, old grocery store ads. But there is something in here. All the way at the bottom.

A gray metal lockbox.

I stare at it. Innocuous enough to be nothing. However, the only thing hidden in a box of packing material at the back of the attic has to be something.

I cough into my arm and curse to myself. The cough is starting to cut up my lungs. I need to figure out how to open this thing as fast as possible because there's no way Mom is going to let me walk out of here holding an unopened box without an explanation.

I grab an old pocketknife from one of the other boxes I just opened and use it to pop the lock without any regard to maintaining the box.

And there it is. A whole world in a single box.

Photos and letters.

Diane and my dad.

My stomach turns as the first photo comes into focus. The two of them in a darkened booth with my dad's arm slung around Diane's shoulder. She's smiling at him the way a woman smiles at a man she adores.

The date is close to the one on Eleanor's photo.

What the hell was going on? How did this happen?

I can't bring myself to read the letters. I don't know if I want to know the story. About a love gone wrong, or a love that could never be, or . . .

I find a cocktail napkin emblazoned with the logo of a bar that no longer exists.

There are words written in blue pen.

I might not get you tomorrow,

But at least I have you today.

And when you see me tomorrow,

That's exactly what I'll say.

There's a kiss mark on the other side.

"Hyacinth" is about my dad. He's the love that could never be.

This is awful. Worse than I could have imagined.

I remember what Eleanor said last night. The idea that a history you thought you knew could be rewritten—how painful that is.

I made her feel the way I feel right now.

I fucking suck.

I already knew that, though.

From small glances here and there, I grip a timeline. Whatever it was, lasted a couple of months in 1991.

Except for a final envelope. One postmarked almost two years ago.

It was never opened.

"Luke!"

I shove the unopened letter in my back pocket, clap the lockbox shut, and throw it back into the packing material. "Yeah?!"

I hear her footsteps on the ladder. "You hungry?"

Shoving the box into the back where it belongs, I call out. "I could eat!"

Mom is moving slowly, so thankfully I'm able to head her off at the pass before she can climb into the attic. She smiles at me. "I just took a meatloaf out of the oven. Your favorite."

Staring down into my mom's face, the tears threaten to return. The story of our family—of my father—what is it really?

Do I even want to know?

Miraculously, I manage to push away the thoughts of my father and Diane while I enjoy lunch with my mother. It's not until I climb into my car that they all hit me at once.

Still nothing from Eleanor. And maybe it's for the best. Because my world just flipped upside down.

I don't have it in me to remain silent, though. So, I send her a text.

I'm sorry I changed our history. It's still the best thing that's ever happened to me.

33

ELEANOR

Luke's text circles in my head throughout the entire workweek.

I never replied to it. And he never texted again.

I'm starting to miss him. In fact, I've missed him since he left my apartment. But I'm not ready to forgive. Not entirely.

"He wanted you so bad that he did anything to get you! Isn't that beautiful?" Jolene says over lunch on Friday when she finally gets the full story out of me.

"Maybe in a rom-com, but not in real life," I reply.

Which is true. The compliment is lost when there's a red flag waving in my face.

I'm a little surprised he hasn't been trying harder to get my attention. On one hand, I respect it, and on the other, I'm annoyed. Grovel! Fight for me! Find me! Show up at my window with a boombox overhead!

Scratch that last one. That's not romantic, either. That's just creepy. It's great in a movie, though.

"Okay, but like, the lie is really harmless at the end of the day," Jolene says.

"Maybe it is, but maybe it isn't. He kept up that lie for a while. What happens when it's actually something that could really hurt?" Make no mistake, *this* really hurts. But I can acknowledge it's not the same as cheating, and it's not violence.

Jolene sighs, chewing a big bite of Caesar salad. Once she gulps it down, she rolls her eyes. "I don't know, no one is perfect."

"True."

"And like, he's perfect in every other way, right?"

I raise my eyebrows in agreement. "I feel like I have a scale in my brain that I keep adding weights to, trying to see if the bad outweighs the good."

"And?"

I shake my head. "Why are women always having to settle? Why do we always have to put up with—"

"Eleanor. What's the scale actually saying?"

That's the thing. I don't like what it's saying. Or I think I *shouldn't* like what it's saying. Luke has mostly pros. He's smart and sexy, charming and sweet, a gentleman, a provider. I never thought I could meet a prince.

Guess I haven't.

"The good technically outweighs the bad."

Jolene pumps her fist. "Yes!"

"*But—*"

"No buts! Only butts."

I sigh. "You're not helping."

"I'm trying to make you see that you can't intellectualize everything, Eleanor. I know that's what has always protected you, but . . ."

"You said no buts."

Jolene smirks and reaches her hands out. I let her grab mine. Our clasped hands rest between us on the table. "I'm not going to say it's not concerning. And I'm not going to devalue how you feel. But have you ever considered that maybe you might see that he's a man who can learn from his mistakes?"

It's a risk. But it's not a bad one.

Her words run through my mind the rest of the day, until I get a call from Harmony Hounds. Not from Claire though. Apparently, they'd like me to come down and see Shortbread. Keep him in good spirits and maybe take him for a test drive. Take him on a walk, feed him, and see how we gel.

I plan to go out there on Sunday. Before I leave the museum, I grab the copy of the photo and load the music onto a USB.

Sunday morning, right as I step out of my apartment, I get another call.

From Luke.

I can't not answer. I'm compelled. I want to hear his voice and find out how he's doing.

Just because he's on my shitlist doesn't mean I don't care.

"Hey," I answer.

Luke blows out a breath. "You picked up."

The relief is evident in his voice, and it makes me want to cry. "I did. Hi."

"Hi."

There's a short pause.

"W-what are you doing right now?"

"Headed out to Harmony Hounds to see Shortbread again," I say.

"Oh . . . that's nice."

I lean on the door frame. "Do you . . . want to come?"

Luke doesn't waste a moment. "Yes, I'd love that."

* * *

255

When Luke gets into my car, there's no wall between us. We both go in for the embrace, sliding our arms around each other and pulling tight.

He smells incredible. I missed his scent on my pillows.

Luke braces a hand against the side of my head and presses his face into my curls. "I've missed you so much."

He still feels safe. It's strange, but he still feels safe even though he broke my trust.

"I've missed you too," I say. And mean it.

We catch up on the whole drive to Harmony Hounds—delicately and slowly. The details come out like breadcrumbs in the forest. He tells me a bit about his gigs, and I talk about the museum. He talks about visiting his mom, and I tell him about going to trivia with Jolene and her friends.

When we get to Harmony Hounds, we're met by the person who called me, a young guy with gauges named Stellan. He eyes Luke warily. "You're Eleanor's partner?"

Luke checks my expression for permission.

I answer for him. "Yeah, he is. Do you think it'd be good for Shortbread to meet him too?"

"Might be. Depends on how he responds. We'll take it slow."

It's hard to take it slow with Shortbread, who bounds up to me when he sees me, clamoring for kisses.

"We gotta work on his jumping," Stellan says.

But I don't mind at all.

Luke hangs back, attacked with love from the other dogs. He plops down on his bottom and lets himself be taken by puppy kisses.

As Shortbread and I reunite, Stellan encourages Luke closer until Shortbread clocks him too.

Luke holds his hand out for Shortbread to approach. And the tentative, shy Shortbread doesn't bat an eye. He goes up and licks Luke's palm.

"Probably helps that you two smell similar," Stellan remarks.

It's an off-handed comment, but it strikes me in the chest. Luke and I have become entangled.

I don't want to lose that. That settles it for me.

After they get acquainted, we head inside with Shortbread to work on leashing him to see how he handles it, if he'll be docile.

"It's possible a muzzle might be good for him," Stellan says as he harnesses Shortbread. "He's good with the dogs around here, but seeing other dogs in a new environment might bring about a different reaction."

Hard to imagine the dog who has his snout in my hand could be snappy. I smooth my thumb down his nose and glance at Luke. "What do you think?"

"Oh, he's perfect," he says, beaming ear to ear, in that tone new parents seem to have when they learn their babies have ten toes and ten fingers.

A shiver goes down my spine when I get a flash of what that might actually be like with Luke, how proud he'd be to have a baby of his own, and not just a fur baby. Yep, the feelings are still there. Not going away any time soon.

"Eleanor?"

I look up to the second level to see Claire. She gives me a wave.

"Hi!"

"Let me come down and say hi."

As Claire descends the steps, I lean into Luke. "That's Diane's daughter."

Luke slides his hands into his pockets. "Yeah, I got that." There's an edge to his voice, which I suppose is only fair.

When Claire comes back into view, I take pause.

Blue eyes. Blonde hair.

I glance at Luke.

His eyes widen. His jaw tics.

The similarities are uncanny. Maybe I'm dreaming it.

But I did swear Claire looked familiar when we first met.

It has to be a coincidence, right?

Right?

34

LUKE

It's like looking in a mirror.

I can't explain it.

I took after Dad—a spitting image people have said.

And this woman . . . Claire . . .

Diane's daughter.

She doesn't look at all like her. She looks like my father.

My heart throbs. I agreed to come out here with Eleanor for this express purpose. Well, not *exactly*. I brought the sealed note from my parents' attic, thinking that maybe, just maybe I would have an opportunity to get a little more information. I didn't think I'd be brave enough to ask.

Seeing Claire doesn't make me braver. Her presence, her *existence* has a gravity, a pull.

I can't ignore the truth here.

Claire doesn't seem to notice. She sticks her hand out in my direction. "Hi, I'm Claire. Nice to meet you."

I shake her hand, at a loss for words. "Luke," I manage.

Eleanor and Claire exchange friendly words, but that all fades into the background as I rush through my thoughts.

If Diane and my dad had an affair, then it's wholly possible that . . .

No, that'd be crazy. A lovechild? My father? Friendly family man Frank Wyatt? An affair *and* a love child? It's too much to fathom.

"I'm glad I was able to stop by today," Eleanor says. "I have the picture for you, and I also brought a thumb drive with your mother's music."

Claire smiles placidly. "That's so kind of you." Her eyes flick to me for a brief moment. Unsure and wary. Sizing me up.

Maybe she notices it too. Although that would be crazy, wouldn't it? To meet a total stranger who has no context for who you might be in their life, and then guess that you might be related?

"Um, I actually did some digging into my records too, for information about Frank."

My stomach flips. I shove my hands into my pockets, lifting my head up and looking for an exit path.

Eleanor touches my arm and squeezes. Her eyes are pleading with me. For what, at first, I'm not sure. And then it occurs to me that she wants me to be truthful. Give the truth I haven't been able to give all these months. But Claire is a stranger and even though Stellan is busy with Shortbread a few strides away, the thought of bringing up the truth makes my mouth dry.

But I've come this far. I either learn and know, or I never know at all. I just keep asking questions.

Can I live a life full of questions? Can I live a life naïve to my own history?

It might be easier not to know, but I also can't imagine living with the itching question in the back of my mind.

What the hell happened between my dad and Diane?

"I knew your mom," I say.

Eleanor's grip tightens on my arm.

Claire's expression is unreadable at first. Her eyes start to widen, and she lifts her chin. "Really?"

"Yep."

"How?"

We all know where this is going. Even if it's a long shot, I think we're all feeling it. "She was friends with . . ." I lick my lips. "She was friends with my parents. With my dad."

Claire freezes. "What was your dad's name?"

It would be foolish to think I can rewind time and back my way out of this moment. I'm already here. Nowhere to fall but forward.

"Frank," I say in a ragged whisper. "Frank Wyatt."

Eleanor goes rigid beside me. Another truth I didn't tell her the entirety of. That one wasn't to hurt her, wasn't to keep her safe. It was to keep me safe. I needed answers before I could hear her questions.

She'd understand that, right?

Claire takes me in, letting her eyes peruse me. It's not the kind of perusal you get in a bar or when you pass someone attractive on the street. She is adding me up, taking in the image of each of my parts, and creating a sum that is more similar to hers than either of us would like to admit. "I have some things to show you."

* * *

Claire's office is silent as she goes to her desk and opens one of the drawers.

Eleanor and I remain in the doorway. I'm afraid to step inside, but Eleanor gives me a small nod. *Go on.* It's not like hanging back is going to change my reality. I step into the office, the wooden floor squeaking underneath me. The wolfhound in the corner raises his head, and when he realizes nothing has changed other than my arrival, he plops back down.

"Well, I guess I'll just rip off the band-aid." Claire reaches into her desk and produces two official-looking documents. She places them in front of me and points to the one on the right. "This is the birth certificate I've always used for government stuff."

She places it in front of me. In the slot where the mother's name is written is Diane Bloom. The place for a father's name is blank.

"And this one . . ."

My eyes travel to the parentage lines again.

And this time the father's slot is not blank.

Francis Wyatt.

There it is. In government ink.

"I found it buried in her stuff. I guess she had his name struck from the record when I was little. My last name has always been Bloom."

I clear my throat in discomfort.

Claire sighs. "I'm sorry, I know this must be hard."

Something surges inside me. "Did you know him? Did you ever—"

"No. Never," Claire answers quickly.

I don't know if that makes it better or worse.

"I have something," I say. "Of my dad's." I reach into my coat.

Claire looks back at Eleanor who is lingering in the corner behind me. Eleanor shakes her head. "I had no idea, I just invited him to come along."

I internally wince at how small her voice sounds.

Later, Wyatt.

I hold the letter out to Claire. "I found this in a locked box that had a bunch of letters and things from their time together. I couldn't take the whole thing from my mom's house. I didn't want to upset her if she doesn't . . . or even if she did . . ."

My poor mom. She's never deserved anything like this.

Claire takes the note and flips it over. "This was recent."

"Yep."

Her thumbs slide over the paper like it's an artifact that she needs to be delicate with. "Should we open it?"

"Sure," I say. "You can do the honors if you want."

Claire takes a letter opener and slices the top of the envelope open in a clean motion. She pulls out a greeting card. On the front is a print of a dog looking up. Claire snickers. "She always had a lot of cards to send to people."

I bite my lip. Claire and I don't just share our father. We share the grief of losing a parent. She technically has lost both, but she never had my father.

We both know how terrible the loss is. How it hollows out your heart. I want to hug her, but I'm afraid that it might open something in me. It might make me weep for all the time I believed my father was a good man, an upstanding man who would never do something like this. Or maybe I would weep to know a part of myself I never knew existed in the world.

When she opens the card, a picture falls out onto the desk.

I look down at it. It's Claire recently wearing a cap and gown standing amidst some trees, arms crossed over her chest, smiling.

"That's my grad school portrait," Claire says. Her eyes travel across the inside of the card. I watch the tears well up. She folds her hand over her face. "Sorry."

"Want me to . . ." I hold my hand out.

She nods and hands the card to me.

The handwriting is the same as the writing on the cocktail napkin I found amongst Dad's memories. I get a tug in my throat. I have to be strong for Claire, though. For me.

I read the note aloud:

> Dear Frank,
> I hope Katie and the kids are well. And I hope you're well too. We're old now, isn't it funny?
> Anyway, I know it's been a while. I just wanted to say thank you. Our girl did good. Better than good. Master's degree in Animal Welfare and Behavior. She's smarter than either of us and definitely prettier.
> All my love,
> Diane

I suck in my cheeks and look up at the light to keep the tears from falling. It's such a simple note, and yet it has stabbed me in the gut and twisted the knife.

Our girl did good.

The birth certificate definitely proved enough, but seeing the words written out like that is somehow so much more real.

Claire rounds the desk and wraps her arms around me. "I'm sorry," she whispers.

I press my hand against her back. "Don't be sorry."

"It's not fair."

"To either of us."

Having her close slots something into me I didn't know was missing. Maybe my body always knew there was another piece of me out there in the world. That our family was a little bit incomplete.

We hold each other tight for a while. The only sound in the room is the tinkling of her dog's tags as he gets up and pushes at her hip with his snout.

Claire pulls back, red-eyed. "You should be mad at me. I think."

"For being born?" I ask.

"I mean, I don't know," she says.

"I'm not mad at you." I'm not even mad at Diane.

All my anger is saved for my father.

He had it all. The house, the kids, the wife.

Perfect. At least that's what I would think if I had all those things. I've *dreamt* of having that. With Eleanor.

And he had to go and fuck it all up. And why?

Because he could. Because he didn't think. Because he didn't care.

And if I'm my father's son, what the hell am I capable of?

Would I fuck it all up too?

35

ELEANOR

The last time we were sitting at this taco truck, we were strangers. I was taking photos of Luke being a charming cowboy. A flash-in-the-pan friendship.

Now, he's my boyfriend, and life is way, way more complicated. Not even the framed photo in my bag can change my mood. I should be celebrating.

How can I, now that Luke's whole world has changed? And maybe mine too.

Across the picnic table, Luke stares at his plate of tacos. Untouched.

"You should eat," I say.

"Not hungry." He swigs his Topo Chico.

It doesn't feel good eating with someone who isn't touching their food, but I'm *starving*. Today, I burned more calories than I know what to do with—all because of this *feeling*.

When Luke revealed his father was Frank, I didn't know what to think. The first thought was that I was an idiot for never asking his dad's name, although I never wanted to pry.

The second thought was . . . why didn't he tell me? Am I not trustworthy? Does he not think I can handle it?

I'm all out of sorts with what to think about our relationship at this point.

"What do you think of Shortbread?" I ask.

Luke manages to crack a smile. A small one, but still a smile. "He's great."

"Yeah, I think so too." I sip my horchata.

More silence. I eat. He doesn't.

This sucks.

"Are we going to talk about . . ."

"I don't really think so," he says in a cool tone.

I've never known this side of him. I didn't even know he was capable of being distant and cold. I know it has nothing to do with me. His world has turned upside down. The man he admired his whole life betrayed him.

Not talking about it, though, isn't going to help.

"I know this is weird, Luke, but Claire's great," I say. "I like her."

Luke says nothing. He chews on his upper lip and looks off to the side.

"You know, she seems like she might be . . ." What? A good addition to the family? A nice friend? "I'm just proud of both of you for how you handled that. Not everyone would be so calm about it."

He purses his lips.

I don't know if I'm making things worse or better. "I really admire you, Luke. You're a good man."

"Eleanor, stop it," he murmurs.

I look down at my half-eaten plate of tacos. Now I don't feel hungry. "I'm just trying to help."

"Yeah, well it's not fucking helping," he says.

I widen my eyes. I wish I could get up and leave, but I'm his ride home. "Don't be mean to me."

"I'm not trying to be mean to you, I'm—"

"You know, you should be grateful I even invited you to come with me today because I'm still pissed off at you," I say.

Luke looks at me again, his blue eyes searing. "I should be grateful you brought me to meet my dad's secret baby?"

"I'm just saying, you should be grateful I wanted to see you because I'm—because you—" I huff, balling up my napkin. "Never mind."

Luke slams his fist against the table.

I jump out of my skin. Where did *that* come from?

He leans across the table and spits out his words low and quick so no one nearby can hear. "I don't feel fucking lucky. I'm pissed off. Because everything I thought I knew is fucking destroyed. So, you don't need to comfort me. And you don't need to remind me that I'm a fucking asshole who ruined our relationship."

"So, I should just shut up?" I shoot back.

"Yeah, that'd be great."

My jaw falls open. "Wow."

Luke shuts his mouth, taking his own advice. He leans an elbow on the table and rests his head in his hand.

"I want to go home," I say.

"Nor, wait." His hand shoots out across the table and grabs mine. His touch still does it for me, still makes my body feel like I shouldn't run away.

When will my body catch up with my mind? When will it start to be unsure?

He peers at me from over his hand. "I'm sorry."

I don't accept his apology.

Luke's thumb skims the back of my hand. "Listen, I'm all kinds of fucked up right now."

"I know," I say.

He wraps my hand in both of his. Lifts it to his lips and kisses it. "Fuck," he mutters.

"Luke, just talk to me, tell me how you're feeling."

"I can't, Eleanor, I can't. What am I supposed to do when the person I always admired turns out to be . . ."

"You aren't your dad, Luke. That's not how admiration works."

Luke's eyes remain on mine. His foot starts tapping, shaking his whole body.

He doesn't believe me.

"Luke, I love you," I say.

"And I don't deserve it." Luke puts my hand back down and grabs the edge of the table. "I need some time, okay?"

"Time to . . . ?"

"To think," he sighs. "To . . . figure myself out."

Alarm bells ring in my brain. "Are you breaking up with me?"

"Not breaking up."

But not *not* breaking up.

"I just need some space and some time to get my head clear."

My face grows taut with concern, anger, and sorrow. I don't know what I'm feeling. "I want to be there for you, baby."

Luke manages a smile. It doesn't reach his eyes. "I don't deserve that. Not after what I did."

"Luke—"

"You're not winning this one, Eleanor."

I didn't know that I had to win the right to be in my boyfriend's life. The right to support him through what might be one of the most dramatic things to happen to him in all his life. His *dead father* has secrets he can never uncover from the horse's mouth. How is he going to wade through that without me?

Maybe I don't mean as much to him as I thought.

Luke pulls out his phone. "I'm going to take a car home, okay?"

I droop further over my uneaten food. Now, I'm the opposite of hungry. I want to expel everything out of my system as if that will somehow purge these emotions too.

I say nothing as he orders an Uber. I say nothing while we wait.

It's not until he gets up from the table and comes over to my side that I let myself look up.

Luke tips my chin up. "This isn't your fault."

I blink and a tear runs down my cheek. "I love you."

He tries to smile.

But he doesn't say it back.

And then he's gone.

36

LUKE

Thankfully, my week is full of gigs and obligations. I'm able to forget myself in the work. As long as I'm busy, I can't think about my dad, Claire, Diane, or Eleanor.

In the slower moments, the ones I dread, it's no longer Eleanor who comes to me for comfort. It's thoughts of my mom and dad. The relationship that I thought they had. The one that, I guess, is a total lie.

Poor Eleanor doesn't deserve my silence. She texts me every day, hoping I'm well, wishing to see me. And I never give her anything in return. I can't. I've already hurt her so deeply. And now that I know the stock I come from, I keep having visions of hurting her even worse. It's only been a few months. Maybe we should call it quits now before we get in too deep; before we're married, and I get restless and have an affair with a family friend.

I don't see that for myself. But I would never have expected that from my dad either.

Mom has been nagging me about what's going on with my girlfriend, and when she'll come out to meet the family. And I don't have the heart to tell her that I don't know when or if Eleanor will ever meet her.

I love her. Still love her with every fiber of my being.

I always thought that was enough.

According to the way my dad lived his life, apparently it wasn't. Apparently, it was a lie.

So, when my mom calls on Saturday to invite Eleanor down for Sunday lunch, I break.

"Mom, I have some questions about dad."

She laughs into the phone. "Why are you sounding so serious?"

"Because I want to know what happened with Aunt Diane."

The line goes quiet for a long time. I half expect her to hang up on me. She's always been the type to suggest there are some conversations parents should never have with their children, and I could see her deciding that this isn't something I have a right to know about.

Mom surprises me with one word. "Alright."

* * *

We sit out in the backyard on a bench. It looks the same as it did when I was a child, with the same tire swing swaying in the breeze. It's worn, but still just the same.

I guess we're all a little worn.

Not the same, though. Not now that I know.

"We all went to school together," Mom says. "College."

Her finger circles the rim of her glass of iced tea.

"She was in my wedding. You saw the pictures." She laughs. *Laughs.* "She hated the dress I made my bridesmaids wear."

I have to rein in my impatience. I want to know the truth, the answers. Not the long winding story.

It's only fair I give her the space to tell it, though. It's her hardship.

"Anyway, she was as close as family. You know that."

I don't know anything anymore.

Mom looks out at the yard. Her expression is even. Not necessarily pained, but intent. "As far as I know, there was never anything between them before . . ." She clears her throat. "Well, Dad got laid off. You remember that."

"Vaguely."

"That's when I started picking up shifts at the library. Put my degree to use for once," she chuckles. "You remember that, too."

The way she keeps pointing out what I know and remember confuses my brain. Are these memories I'm having real, or are they put there by her trying to make this story easier to hear?

Mom laughs out of nowhere. "Idle hands, you know?"

I frown. "What do you mean?"

Her laugh retreats into a sad smile. "The devil's playthings. That's what happened to your father. He had too much time on his hands. He was trying to find a new job, doing what he could here and there to provide. But he was stressed, and he didn't like to talk about it too much. So, he would just explode all at once instead of just expressing what was going on."

Sounds familiar. And not in a good way. My brain flashes to the moment I told Eleanor to shut up, and I want to curl up in a hole and die.

"We almost got divorced," she says almost as easily as she'd say the sky is blue. "But I didn't want that for you kids. And he didn't want that either."

Mom inhales, narrowing her eyes. "It didn't feel like we were married. At least to me. I would have never considered doing what he did, though. That's not how my brain works."

I extend my arm over the back of the bench behind her. "You knew?"

"More or less. I mean, when Diane started dodging my calls, I knew something was going on with her. I thought she was busy with the whole music thing." Mom laughs. "She was such a free spirit. I could never have done that. You know, I wanted to be married after college and feel secure. Happily ever after."

I smile. "Not that easy."

"No, not at all. Not at all." She picks at a thread on her navy dress. "Make no mistake, it was painful when I found out they were . . . behind my back . . ."

I swallow. "Mom?"

"Yes, baby."

"Do you know about . . . about the—"

"Their daughter?"

She's smiling.

"Yes, I know about that."

She should be angry. Furious. Threatening to burn the world down.

"Your dad, for all his faults, told me everything when they realized she was pregnant."

"Oh my god, how did you—how did you . . ."

Mom lifts her chin proudly. "I made him do what a man in that position should do. I made him step up. If he was going to make a bed like that, he was going to sleep in it."

"But didn't that feel awful? Your friend and Dad?"

She nods. "Yes and no. You see, honey, people don't do things with other people in mind. We're all a little bit selfish.

I didn't think any of it really had anything to do with me. Your dad was having a weird life crisis, and I wasn't going to entertain it. Diane did. Until it was too much."

I don't press her with questions, though I have many.

We don't say anything for a while. Birds cry out in the distance. Tree leaves shuffle together in the breeze.

"He came back on his hands and knees begging, and he remained there the rest of his life. The begging just turned into a kind of worship. And let me tell you, there's nothing better than that."

I snort. "*Mom.*"

"What? It's the truth."

"You're a maneater."

"Just the one."

I'm amazed by how proud she remains. Not the bad kind of pride. The kind of pride you have when you can see the things you might regret and say, "Oh well."

"So, anyway, your dad was going to have to cough up the money to support Diane and the baby, and I wasn't going to prevent him from doing that. And that kicked his sorry-for-himself ass into gear. Anyway, she broke off contact before she gave birth."

I chew on the inside of my cheek. "Did you know she passed away?"

"Yes."

"Why didn't you tell me I had a half-sister?"

My mom finally looks at me, hard in the eye. "That's love. It's not always simple."

I wrap my arm around her and bring her to my chest. I hold her the way Dad used to when they'd sit here and watch us playing in the yard.

I am an echo of him in so many ways. My mother was a saint for staying with him after all that bullshit.

I'm grateful my folks stayed together, and that Mom can be happy despite the pain. I'm not going to put someone through that, though. I won't make Eleanor the long-suffering wife who has to deal with my bullshit.

I've already filled my bullshit quota with her. She deserves someone bullshit-free.

I'm not ready to let her go. I'm not sure I can make her stay with me either.

Love might not be simple. But it doesn't have to be hard.

37

ELEANOR

Jolene places a cupcake on my table. "Happy last day!"

I look at the pretty cupcake, my favorite flavor from the bakery nearby.

Then I burst into tears.

"Woah! That's not the reaction I expected!"

I sniffle, wiping at my eyes. "I'm sorry, I'm sorry, I'm just . . ."

Everything that had slotted into place no longer fits. Luke hasn't spoken to me in a week, and I miss him with every fiber of my being. I wake up in the middle of the night with tears running into my ears. I wrap my arms around myself, imagining his embrace. I mourn the future we were supposed to have together.

It feels like the end.

"Honey, come here." Jolene hugs me. "You've had a rough go lately, I know. But it's okay. Things will all work out."

"If he breaks up with me, why the hell did I stay here?"

"You said you loved Austin. *That* was why you were staying."

I roll my eyes. "Who was I kidding?"

"You're being ridiculous. You belong here, Eleanor. With Luke or not."

I want the "with Luke." I don't think I'll survive the "not."

"Tell you what. We'll go out tonight. Go see a show, huh? We'll enjoy ourselves. And you'll remember why you're staying."

"No, Jolene, that's—"

"I'm your boss for one more day. This is my last executive order."

I giggle and mush my face into her shoulder. "What would I do without you?"

"I don't know. There's no one like me back in Chicago."

Truer words were never spoken.

* * *

I've donned my cowboy boots tonight. We're seeing a show at The Yellow Rose. It was a coincidence that Jolene chose this place. Thankfully, Luke's company isn't promoting this event. No chance I'll run into him while he's working. He might think I'm a creep if I did.

Floods of memories come back from the night I met Luke. When he was a stranger.

Tonight, though, we're just in the general admission crowd, no VIP about it. I don't have to sit at that table again and remember how we talked with our bodies bent close so we could hear each other over the music.

That was the night he lied to me. The lie that was the beginning of the end.

We were doomed from the start. An oddly comforting thought. I couldn't have done anything differently. It's all on him.

"Come on, let's get a better spot!" Jolene shouts over the music.

She takes my hand and leads me through the crowd, saying excuse me and pardon me, not the least bit bothered by the glares of people we step in front of. I apologize to each of them as we wade up to the front.

The musical act tonight is a girl group, which would be great any other night, but most of their songs focus on a theme of "fuck that guy," and man do I feel that more now than ever. With each song, I clutch harder to my drink. I want to get out of here. It's not fun. The whole place reminds me of Luke. The wings, the bar, and even the crowd look exactly the same to me.

This is his world. It's always been his world. He invited me into it.

I didn't know I wasn't being invited to stay forever.

I can't ask Jolene to leave, though. She's having the time of her life, flinging her blonde hair around, screaming along to the lyrics. It takes me out of my own grief for a moment here and there.

However, halfway through the set, the lights dim, and the musicians come to the front of the stage for an acoustic set. The first song is a haunting ballad. They've broken out a cello for the song, plangent and tragic. I feel tears coming to my eyes.

"Need another drink?" I say in Jolene's ear.

She nods, her eyes glued to the band.

I am able to wade my way through the crowd, my heart beating with each step. It's suffocating here.

The exposure therapy isn't working.

I need another drink.

I belly up to the bar against the back wall and catch the attention of a bartender.

Purple hair. She served me the first night I was here, and I remember her at the honkytonk too.

Fuck, this night is like déjà vu.

"What can I get you?"

"Another Yellow Rose," I say. "And a shot of . . . something."

She quirks her eyebrow. "You look familiar."

Please, I wish I didn't.

With a snap of her fingers, she places me. "Luke's girlfriend, right?"

"Ha, yeah. I don't know about *girlfriend*, but . . ."

Purple hair gets a serious expression. "Say no more. Yellow Rose and shot coming up."

She works quickly, snatching a bottle of whiskey from a high shelf and pouring a shot. She slides it over to me. "You need the good stuff."

I try to laugh. "You didn't have to—"

"Oh, I did. Trust me. I know how Luke can be."

I swallow. "You and Luke have . . ."

"No, no. But we've known each other for a long time. I've seen the shit he gets up to. Of course, it's been a while since he's broken a heart, but if you're the latest, I'm sorry. I thought he was really getting serious."

I take the shot instead of responding. The whiskey doesn't burn nearly as much as I'd like it to as it slides down my throat.

The bartender works on making my Yellow Rose, managing to field conversation with me as she does. "You know, men in this industry are commitment-phobes. When they're ready, they'll just pick a woman and decide they're ready. It's ridiculous."

"He seemed pretty ready to me," I say, glancing back at the stage where the cellist is really going to town, sawing at her instrument.

"Well, maybe he is, but he scared himself. Isn't that what happens with men? They always talk themselves out of a good thing." She places the drink in front of me. I unzip my fanny pack and fish out my wallet.

"On the house, babe."

I shake my head. "No, really, I—"

"I insist. It's not every day Luke Wyatt fucks up."

It's nice to know I'm not the only one who thinks so.

"Just know, he'll be fine without you. I'm sure if you go off and live your own beautiful life, he'll realize one day you're the one that got away. They always do."

I try to smile and thank her, but all I manage is a grimace and a nod of my head.

He'll be fine without me.

Austin will be fine without me.

Hell, what do I have going for me here, anyway? No job and no prospects. I'm just a person in a sea of people. At least back in Chicago, I own those streets. Here, I'll walk around and see Luke everywhere I go. Especially if I start doing event photography, I'll be in his world, having to deal with the memories of us and his ghosts.

Above it all, maybe I should give up the ghost. He lied. He betrayed my trust.

From the beginning it was wrong.

So, I'm going to make life right again.

38

LUKE

When Claire's name pops up on my phone, I'm surprised by how excited I am. We had decided to stay in contact after the revelations we had in her office. But I didn't expect to hear from her so soon.

I answer, though I'm at my desk: "Claire! Good to hear from you."

"Hey, Luke, do you have a minute?"

"Yeah, of course." Mom and I discussed having Claire come out to the house so she could meet Mom, and maybe go through some of the photo albums and things so she could get an idea of who her father was. It's not a lot to offer, but it's something.

Claire clears her throat. "Well, I'm sorry that things didn't work out with you and Eleanor."

I frown. I didn't know us not working out was public knowledge. Hell, it's not even knowledge to me. I'm still turning that stone over in my head, wondering and wavering. Each day that passes, I change my mind at least a dozen times.

Which isn't fair to Eleanor. She shouldn't be kept waiting like that.

Why does Claire know anything about it? "Oh, yeah. Um, thanks."

"So, I don't normally do this, but Shortbread was really attached to her, and I think it might break his heart if he doesn't get his forever home."

I pause for a moment to collect my thoughts. "I'm . . . not sure I follow."

"Eleanor told me she can no longer adopt him since she's headed out of town."

The record scratch is loud. More like a car crash. "She's leaving town?!"

"Oh, man. I'm sorry, I thought this is something you would have worked out with her since—"

"Claire, I don't know what you're talking about."

"Well, Eleanor told me since things didn't work out, she's moving back to Chicago."

No. No this can't be it. This can't be how it ends.

"She didn't tell you?"

"We . . . haven't been talking." I'm a fucking embarrassment. A disgrace. "I didn't know that she was leaving, though, I thought—"

"God, I'm sorry. I feel like a total jerk."

I swallow hard, like there's a lump of wet newspaper traveling down my throat. "No, you didn't know, how could you have?" I rub a hand over my face. "Um, but Shortbread. You were calling about Shortbread."

"Yeah, well, I thought maybe you'd be interested in adopting him."

I glance out the window of my office. I'd never considered having a pet. I'm too busy. I'd need a dog walker, and I'd probably want to be home more frequently because the poor guy shouldn't be alone too much.

"Like I said," Claire interrupts when my hesitance is too long. "I don't normally do this kind of thing. But since we're—" she cuts herself off with a laugh. "I don't know, it's all kind of topsy turvy. I thought I'd ask. There is no pressure to—"

The answer comes out of me like the starting gun of a race. "I'll do it."

* * *

Claire hands me the leash. "All yours."

I take it, looking down at the dog beside me. Shortbread looks up at me, panting hard with his tongue hanging out.

There wasn't a decision that had to be made. It was instantaneous. No way was I going to let this dog be disappointed. What would be the point of us both missing Eleanor separately if we could be together?

So, the second I was done with my work for the day, I rushed out here to Harmony Hounds.

"What do you think, Shortie?" I ask. "Pretty cool, huh?"

Shortbread licks my hand.

I smile.

Claire crosses her arms. "You can change his name if you want. Might take him some time to adjust, but . . ."

"We'll think of something."

She smiles. "You're a saint, you know that?"

I give her a double take. "No, not a saint." If only you knew the truth.

"I know it killed Eleanor to have to change her mind," Claire says, her voice soft.

"Yeah, well."

Her forehead creases. "You want to talk about it?"

I shrug a shoulder. "There's nothing to talk about." Not really. Eleanor's made the choice. It's only fair after I've ghosted her for this long.

"You two were cute together," Claire says as if it's a consolation.

"Don't remind me."

"Ah, Luke."

I try to smile. Our eyes meet. Reflections. "God, it's still weird," I laugh.

"I know, I'm still getting over the family resemblance myself." Claire nods toward the door. "I'll walk you out."

The walk to my car is quiet. Shortbread is more excited than he knows what to do with, yanking on the leash and jumping. He keeps looking back to me as we go as if he can't believe it.

I'm a dad. A fur dad, but still.

I didn't think I'd be doing this alone, but I'm gonna need all the help I can get as I process how my life has flipped upside down today.

I open the back door for Shortbread and let him leap inside.

"You mind if I ask what happened?" Claire prods.

"You can ask, but I'm not sure I have good answers," I say, my eyes falling to my shoes.

"Is it because of me?"

"What?!"

"I don't know, this is all a lot of drama. Maybe it was too much for her, or . . . I don't know."

I sigh. "No, Claire. It's nothing to do with you and everything to do with me." I glance out at the open landscape beyond the animal sanctuary.

"You love her?" she asks.

I don't reply.

"I'm your sister, it's my job to hold you accountable to your feelings."

I laugh.

Claire does too. "I know, sounds weird. I don't have to call myself that."

"No, that's what you are."

She smiles. Says nothing. Waits for my answer.

I nod once. "Yeah, I love her."

"Then don't be an idiot." She points a finger in my face.

"Damn, you sure you don't have siblings? Because you've got the conversation down pat."

Claire puts her hands in the air. "What can I say? I've always wanted an idiot brother."

I laugh and watch her walk back into the sanctuary. We exchange a laugh just before she disappears inside.

Once I get into the car, Shortbread sticks his head in between the seats and lick my cheek. "Okay, buddy, no distractions while I'm driving." I give him some well-earned chin scratches. "You're so cute."

It was supposed to be the two of us taking Shortbread home. I pictured it. Me driving while Eleanor lavished him with affection. This is *her* dog.

God, what the fuck is going on with us? I know I'm partly to blame, but is she really just going to walk out on our life together, on *her* life in Austin, without even saying anything?

"Goddammit," I say.

Shortbread rests his head on my shoulder.

"I guess I have someone to talk to other than myself now," I say.

He nuzzles harder.

"Maybe . . . should we call her?"

Shortbread looks at me, his ear flopping to the side in an attempt to understand.

That's as good of an answer as any.

I navigate to our last conversation on my phone and pause on her last message. It was sent a couple days ago.

I hope you're okay. I wish you'd talk to me.

"Yeah, maybe not, bud." I turn off the screen and drop my phone in the cupholder.

I've had so many chances to change this outcome. I shouldn't be surprised. And I shouldn't be hurt. I don't deserve to have any emotions other than acceptance. Eleanor has made her decision.

My heartbreak is my own damn fault.

39

ELEANOR

One suitcase down; two more to go. Over the next few days, people will be coming by to pick up the furniture they've purchased. Jolene has offered to be the point of contact for that, so I can get to Chicago as fast as possible. I don't want to waste my time kicking around Austin and making myself more miserable than I already am.

It's bittersweet. On one hand, I was so eager to make this place my home for a long time. On the other, I can't live in a haunted house anymore.

Jolene is helping me sort through things in my bedroom when she pulls up my portfolio of photographs I've printed.

"Oh, I'll take that in my backpack," I say before she can open it.

Jolene ignores me and opens the portfolio. "Oh my god. Eleanor!"

I roll my eyes. "Jolene, please, we have to focus."

"These are amazing!"

She holds up a photo from The Maverick. The nice thing about small venues is that you don't need to have a photography pass to use a nice camera. The picture is of the guitarist I saw with Luke the night everything changed. He's mid-lyric, eyes shut, fingers in an impossible combination. The light pours over him, almost heavenly.

"You could put this one in the museum."

I snort.

"I'm serious."

"Well for every *one* of those, there's hundreds of shitty—"

"Oh my god."

She holds up another one. Luke laying on my floor, wrapped in a blanket.

"Seriously, you need to give me a warning before a jump scare," I grumble.

"Eleanor, listen to me. These aren't just pictures. These are beautiful."

I chuckle. "Yeah, I'm sure the Reeder Music Library would like a picture of my ex-boyfriend wrapped in a blanket on the walls."

"Well, no."

"Mhm."

"But you should have a gallery showing!" Jolene sorts through more photos. I try to ignore them as she spreads the photos out on the bed. So many of them are from times with Luke. The record shop, the boot store, the honkytonk, the lake, and on and on. More confirmation that my life here has always been about him. I'm more resolved than ever that leaving is the right choice.

"Jo, can you please focus?"

Jolene starts sliding the photos back into my portfolio. "I know this isn't easy, Eleanor, but, like, we take chances in life and sometimes they don't work out."

"And sometimes they gut you like a fish," I respond.

"Ha, ha."

"I'm not being funny."

Jolene grabs the shirt I'm folding and tugs on it.

"Hey!" I'm about to give her what for until I see the look in her eyes.

"You're a good photographer, Eleanor. If it's not here in Austin, fine, but you've got to do something with your talent."

I'm not sure how to respond at first. I'm not used to compliments on my work.

That's not true.

I don't know how to *accept* compliments on my work. When you've been rejected so many times, you either have to have a reckless belief in yourself that your work is actually good, or you have to believe that anyone who has ever complimented you is a liar.

I've chosen the latter for a while now.

"I'm not just saying that because I'm your friend, okay?" Jolene grabs a photo off the bed and turns it toward me. It's a photo from 6th Street. The aggressive lights and signage are composed against a swathing sky at sunset. "This is beautiful."

I try to smile. "Then you can have it."

Jolene narrows her eyes. "Great. Thanks."

I laugh, thinking she's joking, but she goes into the living room with the photo to put it with her purse a moment later. I shake my head and smile to myself. I hope we don't lose touch.

From somewhere amongst the messy clothes on the bed, my phone starts buzzing. I haven't shaken the urgency that floods me every time my phone makes the tiniest sound, always thinking it might be Luke. I know that I'm setting myself up for disappointment if I continue to believe that, yet I can't help myself from hoping.

When I find it, I'm surprised to see the number from Harmony Hounds on the screen. I hope they're not calling about Shortbread. The last thing I want is for him to suffer. Although, I'm not sure he'd understand when they tell him that the woman who fell in love with him doesn't want him anymore. He'd probably tip his head back and forth, trying to understand, and then sniff around for a treat.

My baby boy.

Not mine.

I answer the phone. "Hello?"

"Eleanor? It's Claire."

My mouth grows hot. She might not be Luke, but she's a blood relation, and something about that closeness makes me uneasy. "Hey, is everything okay?"

"Yeah, I just wanted to let you know that Luke adopted Shortbread today."

I frown. "Sorry, what?"

"Luke adopted—"

"How did he—what did he—" I only called her this morning to tell her that I was leaving town. It's all happened so fast, I guess I shouldn't be surprised. But still. *Luke?*

"I asked him if he would want to, and he said yes."

I can't help but be annoyed. "You *asked* him to?"

"Yes, I did." Her resolve is impenetrable.

"That's . . ." It's a good thing overall. Shortbread has a home. But with the man I love who won't give me the time of day? It's a betrayal. "That's great. I hope they're very happy together."

"Eleanor, wait—"

How did she know I was just about to hang up?

"Luke told me he didn't know you were leaving Austin. Is that true?"

I sit down on the edge of the bed. "Yeah, that's true."

Jolene appears in the doorway and mouths, "Who is it?"

I wave her off and thankfully, Miss Meddler actually retreats.

"God, Eleanor."

"Look, Claire, I appreciate what you've done, but this is a bit of an overstep, don't you think?"

She ignores what I've said. "It broke his heart when I told him."

I run my hand across my chest where my broken heart sits. Why are we doing this to ourselves? "It did?"

"Yeah." I can sense a smile on her face. "He came this afternoon for Shortbread. Barely any questions asked."

"Why do you care so much, Claire?"

"Because . . . we're family. And I don't have any other family left."

Fucking Claire. As if my heart wasn't already broken enough.

"I know it might be putting the cart before the horse, but I thought I owed it to you to tell you. As thanks for connecting us."

I look into my lap. "Thank you, Claire. I appreciate it."

"You're welcome." She hesitates. "He loves you. I don't know if you love him, but . . . yeah. That's all I've got."

I smile to myself. I love him too.

"Let me know what happens. I'm invested."

I laugh. It feels like the first real smile I've had in weeks.

After we say our goodbyes, Jolene pops her head into the doorway. "What was that about?"

I have so many questions. "Luke adopted my dog."

"The dog you were going to—"

"Yeah."

Jolene eyes me carefully. "How does that make you feel?"

A brick is lifted off my chest. "I feel like I should go talk to him."

Jolene grins. "Atta girl."

* * *

I pull up in front of Luke's house, the house I've never visited.

It's unexpectedly charming in a subdivision much more suited to couples and families than I'd expect for Luke and the life he lives. His home is a white bungalow, shaded by trees, surrounded by a white picket fence. The mailbox juts out an angle toward the street and has been haplessly repainted to obscure the name of the former owners.

A veranda encircles the house with a bench I'd love to sit on as night approaches.

The best part, though, is the blonde dog having the time of his life in the front yard, flipping and flopping. Finally free.

When I climb out of the car, Shortbread clocks me. He starts barking, music to my ears.

I walk up to the gate and reach over to scratch his ears. "Hi, honey. Oh, hi. You look so happy."

He licks and whines, his tail thrumming like a bass drum.

My eyes well up with tears. He'll be happy here. If Luke wants nothing to do with me anymore, Shortbread will be happy here.

A figure moves in my periphery. I lift my eyes and see Luke has come out of the house. He's standing, leaning against one of the columns at the top of the stairs. Looking amazing as always. Not his 6th-Street self. A band T-shirt and a pair of old jeans with frayed cuffs. Damn, the cowboy looks good even when he takes the day off.

Neither of us says anything. Where do you start?

I unlatch the gate, making sure Shortbread can't dart past me into the street. "Excuse me, baby."

As I walk up the front walk, Luke descends the stairs, one at a time. His arms are pressed over his chest defensively, but his expression isn't standoffish. He's trying to read me just as I'm trying to read him.

Neither of us stops until we're close enough to hold one another.

I slide my arms around his waist, and he loops his around my upper back.

I should say hi or something, anything. But I'm mute. I have nothing to say. I'm happy right here, not understanding. If this is the last time I hold him, at least it feels good. At least I know it's right.

Luke's lips brush the crown of my head. I cling to him tighter.

Shortbread yips and leaps up, trying to break us apart.

"Kids," Luke says.

"Yeah, tell me about it." I lift my head and rest my chin against his chest, offering Shortbread a hand as a peace offering.

Luke takes a deep breath. "What are you doing here?"

"Claire called me. To tell me you adopted Shortbread."

"Ah . . . she told me you were going to Chicago."

"Yeah."

Luke nods. "I understand."

"I didn't think I could hack it here. Not just because I don't have a job anymore or a boyfriend, but because all the things I love about Austin have to do with you. I saw you wherever I went. So, I thought the only choice I could make was to leave. But I don't know anymore."

He pinches his eyes shut and shakes his head. "Eleanor, I'm sorry. I've acted like such an asshole."

"At least you know it," I grin.

Luke laughs, chest rumbling against mine. He releases me, keeping a hand on my arm as if I might float away if he lets go. "I didn't know what to do with myself after I found out about my dad and—"

"I get it."

"I thought you might be better off without me. I mean, I lied and then I have a philanderer for a father. I feel like you could do better."

I focus on Shortbread for a moment, scratching his head. "Let's sit, hm?"

Luke and I sit on the top step. Shortbread too, plopping down next to me until he's lying on his belly.

I start. I'm the one who showed up out of the blue. "Look, I think you made a mistake with the picture. I can forgive you for that because life is a whole lot better with you than without."

Luke drops his head and laughs a little at himself.

"As far as what happened with your dad . . . if that's how you always respond to something bad happening, pushing me away, then I have to walk away, Luke."

Luke grabs my hand. "I promise, I won't. Never again. It was—I'd say it wasn't like me, but the truth is, I don't know myself in a relationship like this. Not with someone who—"

He stops. "Goddammit, Eleanor, I think you're the love of my life."

"And you couldn't even bother to call and tell me?" I ask with a stupid smile.

He brings my hand to his mouth, his lips ghosting across my knuckles. "Is it too little too late to tell you I need you? That I don't want you to go?"

"Not too late," I say.

Luke leans closer to my ear. "I need you. I don't want you to go to Chicago."

Before he can pull away, I turn my face into his and let my lips press against his. I've needed this. Badly.

Luke cups my cheek and when the kiss breaks, he leans his forehead against mine. "I'm sorry. I can't say it enough."

"It's okay. We're here now. We'll try again."

"You'll stay?"

"I'll stay."

He kisses my forehead.

"I like your house," I say.

"It's . . . intense, isn't it?"

"Intense?"

Luke glances up at it. "I don't know. I bought it because I knew I wanted to have a home and a family someday. But then I realized when women learn you have a house, they start thinking you're trying to rush things and—"

"I love it," I interrupt. "Perfect for a man and his dog."

"Speaking of . . ." Luke reaches around me and pats Shortbread. "Claire mentioned I could rename him."

I quirk an eyebrow. "You don't like the name Shortbread?"

Luke grimaces.

"Say no more."

"It doesn't really roll off the tongue. Shortie's cute, but that feels like a hit to his ego."

I scritch behind Not-Shortbread's ears. "I guess it is a little demoralizing for a mid-sized dog."

Not-Shortbread's eyes roll toward us. He licks his lips, pink tongue darting out before he settles again and sighs. It truly is a dog's life.

"How about Frank?" I tease.

Luke guffaws. "Are you being serious?"

I shrug. "Yes, I mean no, but . . . it's not a bad name."

Luke leans over me. "Let's see . . . Yo, Frank."

Not-Shortbread's ears perk.

We exchange a look, eyebrows launching up.

"Maybe it was meant to be," I say. "But he's your dog, you should name him."

I lean into Luke as we both gaze down at Not-Shortbread. Or *Frank,* I should say.

"No, he's ours."

Luke presses a kiss to the side of my head.

"I think Frank suits him perfectly."

Luke considers for a moment. He squeezes my shoulder. "Frank it is."

Frank's ears twiddle, and he side-eyes us both before licking his lips and yawning.

We both laugh at the abject cuteness. Our eyes return to each other's.

"I love you," he says. "Everything I've done, as stupid as it has sometimes been, has come from loving you."

I cup his chin, unable to hide my smile.

"What's that look?" he asks.

I take a deep inhale. His musk intermingles with the freshness of the air, a sweetness on the breeze. "I'm taking a picture, so I never forget this moment."

Luke moves in to kiss me, but he stops an inch away. "You're going to have thousands of moments like this with me, Eleanor."

I close the space between us, indulging in his lips.

Yep. I'm exactly where I'm supposed to be.

Epilogue

LUKE

A year and a half later . . .

"Frank!"

Dogs don't make good ring bearers, but they sure are cute.

I already have enough to be stressed out about today, and now my darn, effortlessly adorable dog is fumbling down the aisle toward me, zigzagging to get pats from the people on either side. He gets caught up with one of the guest's kids, who he's enchanted by since they're close to him in size.

I squat down as best I can in my suit pants and clap my hands at him. "Come on, Frankie!"

Frank's body alerts and he hurries over to me, shoving himself up against me, blonde hairs attaching themselves to my black suit.

They're right about pets being good for cortisol levels. The second I lay my hands on him, I realize how badly my hands have been shaking. My nerves settle, if only for a moment, and

I focus on giving my dog all the love for the work he's done. "Good boy, buddy."

Sure, the weather turned out perfectly, a balmy seventy degrees, not too hot and not too cool. I shouldn't be sweating bullets and yet I am, the nerves grinding through me without any sign of stopping. And, *yes,* the setting is perfect. Claire offered up the perfect patch of land at the sanctuary the second she learned Eleanor and I were engaged. A weeping willow swoons above us, serving as an almost natural altar. From time to time, you can hear the barking of dogs down the hill as they romp around in the field.

Everything is perfect with a capital P, and yet I am vibrating with the anxiety of the next moment.

I thought I'd be fine. Who cares? It's just a wedding? Eleanor and I are basically married. We live together, our lives completely entangled in every way. This is just another day. Right?

Wrong. Dead wrong.

Frank goes in for face kisses, and I have to hold him back. "Easy, boy! I'm saving my lips for someone else!"

There's laughter from the guests and, thankfully, Claire rushes over, navy bridesmaids dress and all, and grabs Frank by the harness. She chides him for stealing the spotlight and gives me a smile over her shoulder before returning to her place in the grouping of bridesmaids.

I pat my knees and push myself back up to standing. The second I do, the music shifts, and my stomach *drops.* The good kind of drop, like the kind you get on a rollercoaster.

It's happening. It's really happening.

All the guests rise in preparation for Eleanor's entrance. I try to steady my breath. Is it hot out here, or is it just me?

Everyone acts like the bride is the one who is doing all the work, walking down the aisle, but I've been standing up here with eyes on me for what feels like hours. I'm more than ready for the star of the show.

As I wait for Eleanor to appear from the tent at the end of the aisle where she's been hidden for far too long, I scan the faces of those who have come today to celebrate, landing on the face of my mother in the front. She's already gone through half a box of Kleenex. Beside her is an empty seat where my father would be.

"I love you," I mouth.

She only smiles bigger, though the tears keep coming.

Yeah, that will be me pretty soon.

The tent flaps part, and Eleanor emerges on the arm of her father. As if in a movie, a breeze washes across all of us, fluttering through her wildflower-adorned curls. I don't know where to begin with how fantastic she looks. Her dress is simple and elegant, classically her. The sleeves are fluttering over her shoulders, lace appliques dancing down the front.

She could have worn a paper bag and still be the most beautiful woman in the world.

Eleanor and her dad walk down the aisle, thanks to the stylings of Bobby Sutton and his band. The jazziest wedding march you've ever heard.

From beside me, Randy holds out a handkerchief.

"Dammit, man," I say. "I'm trying to hold it in."

He just grins.

I snatch the handkerchief and dab at my eyes just as the tears are about the fall. I can't stop smiling so hard it hurts, but the pain is completely irrelevant to how perfect this moment is. I never thought I'd care this much about my wedding, and now here I am.

I guess that goes to show you what it means to meet the right person.

Though I'm tired of being up here alone, I could live in this moment forever. Eleanor walks toward me, ready to join me in stepping into our future.

When Eleanor and her dad arrive at the end of the aisle, it takes everything in me not to grab her and kiss her until her glasses are foggy. But I'm a gentleman and this is our wedding day. I'll have forever to do that.

Her father and I shake hands before he retreats, and it's just me and Eleanor at the end of the aisle.

Well, and Jolene. When it came to picking an officiant, there was only one woman for the job.

Eleanor's smile is full of mischief. I narrow my eyes at her. *What are you up to?*

The smile turns into a full-on grin. She grabs the front of her dress and lifts it just an inch, revealing the tips of blue cowboy boots.

"Something blue," she whispers.

I shake my head in disbelief. She's perfect. "I love you."

* * *

After the ceremony, Eleanor and I only have a moment to celebrate before the marathon of entertaining our guests.

We disappear into the tent, the flaps closing behind us. I pull her into my arms and kiss her the way I wish I could have at the end of the aisle, but it would have absolutely scandalized my mother. "Oh my god, you look amazing," I say, scrunching my fingers through her hair.

She giggles. "You fogged up my glasses."

You bet I did. I pull her glasses off and polish them off on my jacket before placing them back on her nose. "That's better."

"Hi, husband," she says, now able to look up at me like I've hung the moon.

My heart's flopping like a fish on a dock. "Hi, wife."

She grins. "Ooh, that's fun!"

We both laugh and find ourselves chatting excitedly about everything leading to the big moment, rather than tearing each other's clothes off which was my original plan. I can't help it though. I want to know everything.

Sooner than I'd like, we have to go out and greet our public. I make a note to get her alone later to show her *just* how beautiful she is to me.

We wade through our guests, flashing smiles, sharing conversations, and convincing them to go visit the main cabin to check out all the animals up for adoption. We ply them with enough champagne that some of those fur babies are definitely getting their forever homes tonight.

"God, I'm starving," she says before swiping some canapes off a passing tray, giving the server a grateful smile. "I haven't eaten all day."

"Neither have I," I reply.

She hip-checks me. "Were you nervous, Luke Wyatt?"

"Obviously."

Eleanor sips her champagne, eyes rolling up, knowing how I exist always in the palm of her hand. "Mm! The truck!"

Everyone has worked on making our day as special as possible, including my mom, who had my dad's old truck all tuned up to make the drive out here. It's currently adorned with garlands of flowers and tin cans tied to the tires, with a sign hanging off the back that says "Eleanor and Luke's Wedding."

It's serving as a photo op for our guests to have a photo memento of our day.

My mother pops between us and squeezes us to her sides. "If you flip the sign around, it says 'Just Married!'" she squeals.

"We're not driving home in that, Mom," I snort.

"Why not? It was your father's!"

"Because look at her! She's in a wedding dress."

Eleanor scoffs. "So?" She sticks a foot out from under her dress. "I'm in my boots. I'm not too good for a pickup."

My mom beams up at me. "I love her."

Lots of friends from the music scene are here, so many friendly faces from my years of music promoting. I've scaled back on how much promotion work I'm taking on. I've got plans. Big plans. Ideas I never would have had if I hadn't met Eleanor Hayes.

After dinner, as I promised myself, I manage to get her alone in the main Harmony Hounds cabin, stealing kiss after kiss after kiss.

Eleanor giggles. "Careful, or we won't be able to stop."

I cage her against the wall. "That's my plan."

"*Luke* . . ." she admonishes me.

I wrap a hand around her waist, pull her to me so our hips are locked. "Tell me to stop."

Eleanor tilts her head back. "Why would I do that?"

Before our lips connect again, someone shouts out, "There you are!"

Eleanor and I jerk apart so violently that I knock a picture frame off the wall. "Dammit," I mutter.

Claire is standing in the entryway of the cabin, a hand on her hip, eyebrow raised. "Did I interrupt?"

"You're making up for lost time with this annoying younger sister routine," I mumble, picking the picture up off the ground. Thankfully, when I flip it, the glass is still intact. I smile to myself at the image of a cat languishing on the windowsill of Claire's office. Eleanor took it. She's taken the freelancing photographer thing to heart, and thanks to all of our friends in high places, she's been able to gain a lot of traction quickly.

It's my goal to open an event space. Yes, primarily for concerts. But one that is easily convertible for other artistic endeavors such as photography showings. You know, for Eleanor's work.

My wife's work.

I like the sound of that.

"It's time for your first dance," Claire explains. "Unless you want me to go back and tell everyone that you've got more important things to do."

Eleanor snickers and grabs my hand. "You wouldn't dare."

"You never know, I *am* an annoying younger sister," Claire replies with a grin.

As Eleanor and I pass Claire, I give her a soft punch on the shoulder. Since we've met, Claire and I have gotten along like gangbusters. The Diane I miss is in her, but she's also a chip off the old Wyatt block. Guess some things about a personality are just inherited.

Mom welcomed Claire with open arms, and since Claire was kind of on her own, she fell right in step with our family. The story might be strange, but for us, it slotted into place just as it should.

When we arrive at the tent, all of our guests cheer as we go to the dance floor.

The opening notes of "Hyacinth" begin to play through the speakers.

Eleanor and I assume a dancing position and begin to sway across the floor. It's like we're in our own little world, though we're surrounded by friends and family.

"*I've got arms to hold you too tight / I've got words to keep you up all night,*" Diane sings. It seems only right that the woman who brought us together has a place in our wedding.

"Are you ready to admit that maybe it wasn't such a bad idea that I lied about the photo?" I tease in Eleanor's ear.

She squeezes my shoulder. "In your dreams, Wyatt."

"*Something told me you were mine / But the world had a different plan*"

The song is about lost love. It's heartrending and complicated. But it's not what the song says, it's what it does that makes it our song.

I pull Eleanor closer to me, kissing the shell of her ear.

"*In the morning, please remember me / Beautiful and brilliant, the way we used to be*"

"The way we'll always be," I whisper.

Eleanor leans her head on my shoulder.

My mother is right. Love isn't simple.

Not by a long shot.

But dammit, it's amazing.